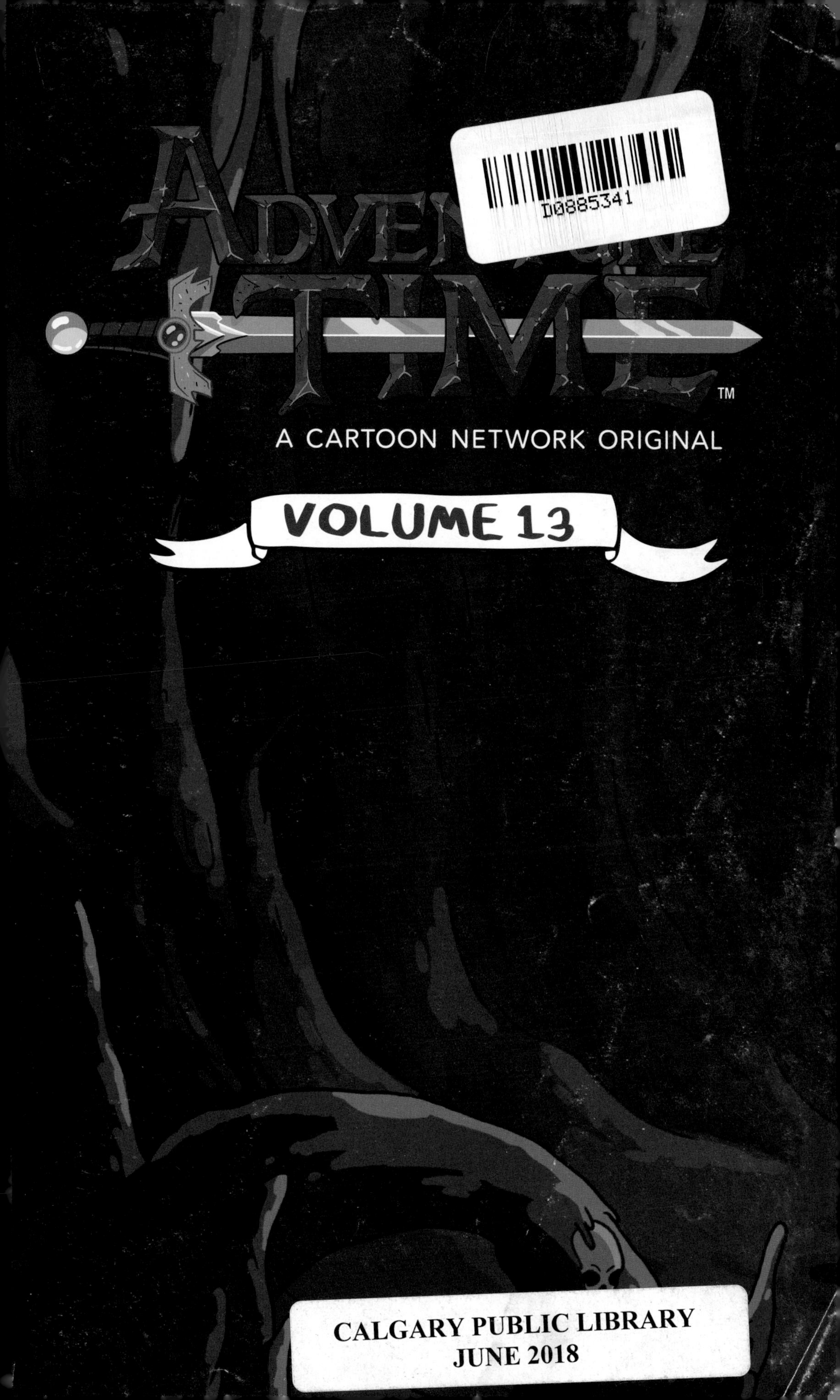
ADVEN[...]
TIME™
A CARTOON NETWORK ORIGINAL
VOLUME 13

ROSS RICHIE CEO & Founder • MATT GAGNON Editor-in-Chief • FILIP SABLIK President of Publishing & Marketing • STEPHEN CHRISTY President of Development • LANCE KREITER VP of Licensing & Merchandising
PHIL BARBARO VP of Finance • ARUNE SINGH VP of Marketing • BRYCE CARLSON Managing Editor • MEL CAYLO Marketing Manager • SCOTT NEWMAN Production Design Manager • KATE HENNING Operations Manager
SIERRA HAHN Senior Editor • DAFNA PLEBAN Editor, Talent Development • SHANNON WATTERS Editor • ERIC HARBURN Editor • WHITNEY LEOPARD Editor • JASMINE AMIRI Editor • CHRIS ROSA Associate Editor • ALEX GALER Associate Editor
CAMERON CHITTOCK Associate Editor • MATTHEW LEVINE Assistant Editor • SOPHIE PHILIPS-ROBERTS Assistant Editor • KATALINA HOLLAND Editorial Administrative Assistant • AMANDA LaFRANCO Executive Assistant
JILLIAN CRAB Production Designer • MICHELLE ANKLEY Production Designer • KARA LEOPARD Production Designer • MARIE KRUPINA Production Designer • GRACE PARK Production Design Assistant
CHELSEA ROBERTS Production Design Assistant • ELIZABETH LOUGHRIDGE Accounting Coordinator • STEPHANIE HOCUTT Social Media Coordinator • JOSÉ MEZA Event Coordinator • HOLLY AITCHISON Operations Assistant
MEGAN CHRISTOPHER Operations Assistant • MORGAN PERRY Direct Market Representative • CAT O'GRADY Marketing Assistant • LIZ ALMENDAREZ Accounting Administrative Assistant • CORNELIA TZANA Administrative Assistant

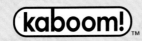

ADVENTURE TIME Volume Thirteen, December 2017. Published by KaBOOM!, a division of Boom Entertainment, Inc. ADVENTURE TIME, CARTOON NETWORK, the logos, and all related characters and elements are trademarks of and © Cartoon Network. (S17) Originally published in single magazine form as ADVENTURE TIME No. 58-61. © Cartoon Network. (S16) All rights reserved. KaBOOM!™ and the KaBOOM! logo are trademarks of Boom Entertainment, Inc., registered in various countries and categories. All characters, events, and institutions depicted herein are fictional. Any similarity between any of the names, characters, persons, events, and/or institutions in this publication to actual names, characters, and persons, whether living or dead, events, and/or institutions is unintended and purely coincidental. KaBOOM! does not read or accept unsolicited submissions of ideas, stories, or artwork.

BOOM! Studios, 5670 Wilshire Boulevard, Suite 450, Los Angeles, CA 90036-5679. Printed in China. First Printing.

ISBN: 978-1-68415-051-9, eISBN: 978-1-61398-728-5

CREATED BY
Pendleton Ward

WRITTEN BY
Christopher Hastings

ILLUSTRATED BY
Ian McGinty

COLORS BY
Maarta Laiho

LETTERS BY
Mike Fiorentino

COVER BY
Shelli Paroline & Braden Lamb

DESIGNER	ASSOCIATE EDITOR	EDITOR
Chelsea Roberts	**Alex Galer**	**Whitney Leopard**

With Special Thanks to Marisa Marionakis, Janet No, Curtis Lelash, Conrad Montgomery, Kelly Crews, Scott Malchus, Adam Muto and the wonderful folks at Cartoon Network.

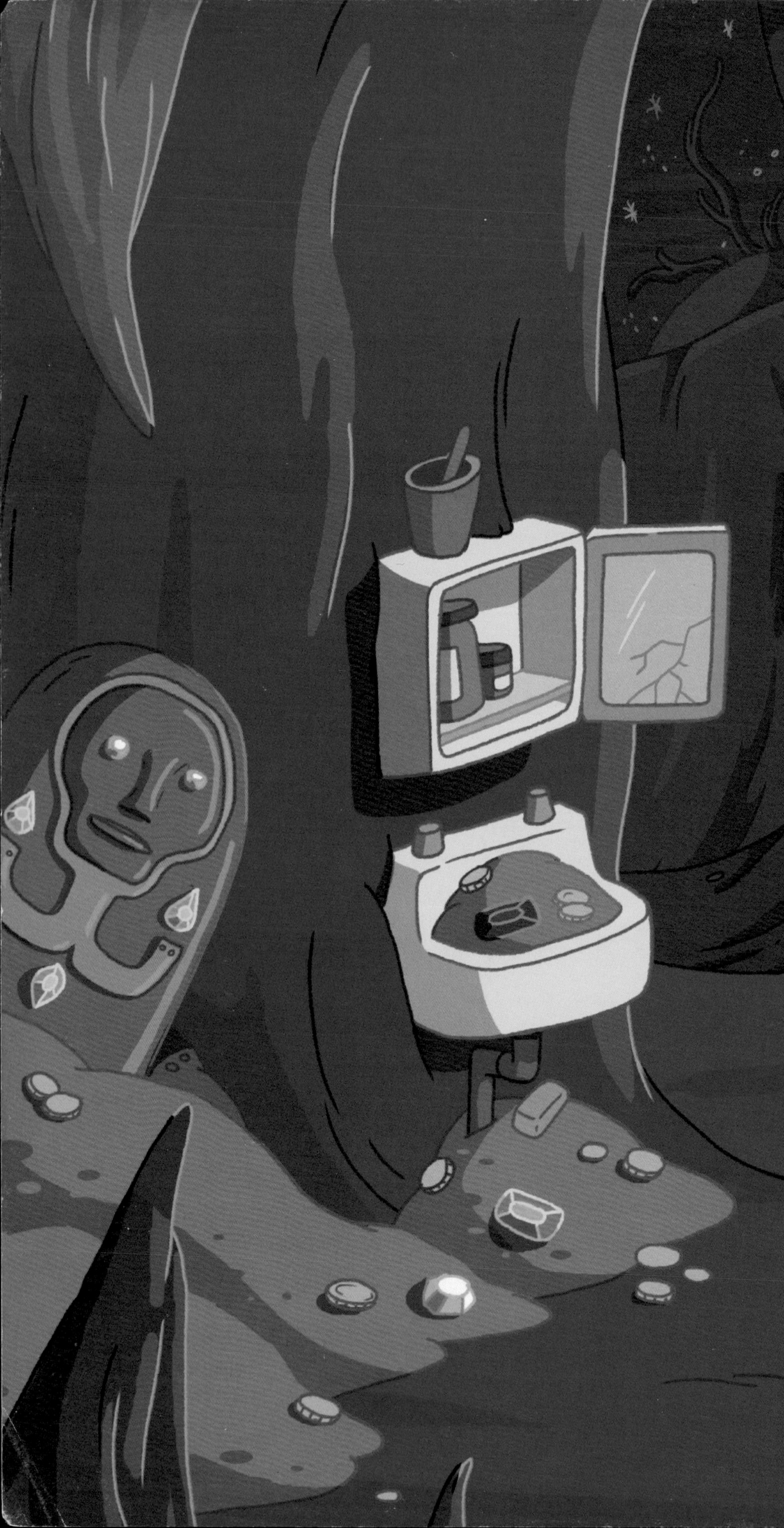

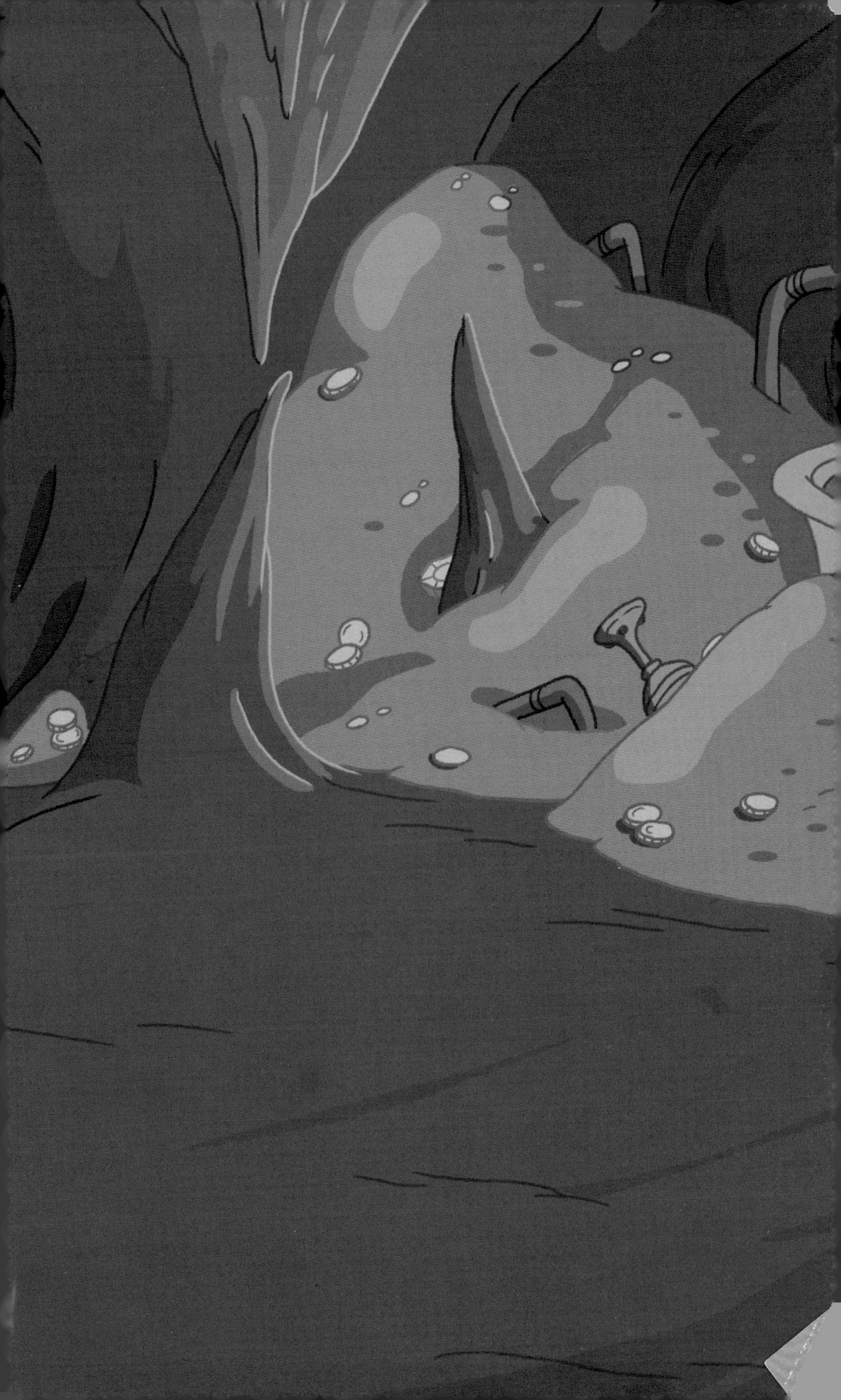

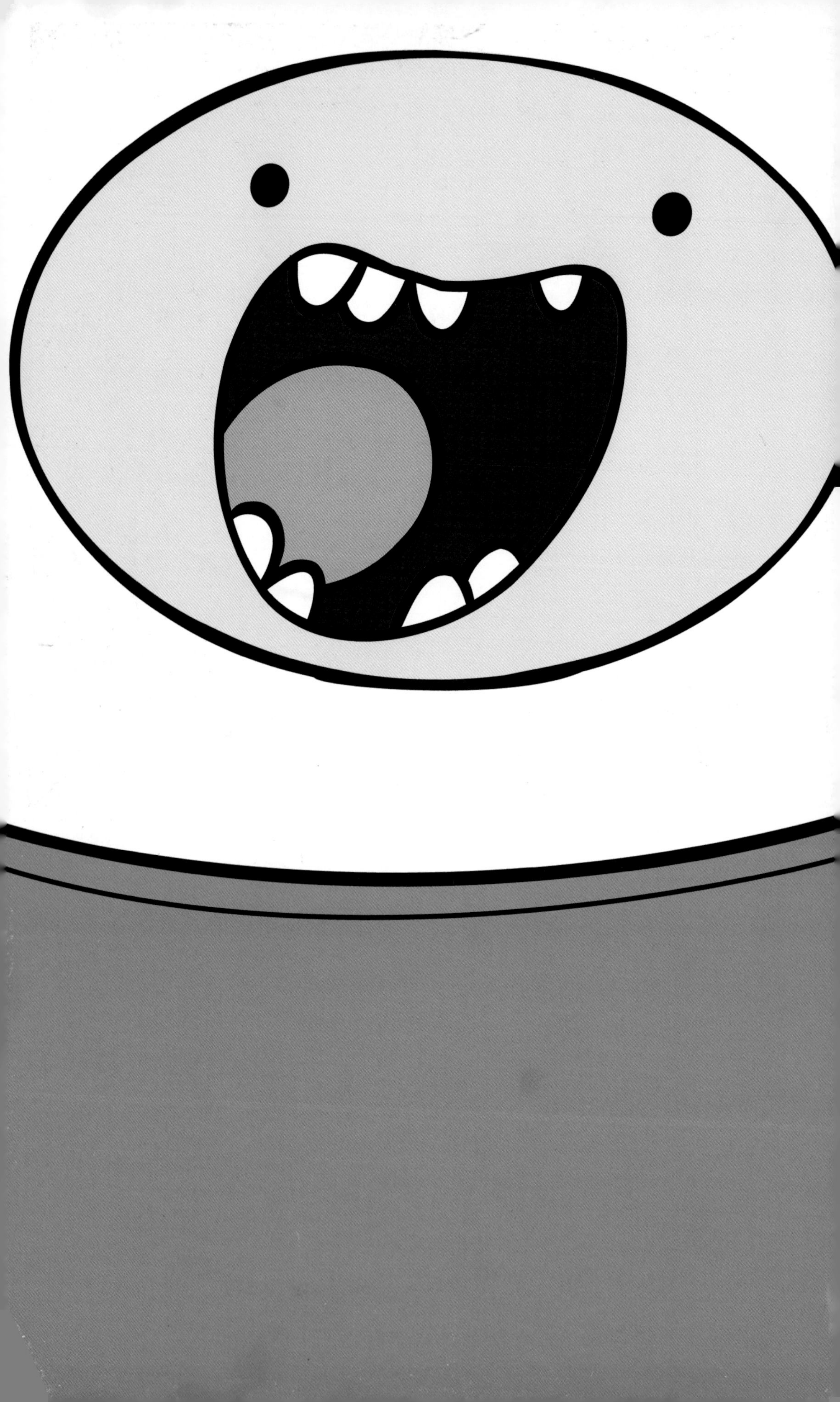

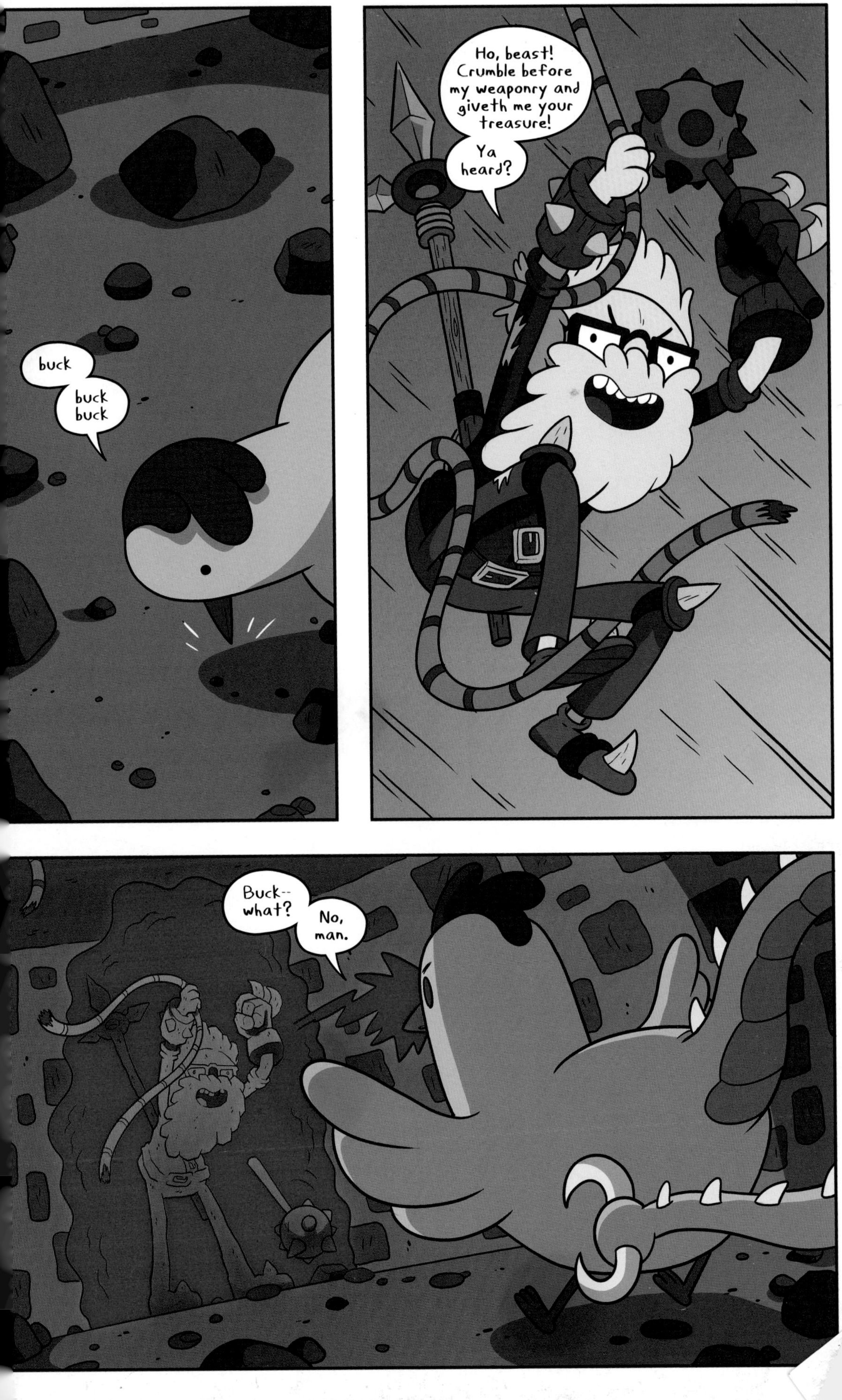
buck
buck buck
Ho, beast! Crumble before my weaponry and giveth me your treasure!
Ya heard?
Buck--what?
No, man.

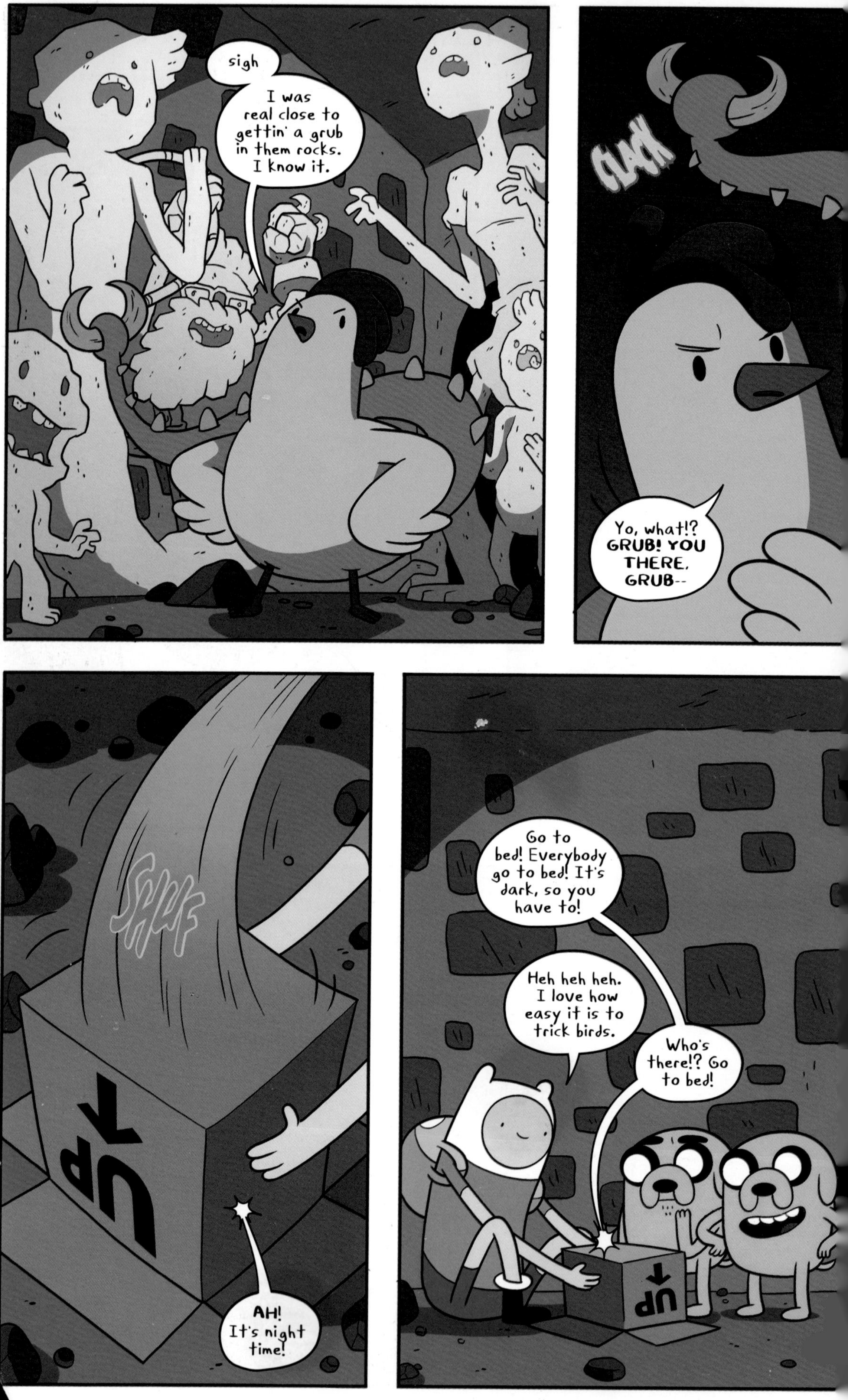
sigh
I was real close to gettin' a grub in them rocks. I know it.
CLACK
Yo, what!? GRUB! YOU THERE, GRUB--
SHLF
AH! It's night time!
UP
Go to bed! Everybody go to bed! It's dark, so you have to!
Heh heh heh. I love how easy it is to trick birds.
Who's there!? Go to bed!
UP

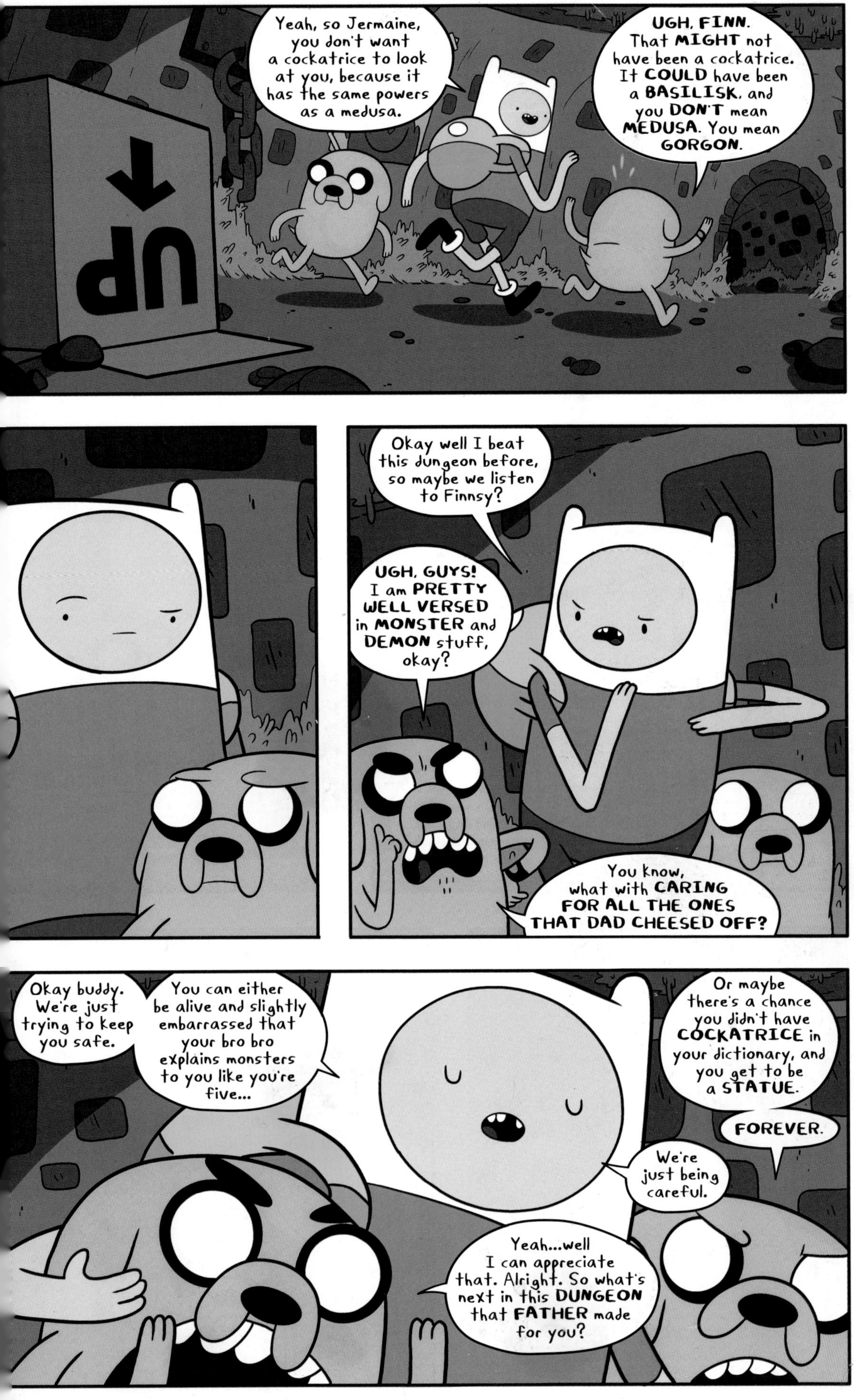

dn
Yeah, so Jermaine, you don't want a cockatrice to look at you, because it has the same powers as a medusa.
UGH, FINN. That MIGHT not have been a cockatrice. It COULD have been a BASILISK, and you DON'T mean MEDUSA. You mean GORGON.
Okay well I beat this dungeon before, so maybe we listen to Finnsy?
UGH, GUYS! I am PRETTY WELL VERSED in MONSTER and DEMON stuff, okay?
You know, what with CARING FOR ALL THE ONES THAT DAD CHEESED OFF?
Okay buddy. We're just trying to keep you safe.
You can either be alive and slightly embarrassed that your bro bro explains monsters to you like you're five...
Or maybe there's a chance you didn't have COCKATRICE in your dictionary, and you get to be a STATUE.
FOREVER.
We're just being careful.
Yeah...well I can appreciate that. Alright. So what's next in this DUNGEON that FATHER made for you?

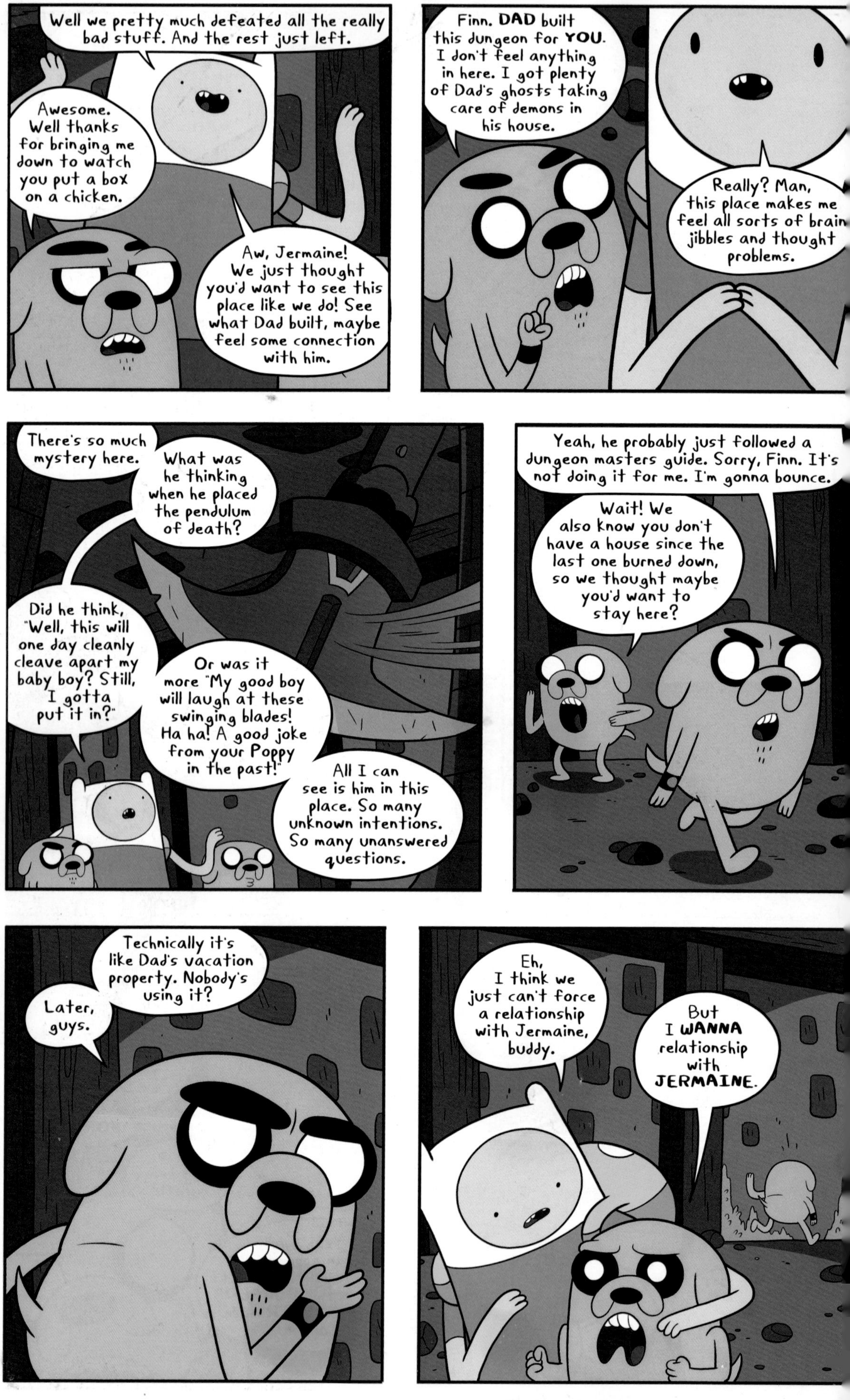

Well we pretty much defeated all the really bad stuff. And the rest just left.
Awesome. Well thanks for bringing me down to watch you put a box on a chicken.
Aw, Jermaine! We just thought you'd want to see this place like we do! See what Dad built, maybe feel some connection with him.
Finn. DAD built this dungeon for YOU. I don't feel anything in here. I got plenty of Dad's ghosts taking care of demons in his house.
Really? Man, this place makes me feel all sorts of brain jibbles and thought problems.
There's so much mystery here.
What was he thinking when he placed the pendulum of death?
Did he think, "Well, this will one day cleanly cleave apart my baby boy? Still, I gotta put it in?"
Or was it more "My good boy will laugh at these swinging blades! Ha ha! A good joke from your Poppy in the past!"
All I can see is him in this place. So many unknown intentions. So many unanswered questions.
Yeah, he probably just followed a dungeon masters guide. Sorry, Finn. It's not doing it for me. I'm gonna bounce.
Wait! We also know you don't have a house since the last one burned down, so we thought maybe you'd want to stay here?
Technically it's like Dad's vacation property. Nobody's using it?
Later, guys.
Eh, I think we just can't force a relationship with Jermaine, buddy.
But I WANNA relationship with JERMAINE.

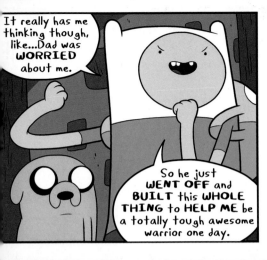

It really has me thinking though, like...Dad was **WORRIED** about me.

So he just **WENT OFF** and **BUILT** this **WHOLE THING** to **HELP ME** be a totally tough awesome warrior one day.

Which I did not need.

Which you did not need.

Obviously

But **STILL.** I wish I knew him better, and all I have are some crummy video messages, and this...

...what did all this mean...

Maybe you should do it yourself.

Hm?

Why not make your own dungeon, man? Go through the whole process, just like he did. It'll like... **CONNECT** the two of you...**ACROSS TIME!**

Build my own dungeon, eh?

Yes! Yes, eh!

I think I'm into that! **I THINK I'M REAL INTO IT, BRO!**

Ha ha! Yeah! D. I. Y. **DUNGEON!**

I wanna do it too.

Natch.

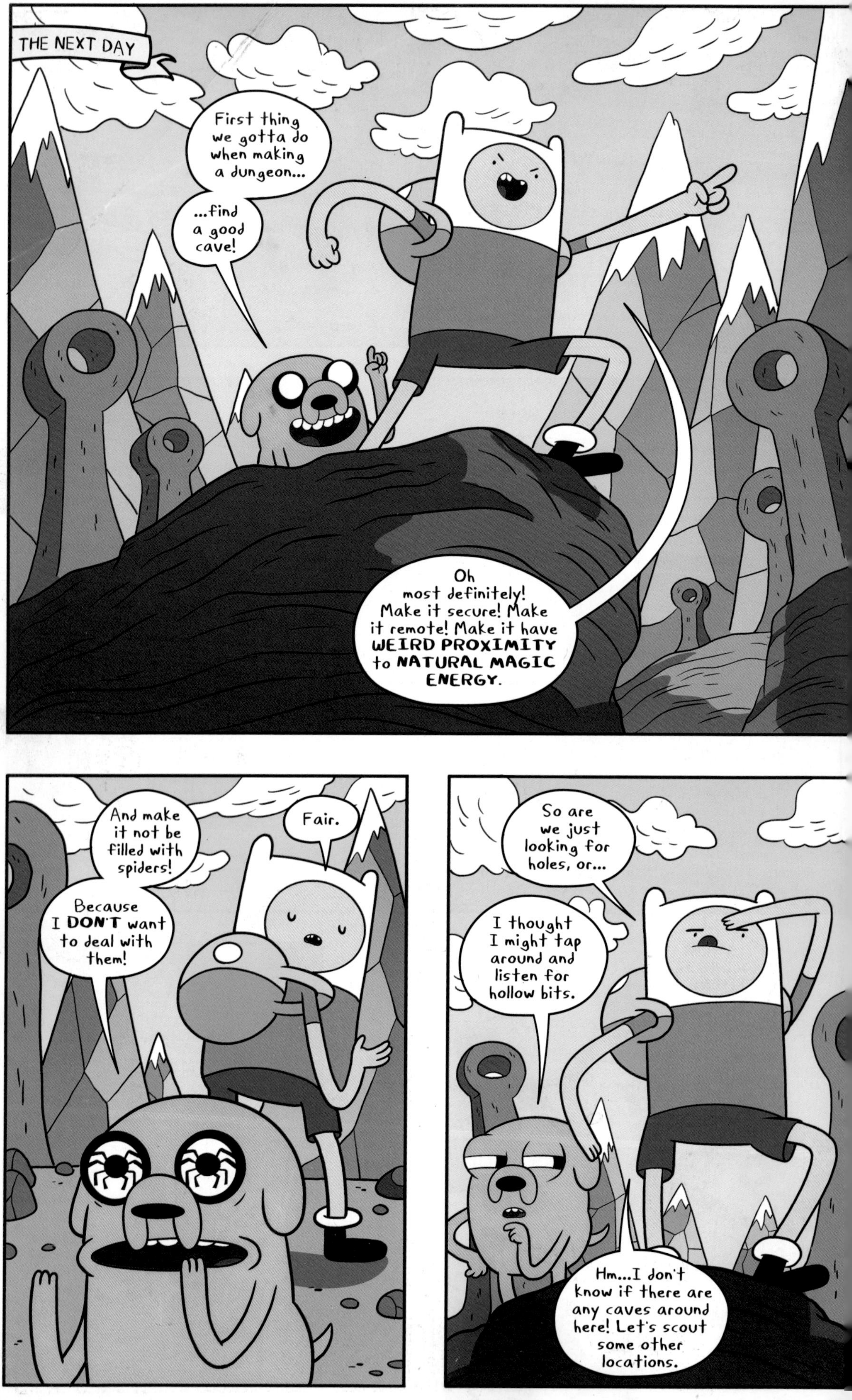
THE NEXT DAY
First thing we gotta do when making a dungeon...
...find a good cave!
Oh most definitely! Make it secure! Make it remote! Make it have **WEIRD PROXIMITY** to **NATURAL MAGIC ENERGY**.
And make it not be filled with spiders!
Because I **DON'T** want to deal with them!
Fair.
So are we just looking for holes, or...
I thought I might tap around and listen for hollow bits.
Hm...I don't know if there are any caves around here! Let's scout some other locations.

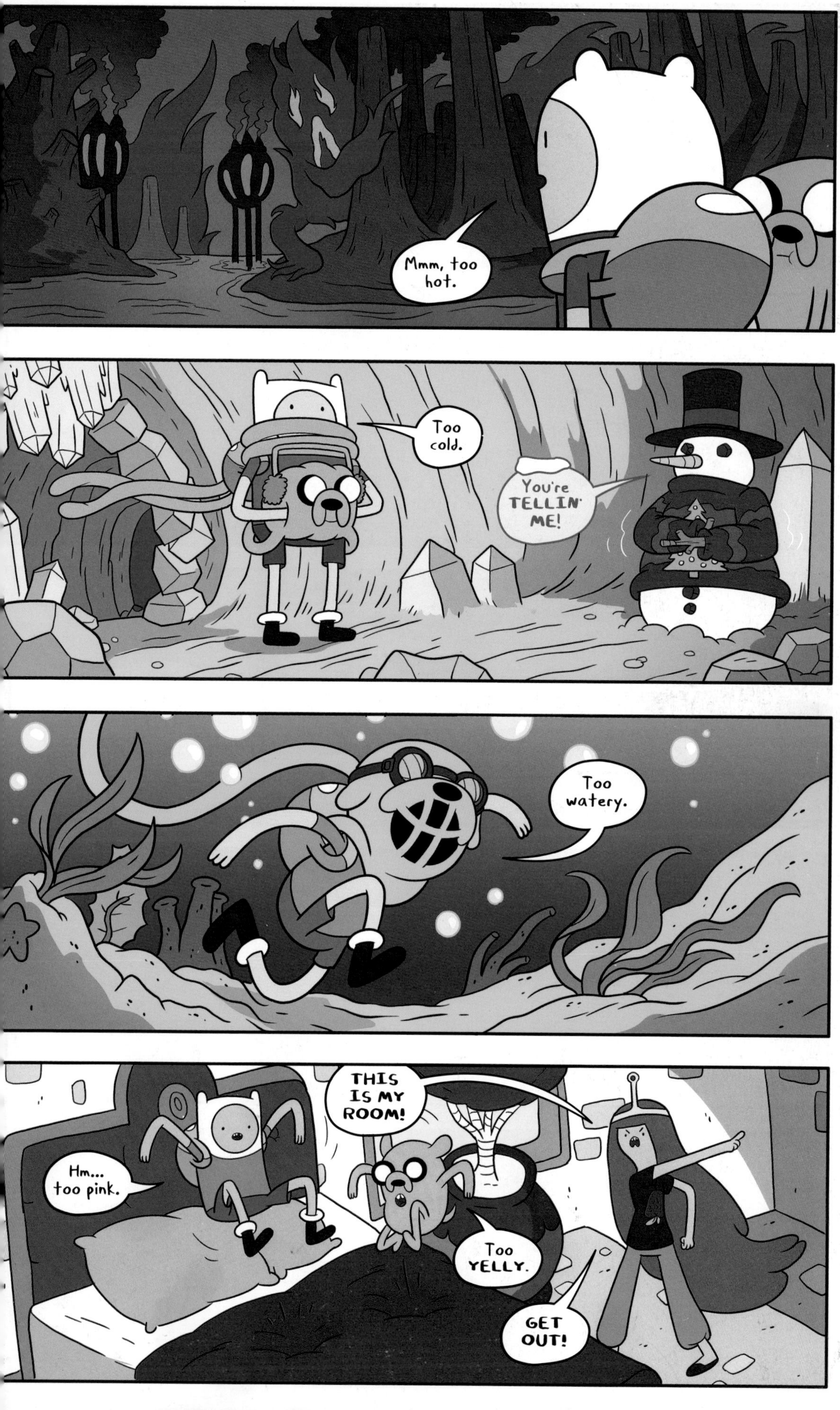

Mmm, too hot.
Too cold.
You're TELLIN' ME!
Too watery.
THIS IS MY ROOM!
Hm... too pink.
Too YELLY.
GET OUT!

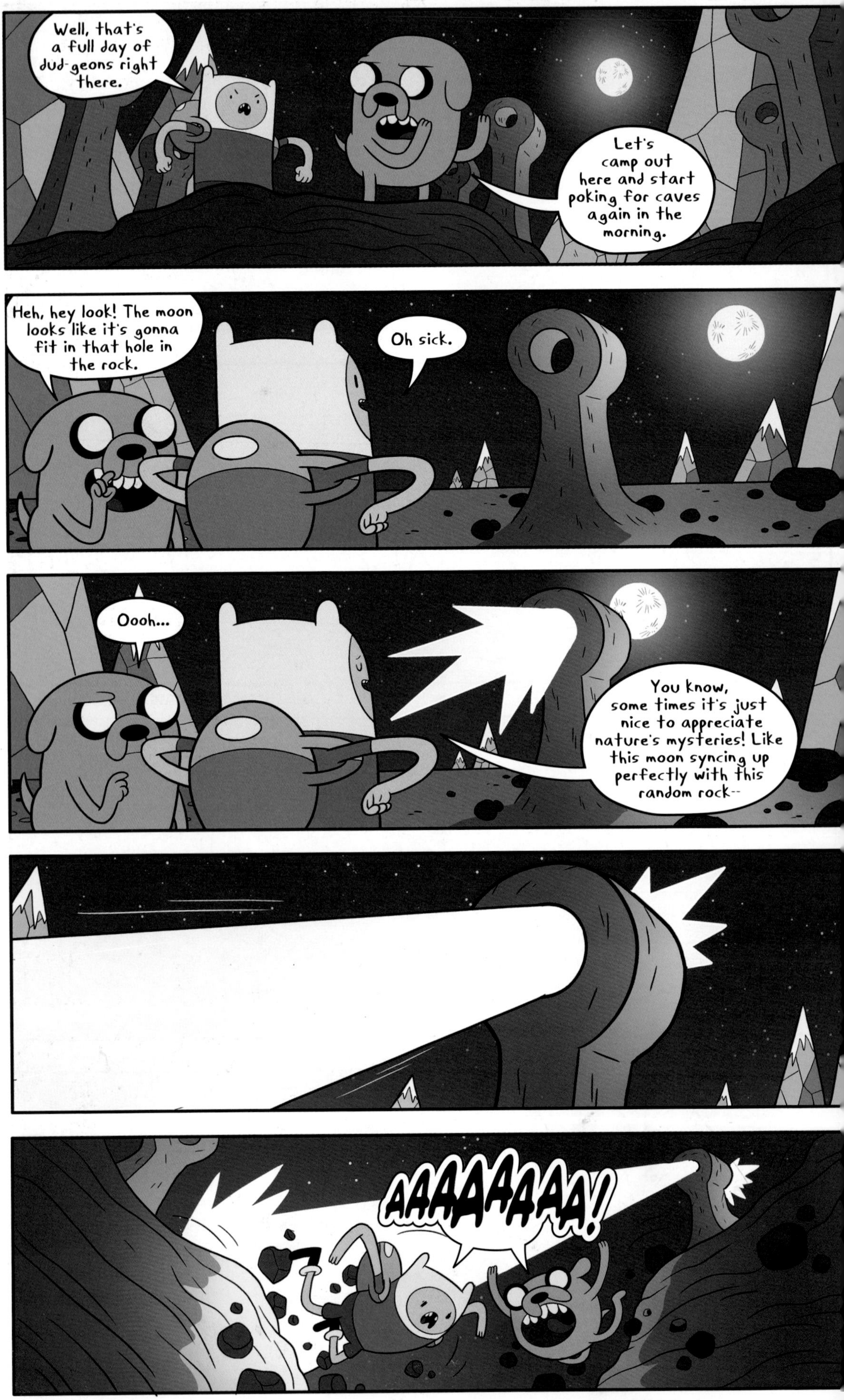
Well, that's a full day of dud-geons right there.
Let's camp out here and start poking for caves again in the morning.
Heh, hey look! The moon looks like it's gonna fit in that hole in the rock.
Oh sick.
Oooh...
You know, some times it's just nice to appreciate nature's mysteries! Like this moon syncing up perfectly with this random rock--
AAAAAAAA!

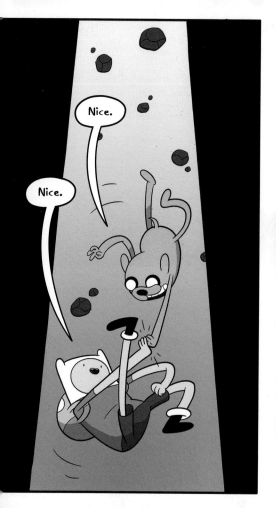

Nice.

Nice.

Whoah, buddy! I think...this might be IT!

You tryin' to tell me a hole that opened up because of the placement of the moon **MIGHT BE AN INDICATION OF PROXIMITY TO NATURAL MAGICAL ENERGY?**

WHICH WAS ONE OF OUR CRITERIA FOR A DUNGEON SPOT?

I MIGHT BE, BUDDY MAN!

OOOH THAT'S WHAT I LIKE!

Okay so like, let's scope it out, then we can start planning--

Wait, shush.

We're not alone.

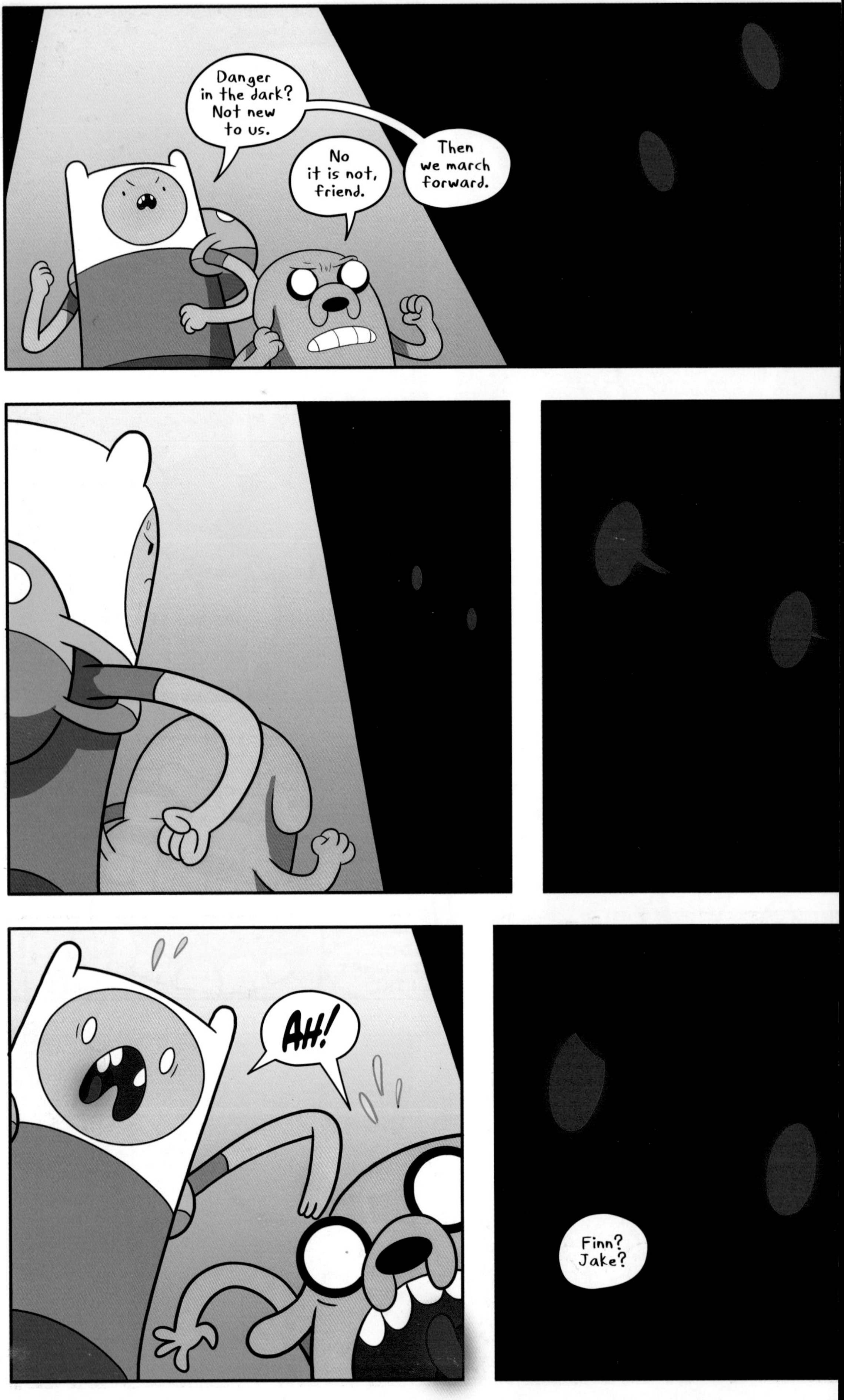
Danger in the dark? Not new to us.
No it is not, friend.
Then we march forward.
AH!
Finn? Jake?

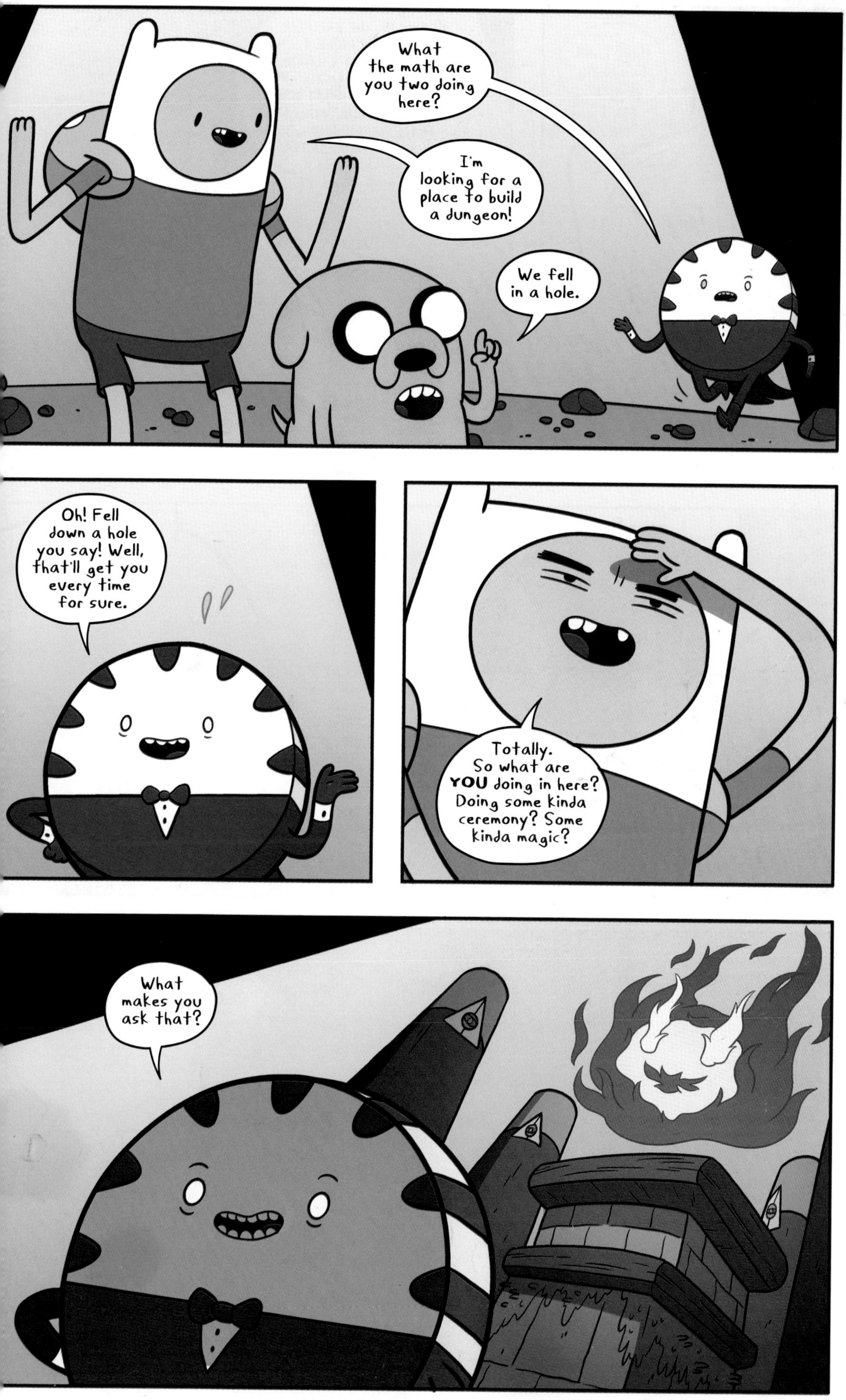

What the math are you two doing here?
I'm looking for a place to build a dungeon!
We fell in a hole.
Oh! Fell down a hole you say! Well, that'll get you every time for sure.
Totally. So what are **YOU** doing in here? Doing some kinda ceremony? Some kinda magic?
What makes you ask that?

Hey, that fire looks like m--

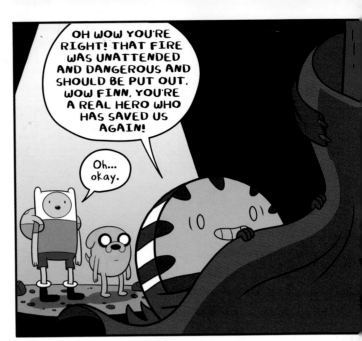

OH WOW YOU'RE RIGHT! THAT FIRE WAS UNATTENDED AND DANGEROUS AND SHOULD BE PUT OUT. WOW FINN, YOU'RE A REAL HERO WHO HAS SAVED US AGAIN!

Oh... okay.

Well I should go. There's a real nice natural magic flowing through this place. It's why I was here. Gave a clarity like no other. Enjoy it in your dungeoning!

Nice, man. REAL nice.

Yeah... hey how did HE get in there before us?

Ah, a dungeon of mystery.

Nice.

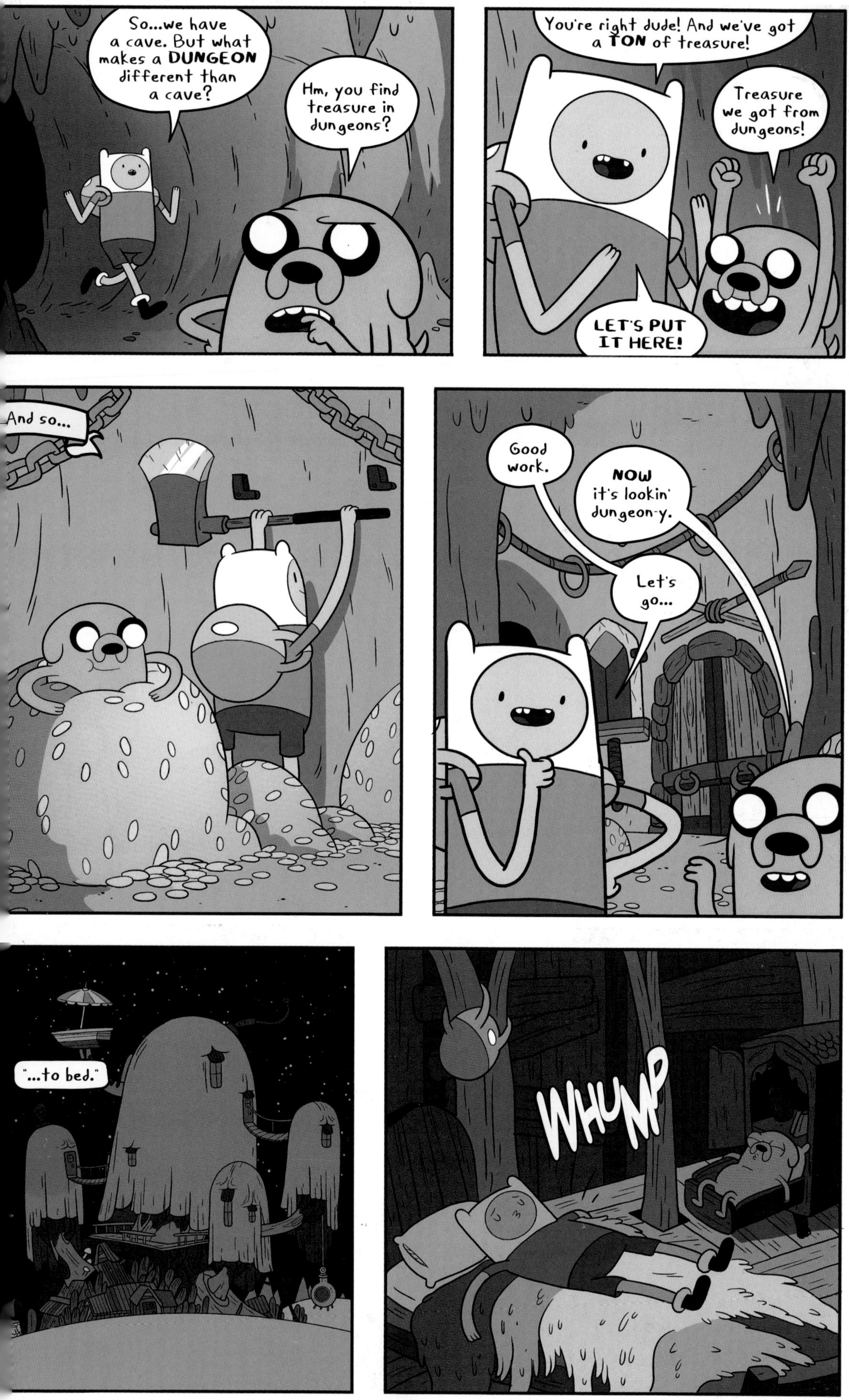
So...we have a cave. But what makes a DUNGEON different than a cave?
Hm, you find treasure in dungeons?
You're right dude! And we've got a TON of treasure!
Treasure we got from dungeons!
LET'S PUT IT HERE!
And so...
Good work.
NOW it's lookin' dungeon-y.
Let's go...
"...to bed."
WHUMP

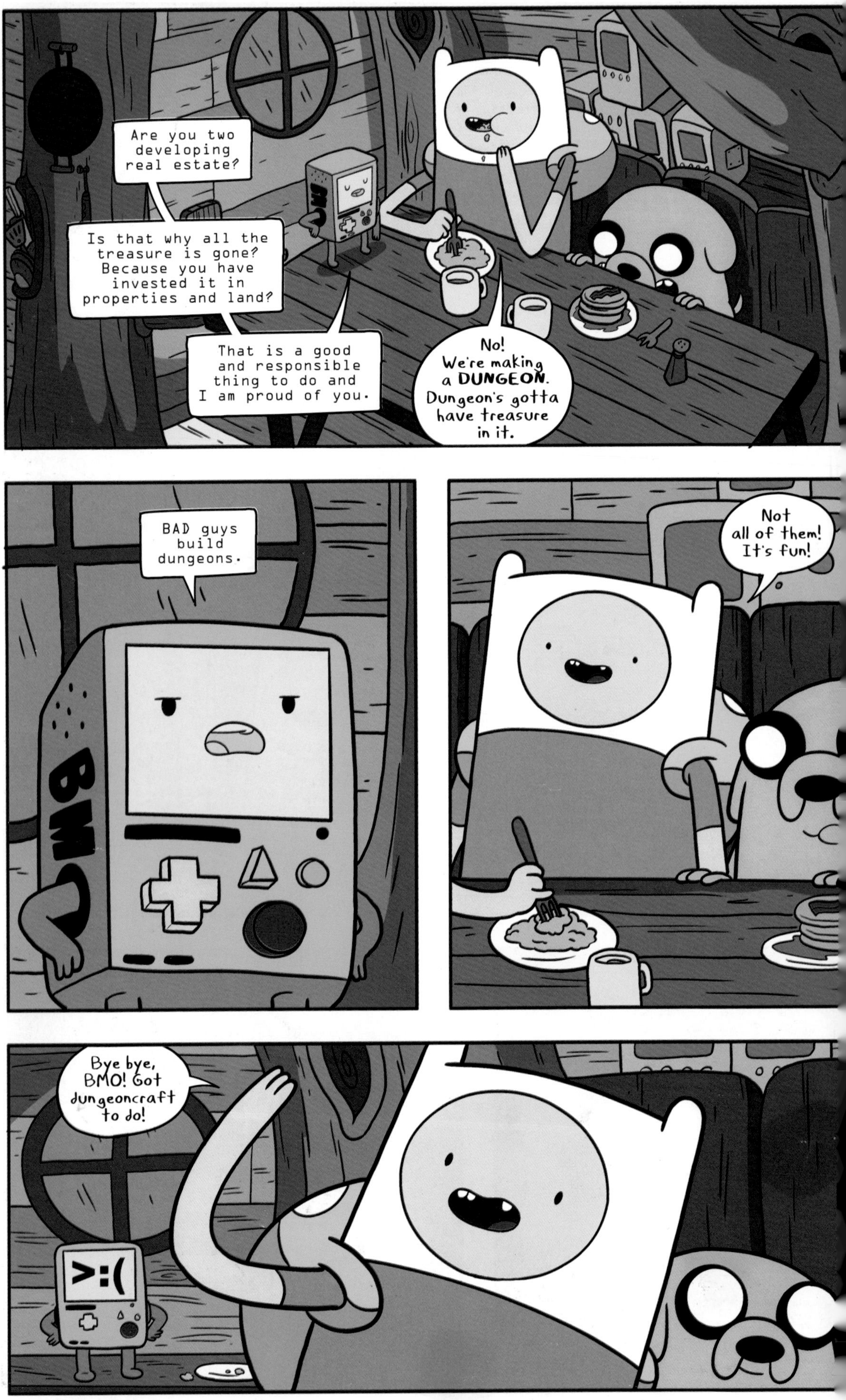
Are you two developing real estate?
Is that why all the treasure is gone? Because you have invested it in properties and land?
That is a good and responsible thing to do and I am proud of you.
No! We're making a DUNGEON. Dungeon's gotta have treasure in it.
BAD guys build dungeons.
Not all of them! It's fun!
Bye bye, BMO! Got dungeoncraft to do!
BMO
>:(

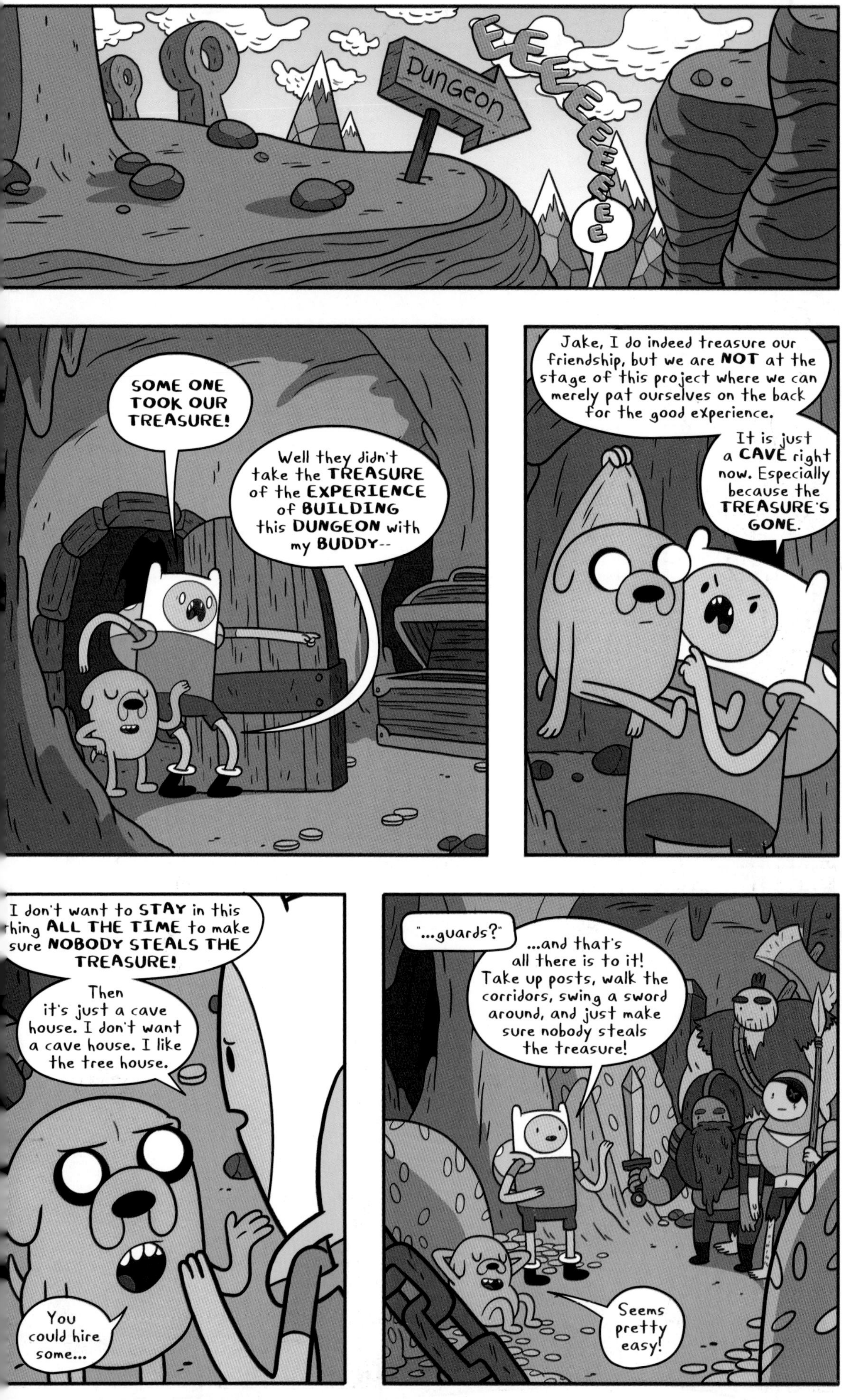

DUNGEON
EEEEEEEEE
SOME ONE TOOK OUR TREASURE!
Well they didn't take the TREASURE of the EXPERIENCE of BUILDING this DUNGEON with my BUDDY--
Jake, I do indeed treasure our friendship, but we are NOT at the stage of this project where we can merely pat ourselves on the back for the good experience.
It is just a CAVE right now. Especially because the TREASURE'S GONE.
I don't want to STAY in this thing ALL THE TIME to make sure NOBODY STEALS THE TREASURE!
Then it's just a cave house. I don't want a cave house. I like the tree house.
You could hire some...
"...guards?"
...and that's all there is to it! Take up posts, walk the corridors, swing a sword around, and just make sure nobody steals the treasure!
Seems pretty easy!

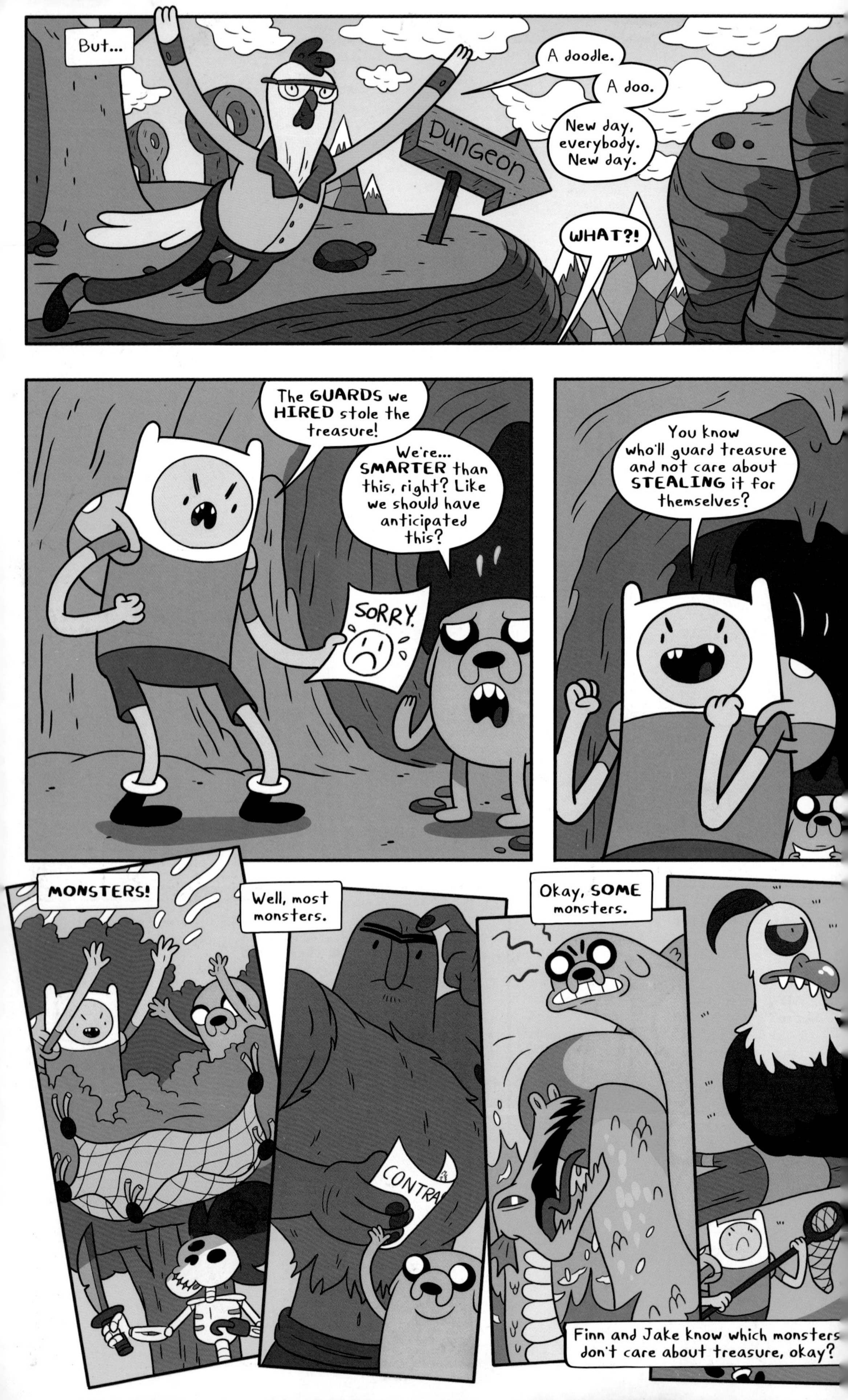

But...
A doodle.
A doo.
New day, everybody. New day.
DUNGEON
WHAT?!
The GUARDS we HIRED stole the treasure!
We're... SMARTER than this, right? Like we should have anticipated this?
SORRY.
You know who'll guard treasure and not care about STEALING it for themselves?
MONSTERS!
Well, most monsters.
CONTRA
Okay, SOME monsters.
Finn and Jake know which monsters don't care about treasure, okay?

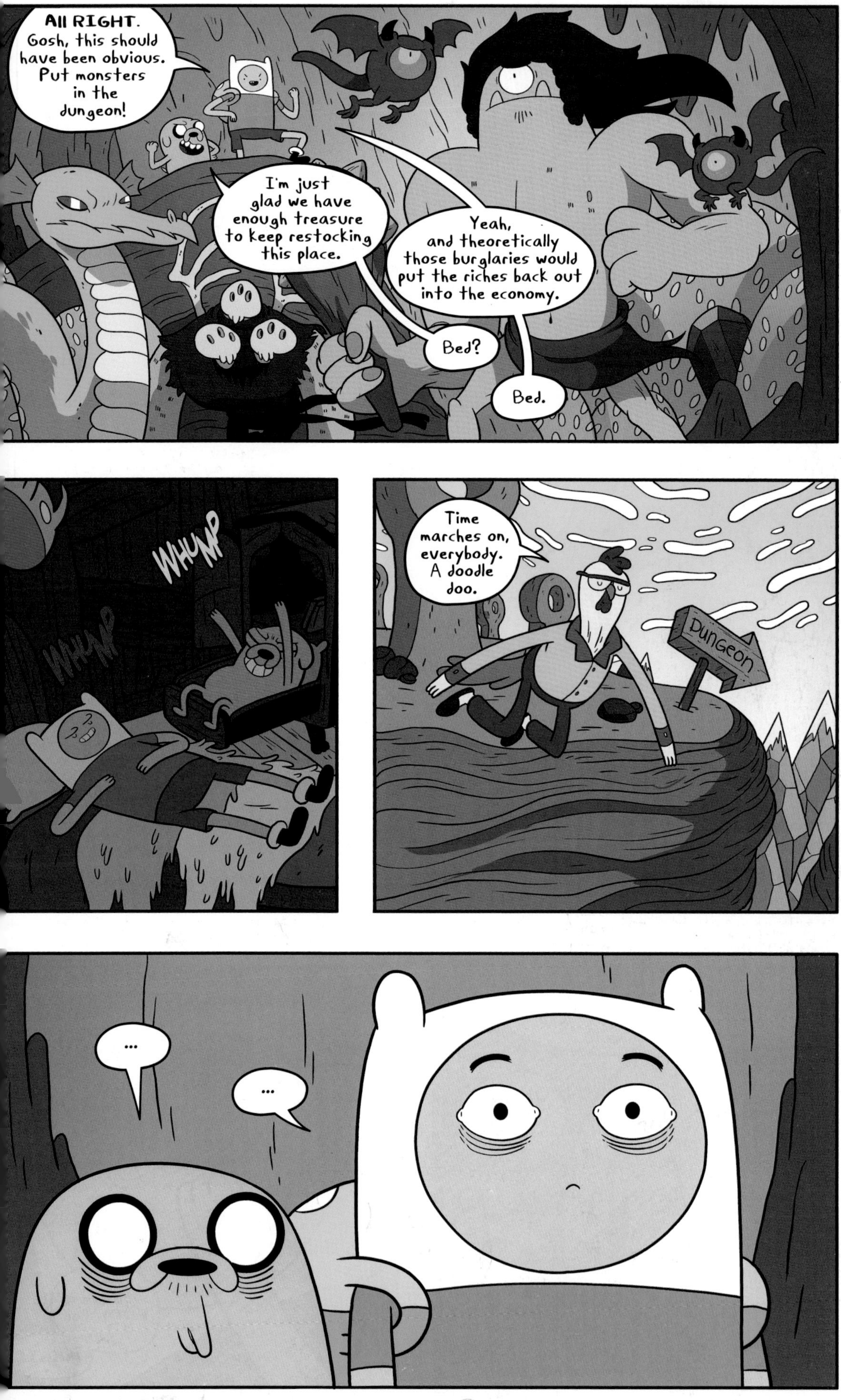

All RIGHT. Gosh, this should have been obvious. Put monsters in the dungeon!
I'm just glad we have enough treasure to keep restocking this place.
Yeah, and theoretically those burglaries would put the riches back out into the economy.
Bed?
Bed.
WHUMP
WHUMP
Time marches on, everybody. A doodle doo.
Dungeon
...
...

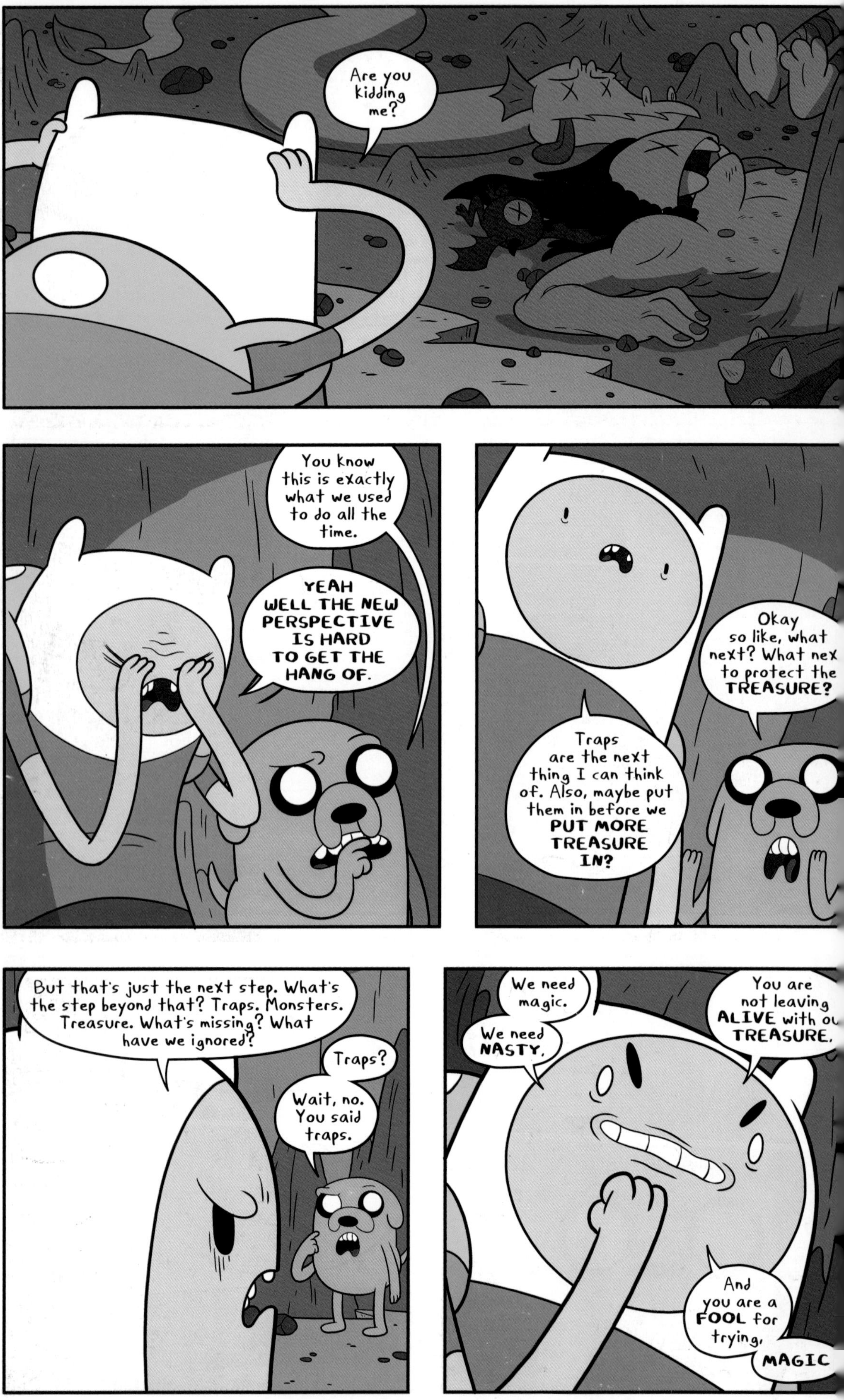
Are you kidding me?
You know this is exactly what we used to do all the time.
YEAH WELL THE NEW PERSPECTIVE IS HARD TO GET THE HANG OF.
Okay so like, what next? What nex to protect the TREASURE?
Traps are the next thing I can think of. Also, maybe put them in before we PUT MORE TREASURE IN?
But that's just the next step. What's the step beyond that? Traps. Monsters. Treasure. What's missing? What have we ignored?
Traps?
Wait, no. You said traps.
We need magic.
We need NASTY.
You are not leaving ALIVE with ou TREASURE.
And you are a FOOL for trying,
MAGIC

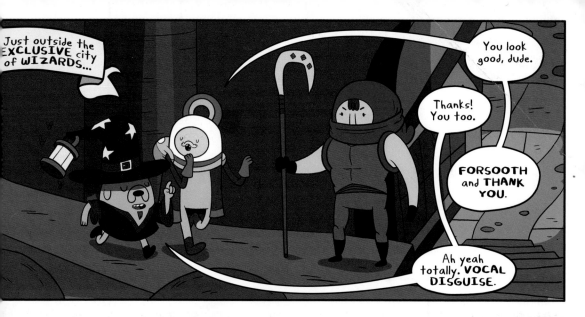

Just outside the **EXCLUSIVE** city of **WIZARDS**...

You look good, dude.

Thanks! You too.

FORSOOTH and **THANK YOU.**

Ah yeah totally. **VOCAL DISGUISE.**

"Wizards only, fools."

That's the password, boys! Have a magical day!

HA HA! BUT WE MUST! As we are **WIZARDS!** Every **DAY** is magical for **US!**

...

It's just a courtesy, man.

Eh, not great for a **DUNGEON**...

I don't know what **THIS** even does...

Ah can I **HELP** you?

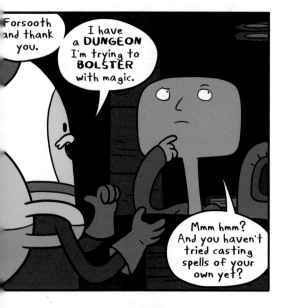

Forsooth and thank you.

I have a **DUNGEON** I'm trying to **BOLSTER** with magic.

Mmm hmm? And you haven't tried casting spells of your own yet?

Uh, forsooth! I have tried! But it simply isn't **STRONG** enough magic. You understand. Very embarrassing.

Ah, well I might not have anything here but perhaps you should visit...

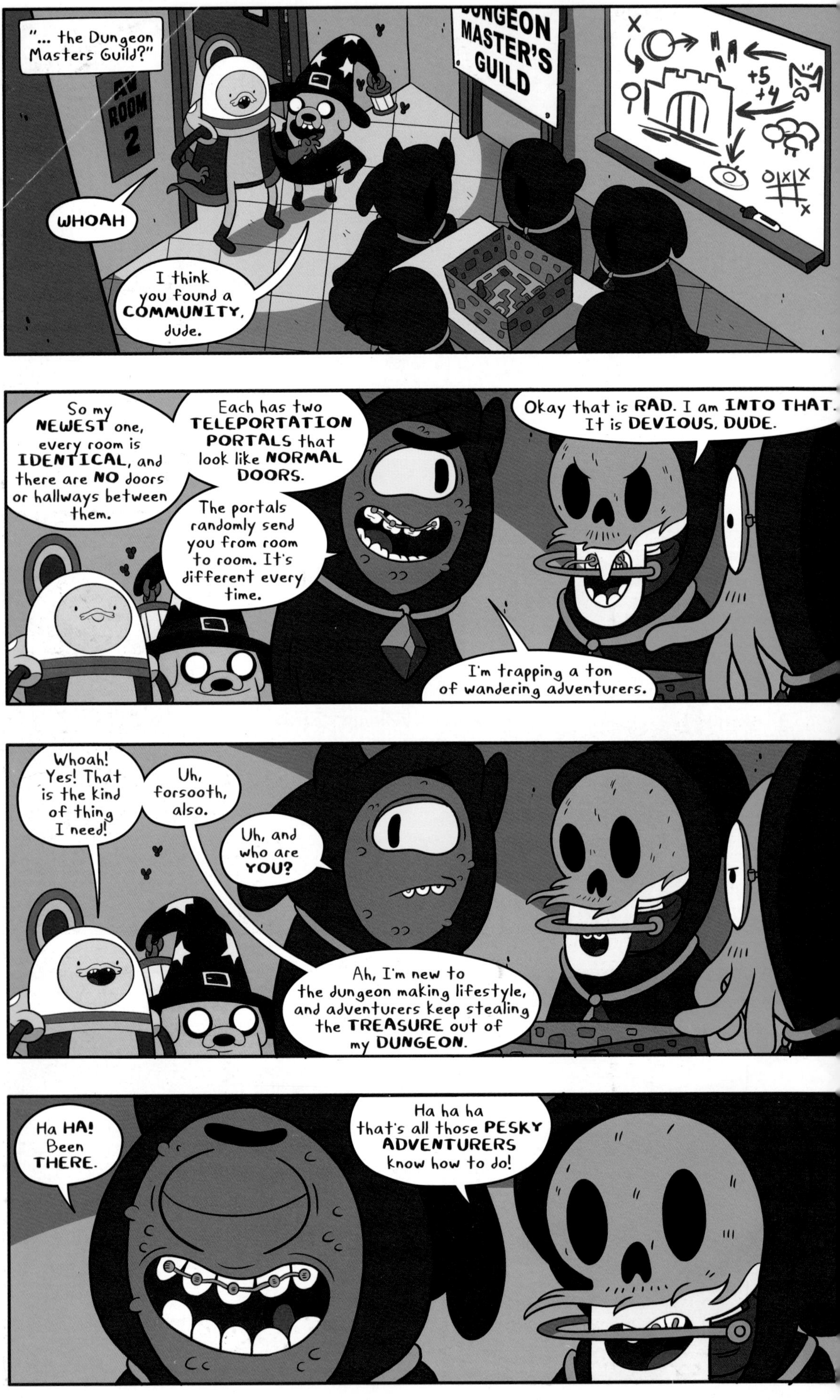
"... the Dungeon Masters Guild?"
AV ROOM 2
DUNGEON MASTER'S GUILD
+5 +4
WHOAH
I think you found a COMMUNITY, dude.
So my NEWEST one, every room is IDENTICAL, and there are NO doors or hallways between them.
Each has two TELEPORTATION PORTALS that look like NORMAL DOORS.
The portals randomly send you from room to room. It's different every time.
Okay that is RAD. I am INTO THAT. It is DEVIOUS, DUDE.
I'm trapping a ton of wandering adventurers.
Whoah! Yes! That is the kind of thing I need!
Uh, forsooth, also.
Uh, and who are YOU?
Ah, I'm new to the dungeon making lifestyle, and adventurers keep stealing the TREASURE out of my DUNGEON.
Ha HA! Been THERE.
Ha ha ha that's all those PESKY ADVENTURERS know how to do!

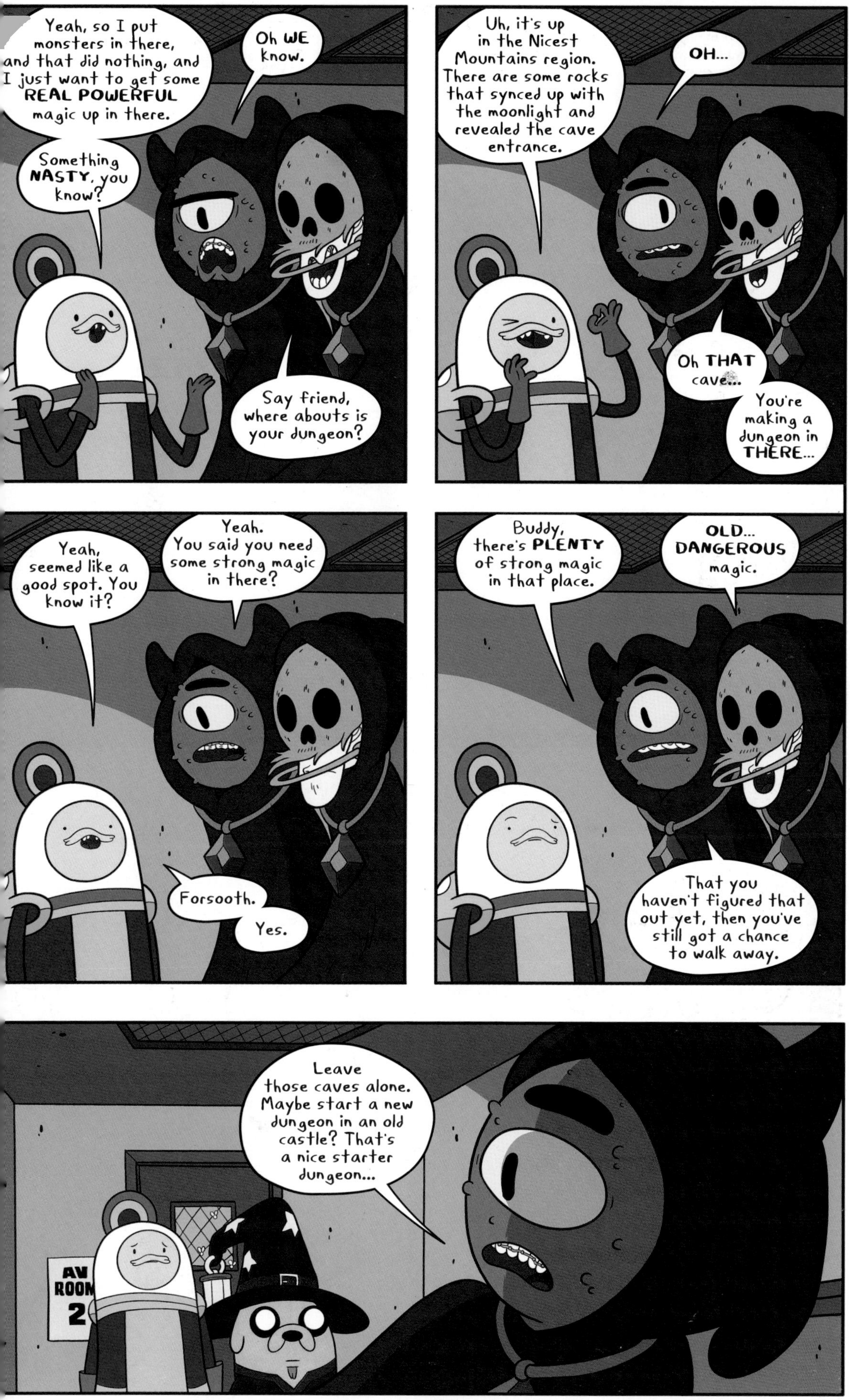
Yeah, so I put monsters in there, and that did nothing, and I just want to get some REAL POWERFUL magic up in there.
Oh WE know.
Something NASTY, you know?
Say friend, where abouts is your dungeon?
Uh, it's up in the Nicest Mountains region. There are some rocks that synced up with the moonlight and revealed the cave entrance.
OH...
Oh THAT cave...
You're making a dungeon in THERE...
Yeah, seemed like a good spot. You know it?
Yeah. You said you need some strong magic in there?
Forsooth.
Yes.
Buddy, there's PLENTY of strong magic in that place.
OLD... DANGEROUS magic.
That you haven't figured that out yet, then you've still got a chance to walk away.
Leave those caves alone. Maybe start a new dungeon in an old castle? That's a nice starter dungeon...
AV ROOM 2

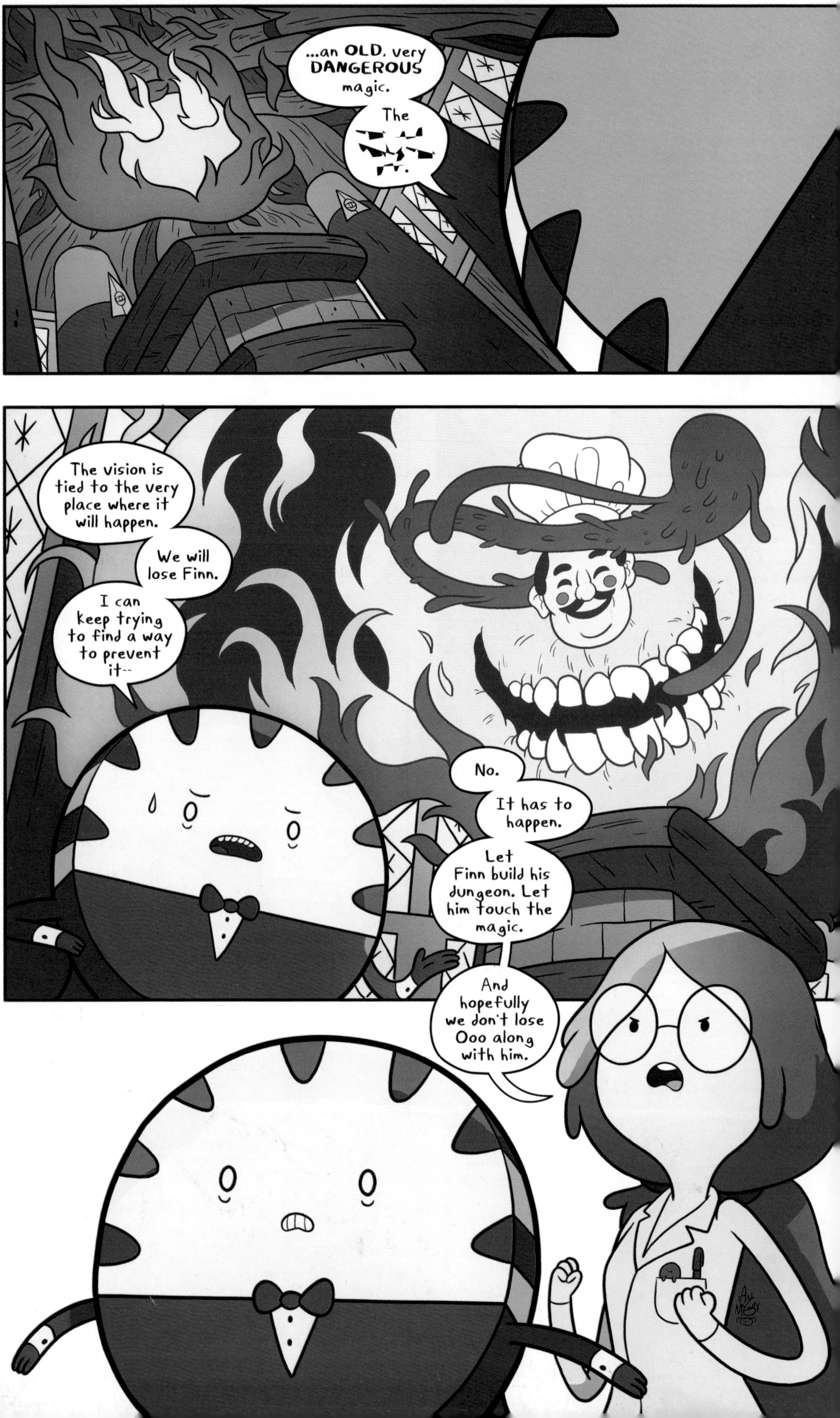

...an OLD, very DANGEROUS magic.
The
The vision is tied to the very place where it will happen.
We will lose Finn.
I can keep trying to find a way to prevent it--
No.
It has to happen.
Let Finn build his dungeon. Let him touch the magic.
And hopefully we don't lose Ooo along with him.

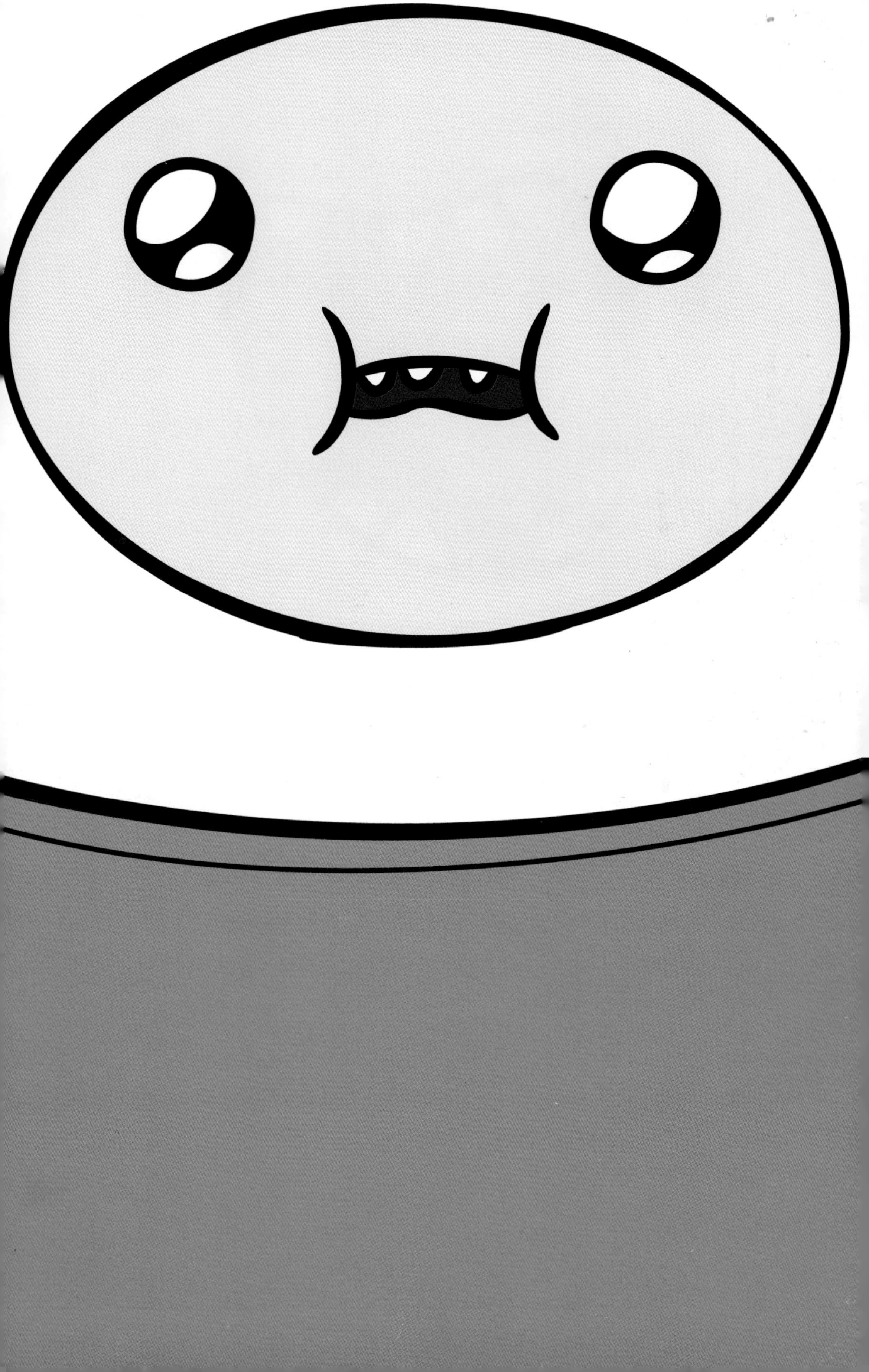

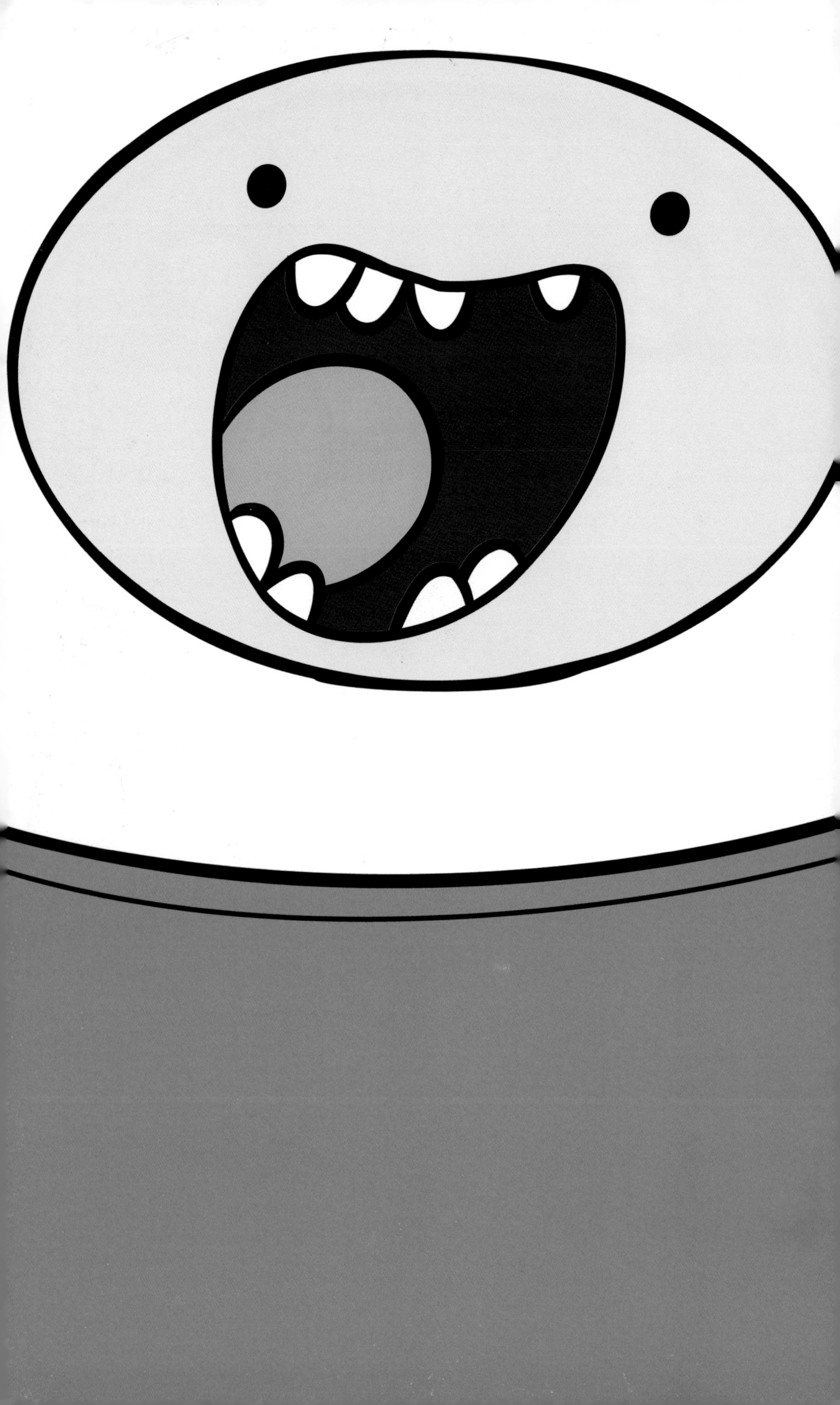

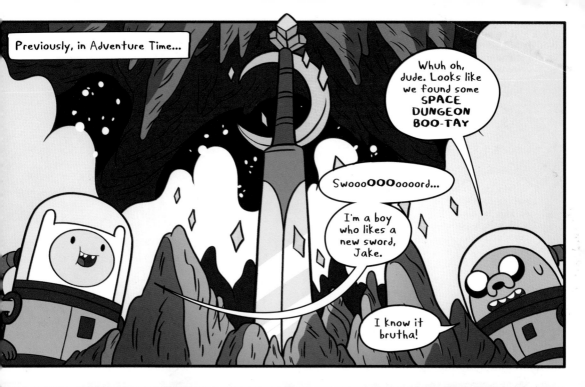

Previously, in Adventure Time...

Whuh oh, dude. Looks like we found some **SPACE DUNGEON BOO-TAY**

SwoooOOOoooord...

I'm a boy who likes a new sword, Jake.

I know it brutha!

Ha ha ha

WOWMP

SKA BOOOM

Catch you later, giant weirdo that wanted to cook **ALL OF OOO**.

We gotta worry about you pulling any more shenanigans, ma'am?

Maybe? I'm not going to stop trying to do nice things! I think Arklothac cooking Ooo would have been **VERY NICE.**

Ha ha, but seriously, do this again, I'm-ah punch you up for real.

MUMBLE.

AND DON'T FORGET ABOUT **ME!**

I POSSESSED YOUR SWORD. BEEN HERE THIS WHOLE TIME.

AAAAAAAA!

AAAAAAAA!

SPLOOSH!

Hope that thing doesn't possess a **SHARK** or something now.

It said it couldn't possess living things.

Shark **SKELETON** then.

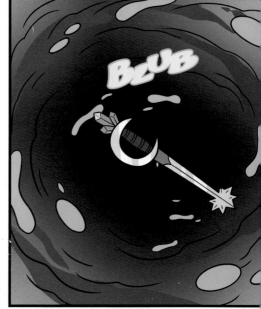

BLUB

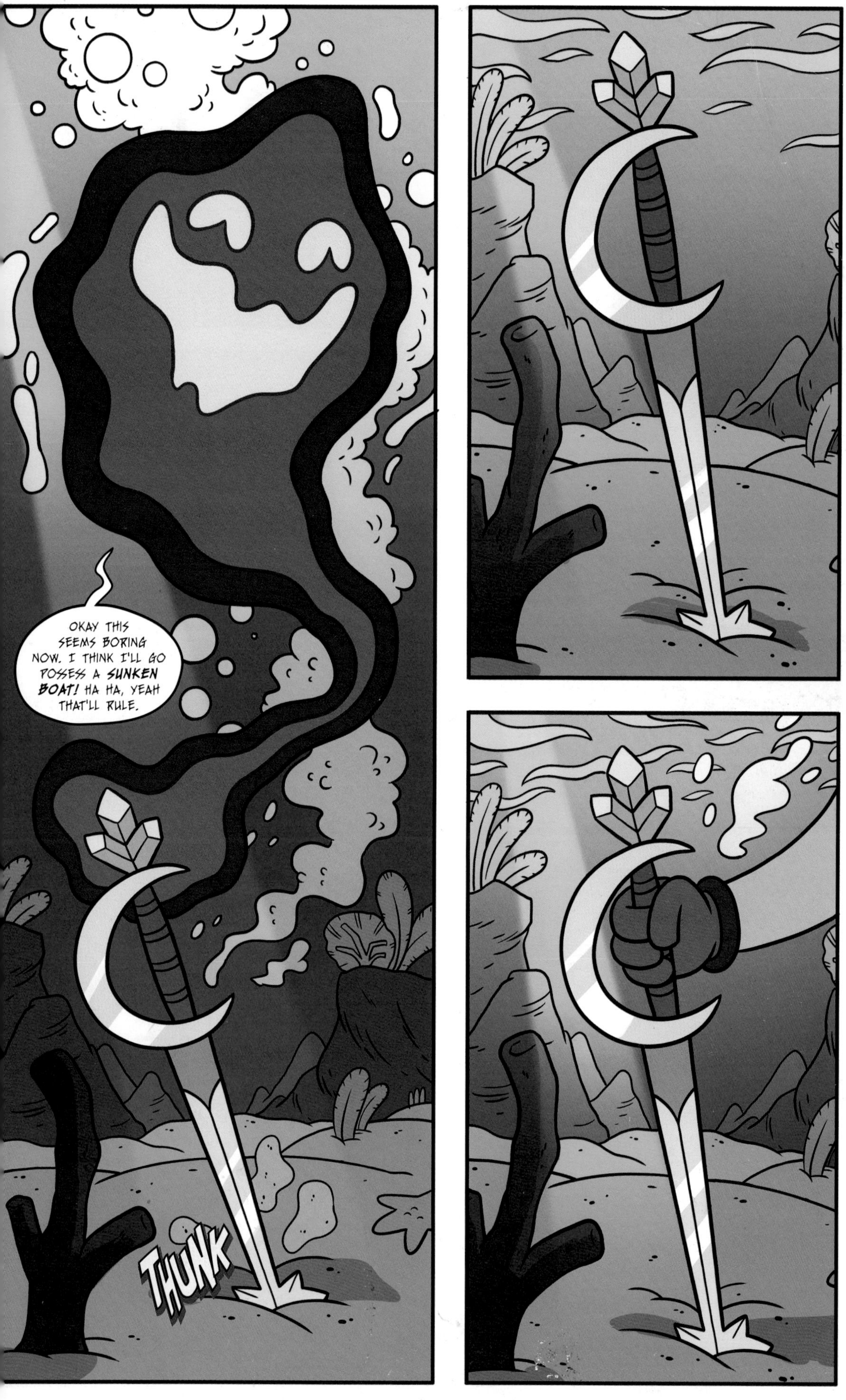
OKAY THIS SEEMS BORING NOW. I THINK I'LL GO POSSESS A SUNKEN BOAT! HA HA, YEAH THAT'LL RULE.
THUNK

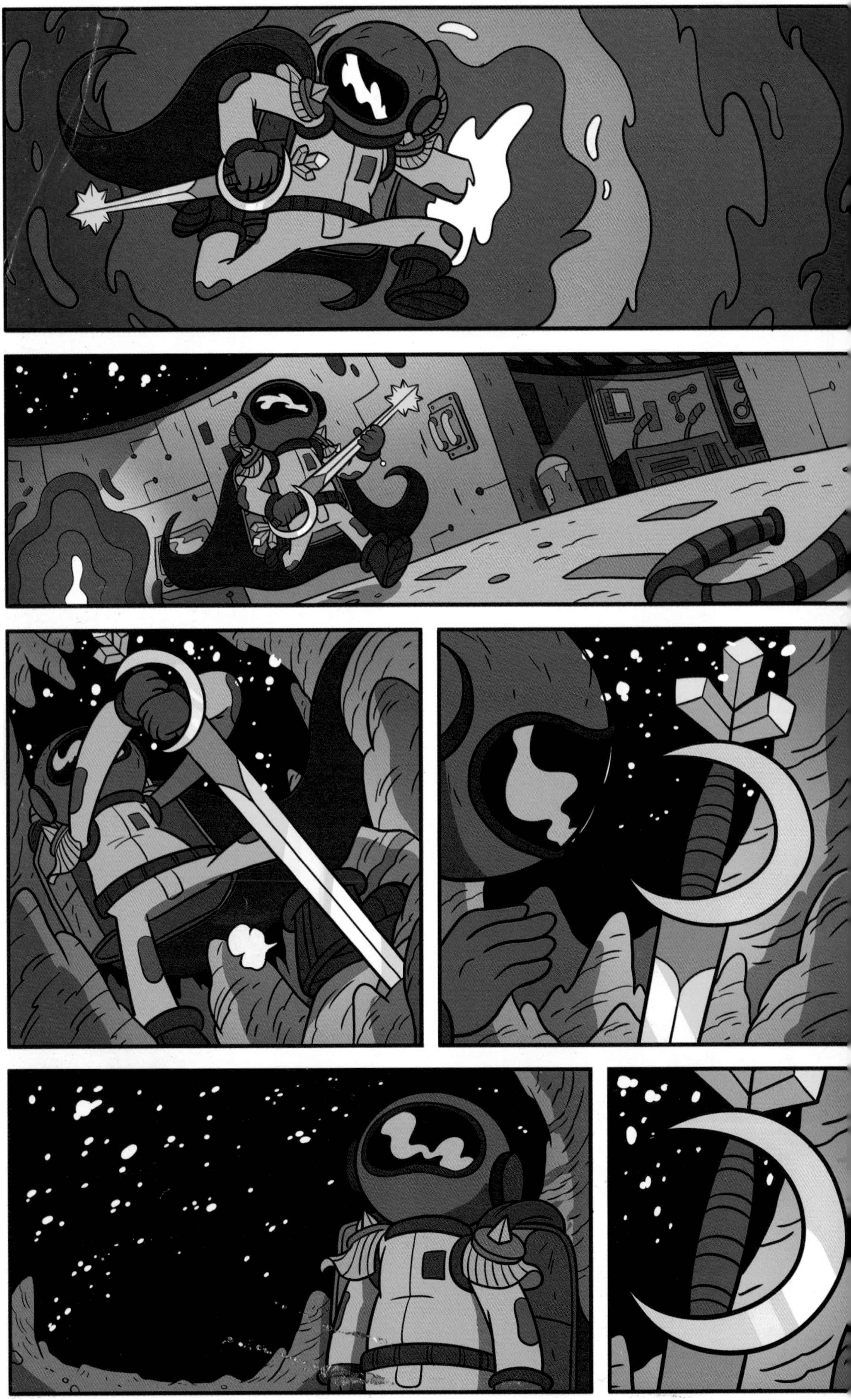

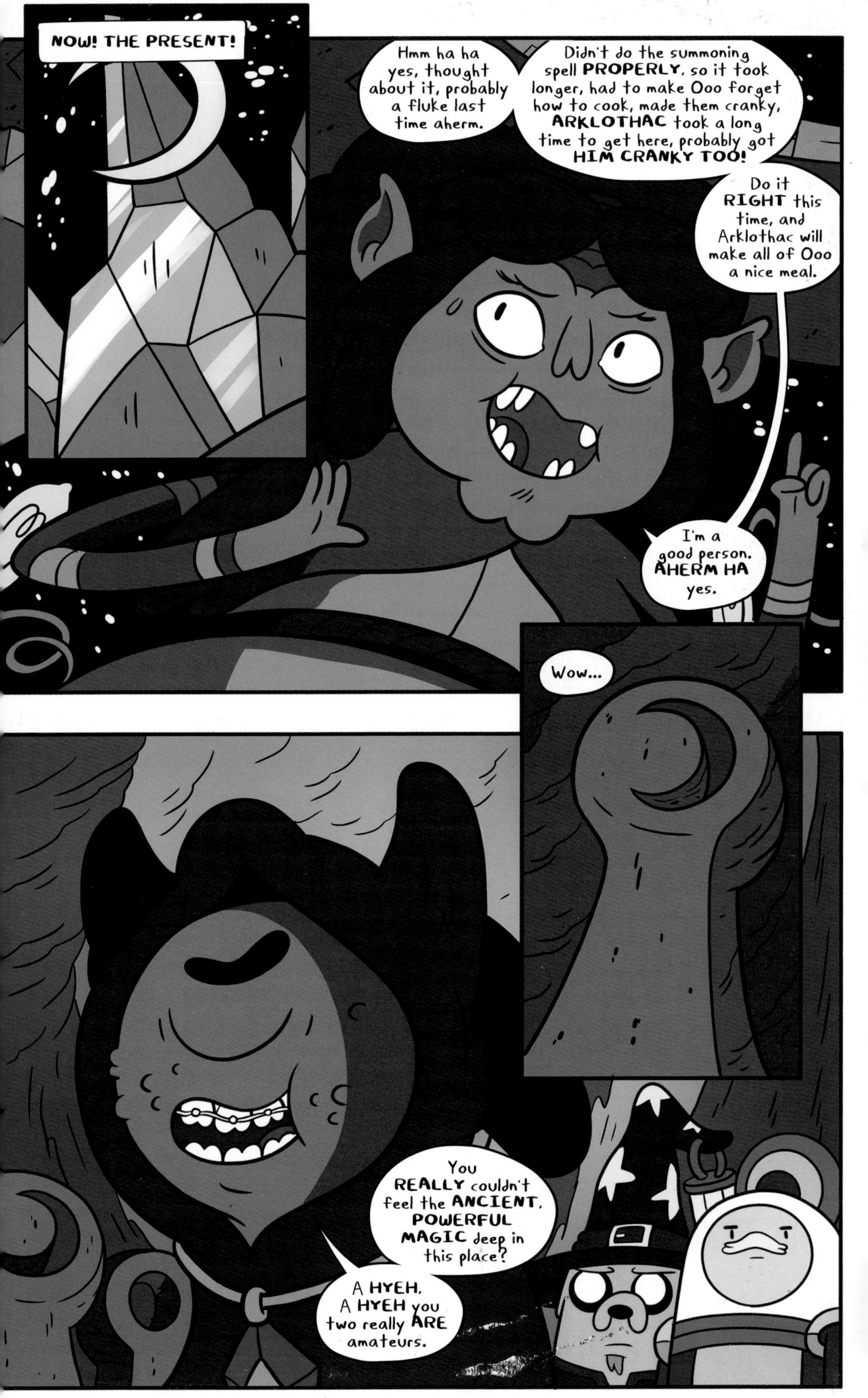

NOW! THE PRESENT!
Hmm ha ha yes, thought about it, probably a fluke last time aherm.
Didn't do the summoning spell PROPERLY, so it took longer, had to make Ooo forget how to cook, made them cranky, ARKLOTHAC took a long time to get here, probably got HIM CRANKY TOO!
Do it RIGHT this time, and Arklothac will make all of Ooo a nice meal.
I'm a good person. AHERM HA yes.
Wow...
You REALLY couldn't feel the ANCIENT, POWERFUL MAGIC deep in this place?
A HYEH, A HYEH you two really ARE amateurs.

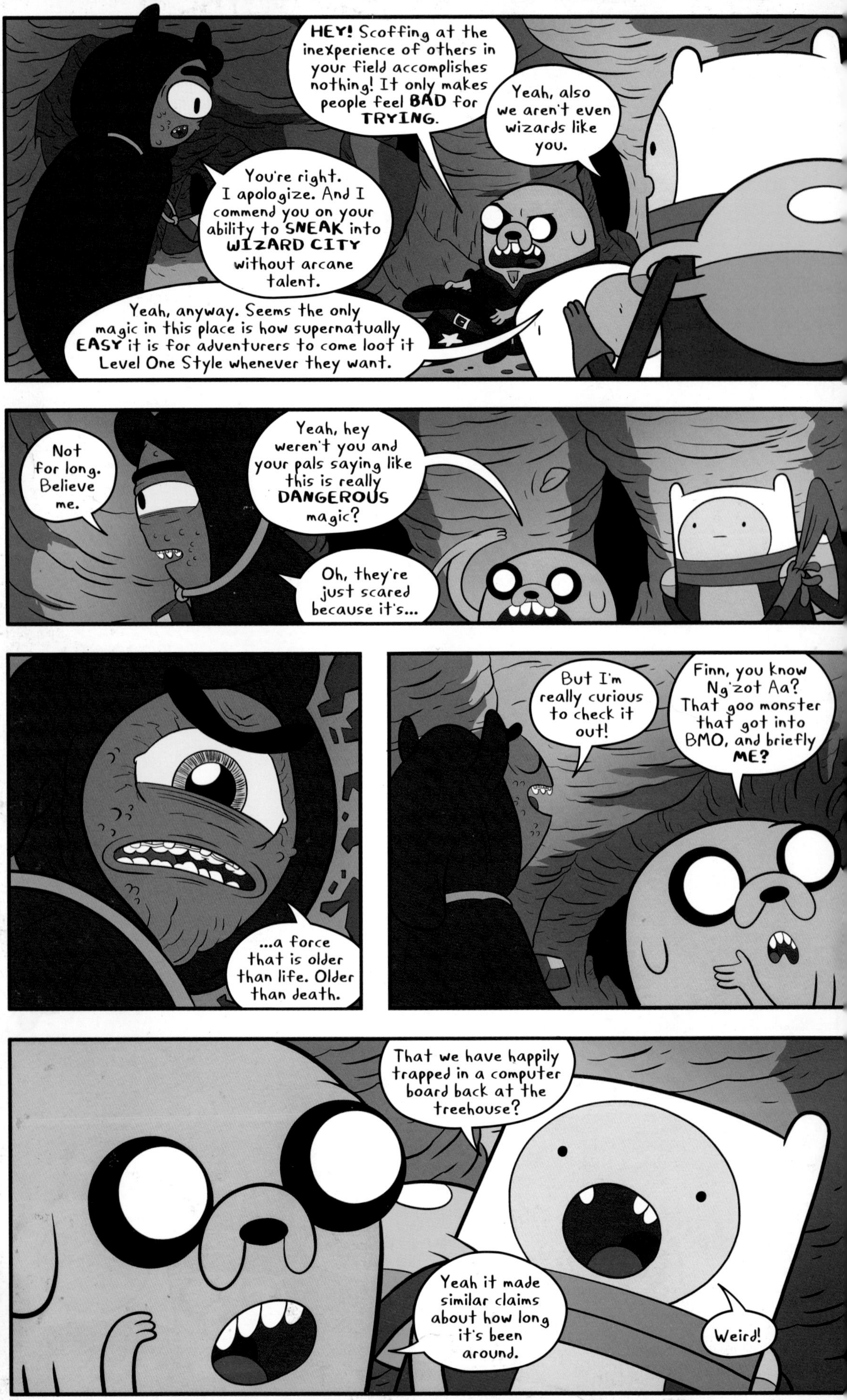

HEY! Scoffing at the inexperience of others in your field accomplishes nothing! It only makes people feel BAD for TRYING.
Yeah, also we aren't even wizards like you.
You're right. I apologize. And I commend you on your ability to SNEAK into WIZARD CITY without arcane talent.
Yeah, anyway. Seems the only magic in this place is how supernatually EASY it is for adventurers to come loot it Level One Style whenever they want.
Not for long. Believe me.
Yeah, hey weren't you and your pals saying like this is really DANGEROUS magic?
Oh, they're just scared because it's...
...a force that is older than life. Older than death.
But I'm really curious to check it out!
Finn, you know Ng'zot Aa? That goo monster that got into BMO, and briefly ME?
That we have happily trapped in a computer board back at the treehouse?
Yeah it made similar claims about how long it's been around.
Weird!

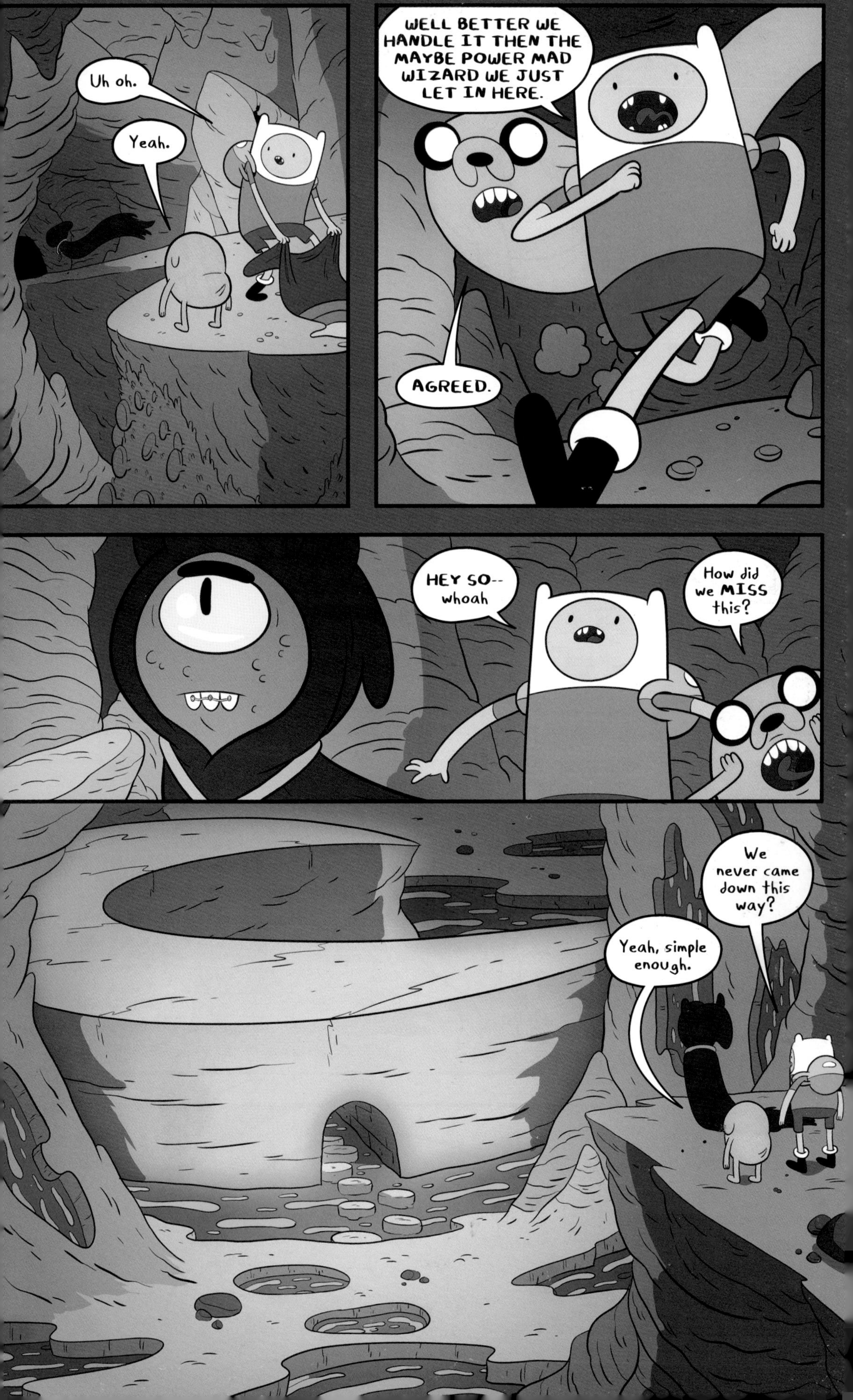

Uh oh.
Yeah.
WELL BETTER WE HANDLE IT THEN THE MAYBE POWER MAD WIZARD WE JUST LET IN HERE.
AGREED.
HEY SO-- whoah
How did we MISS this?
We never came down this way?
Yeah, simple enough.

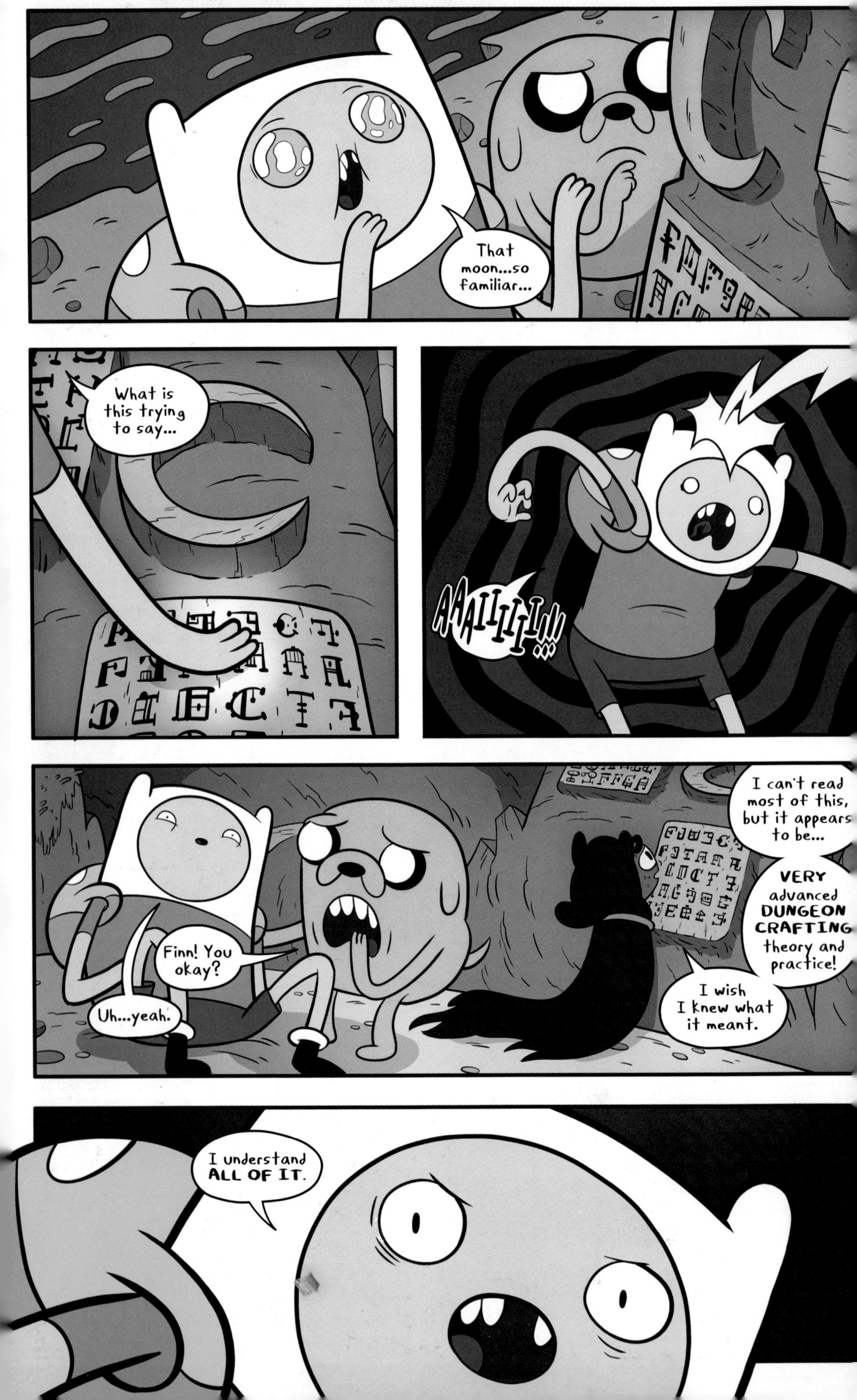
That moon...so familiar...
What is this trying to say...
AAAIIIIII!!!
Finn! You okay?
Uh...yeah.
I can't read most of this, but it appears to be...
VERY advanced DUNGEON CRAFTING theory and practice!
I wish I knew what it meant.
I understand ALL OF IT.

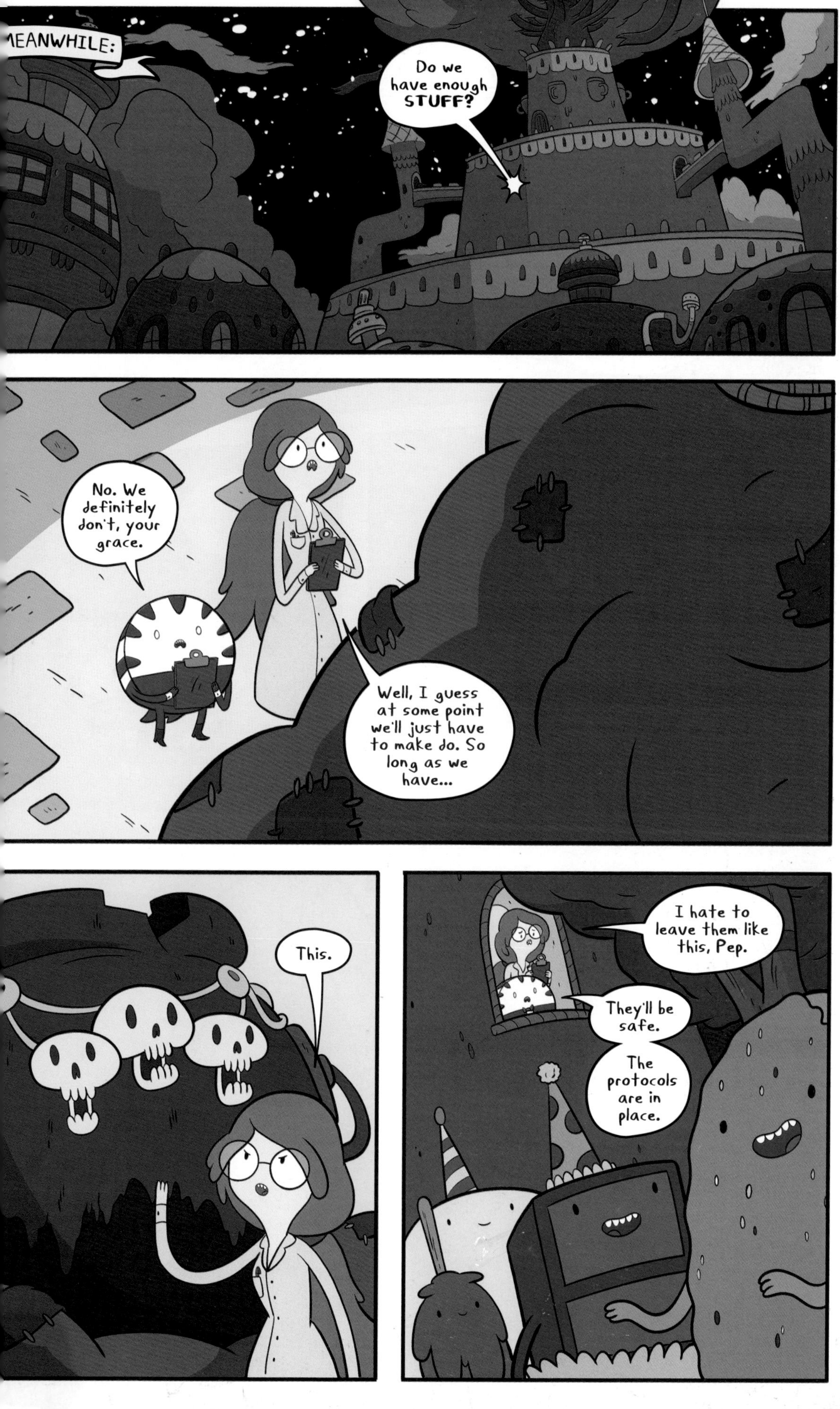
MEANWHILE:
Do we have enough STUFF?
No. We definitely don't, your grace.
Well, I guess at some point we'll just have to make do. So long as we have...
This.
I hate to leave them like this, Pep.
They'll be safe.
The protocols are in place.

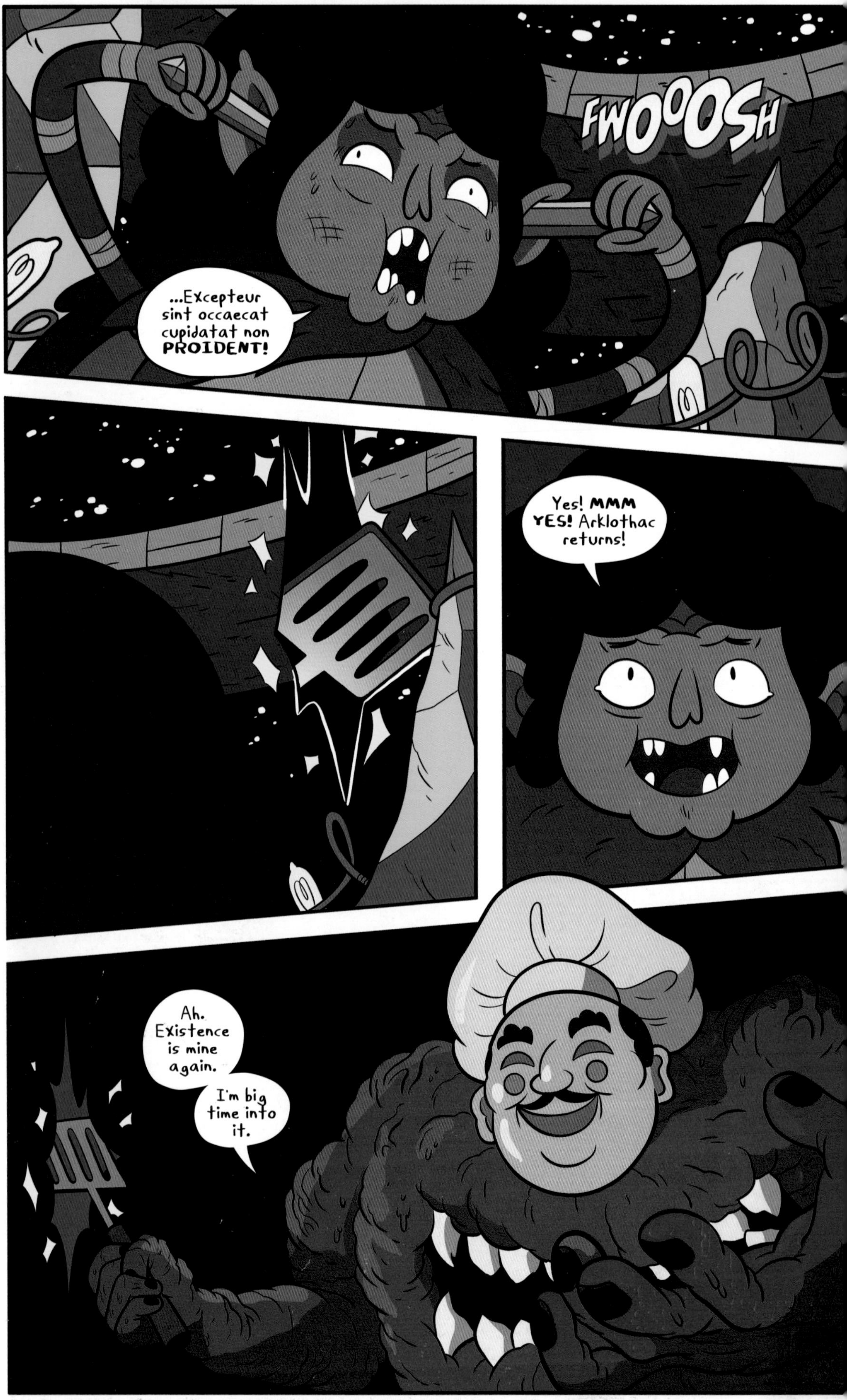
FWOOOSH
...Excepteur sint occaecat cupidatat non PROIDENT!
Yes! MMM YES! Arklothac returns!
Ah. Existence is mine again.
I'm big time into it.

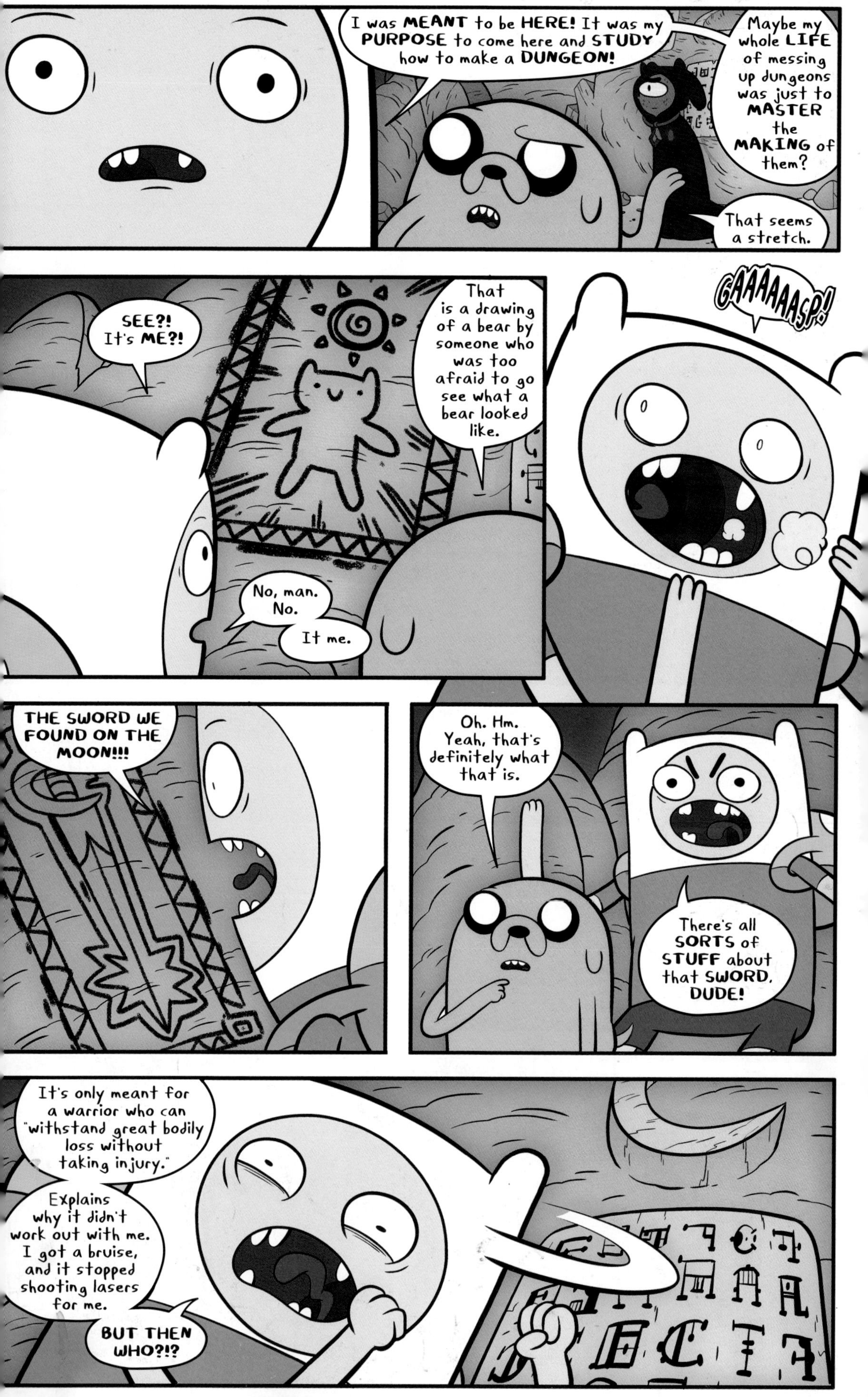

I was MEANT to be HERE! It was my PURPOSE to come here and STUDY how to make a DUNGEON!
Maybe my whole LIFE of messing up dungeons was just to MASTER the MAKING of them?
That seems a stretch.
SEE?! It's ME?!
That is a drawing of a bear by someone who was too afraid to go see what a bear looked like.
GAAAAAASP!
No, man. No.
It me.
THE SWORD WE FOUND ON THE MOON!!!
Oh. Hm. Yeah, that's definitely what that is.
There's all SORTS of STUFF about that SWORD, DUDE!
It's only meant for a warrior who can "withstand great bodily loss without taking injury."
Explains why it didn't work out with me. I got a bruise, and it stopped shooting lasers for me.
BUT THEN WHO?!?

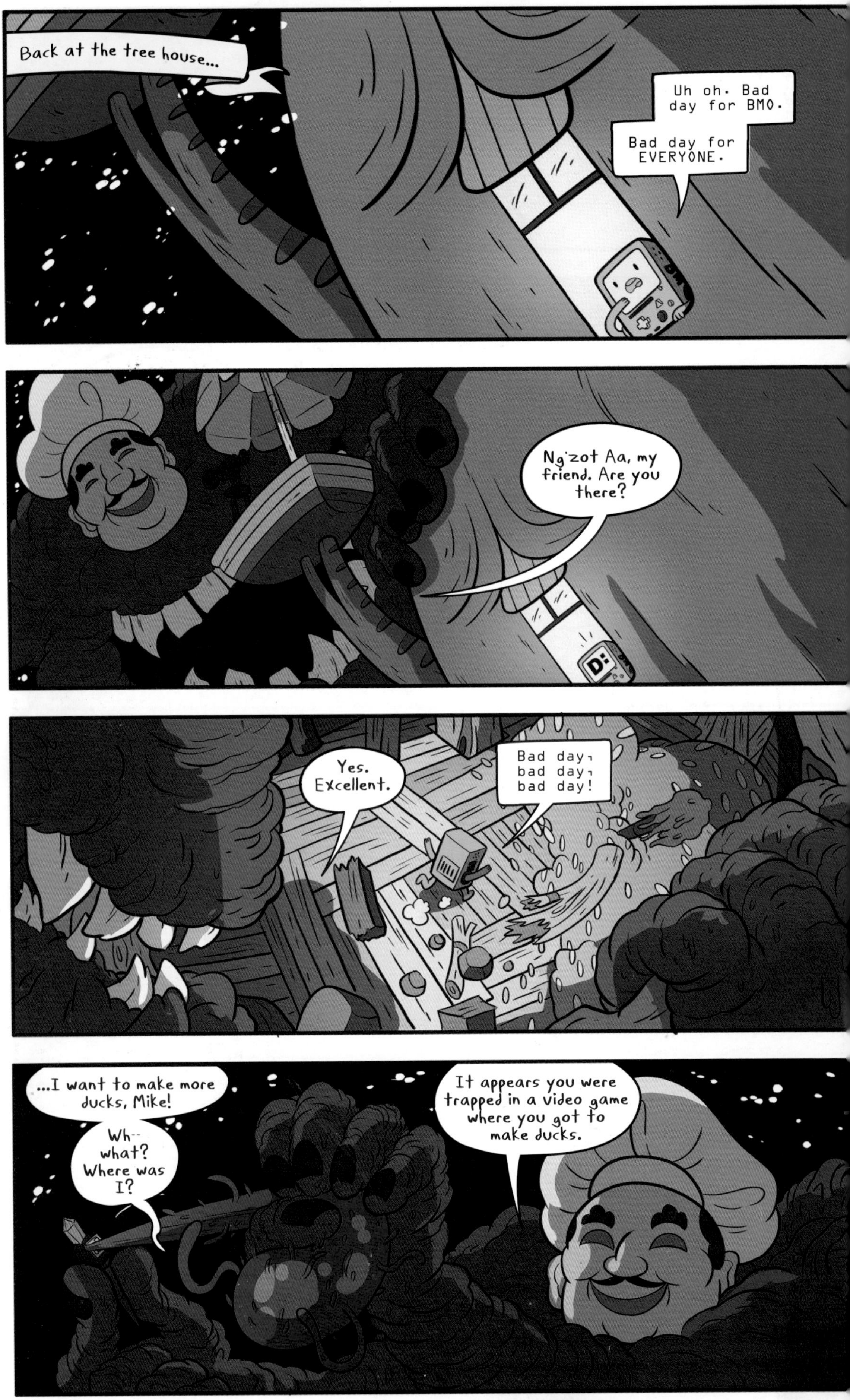
Back at the tree house...
Uh oh. Bad day for BMO.
Bad day for EVERYONE.
Ng'zot Aa, my friend. Are you there?
D:
Yes. Excellent.
Bad day, bad day, bad day!
...I want to make more ducks, Mike!
Wh-- what? Where was I?
It appears you were trapped in a video game where you got to make ducks.

I was...

Arklothac, it is good to see you. The universe is small, and it bores me. To greet a peer again is a comfort.

Same.

Though I am...

Hungry?

I will soothe you with feast soon. But perhaps, the last of us should join too?

Indeed.

Zon? Would you awaken, and join the ◢◣◥◤

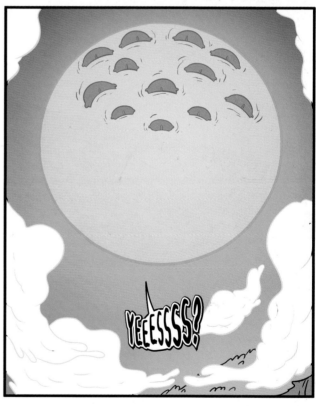

YEEESSSS?

Cock-a-doodle-what-the--WHAT?!

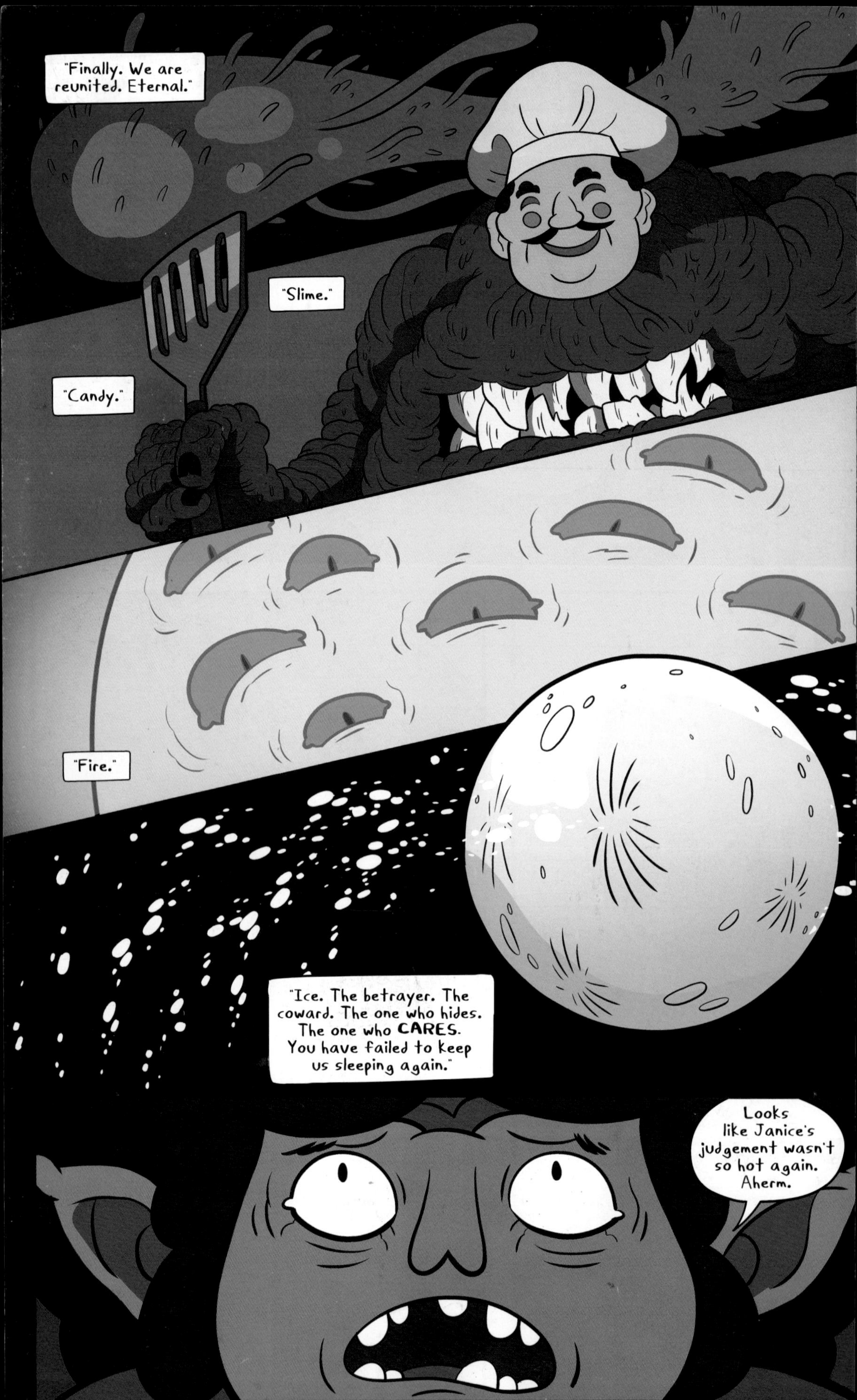
"Finally. We are reunited. Eternal."
"Slime."
"Candy."
"Fire."
"Ice. The betrayer. The coward. The one who hides. The one who CARES. You have failed to keep us sleeping again."
Looks like Janice's judgement wasn't so hot again. Aherm.

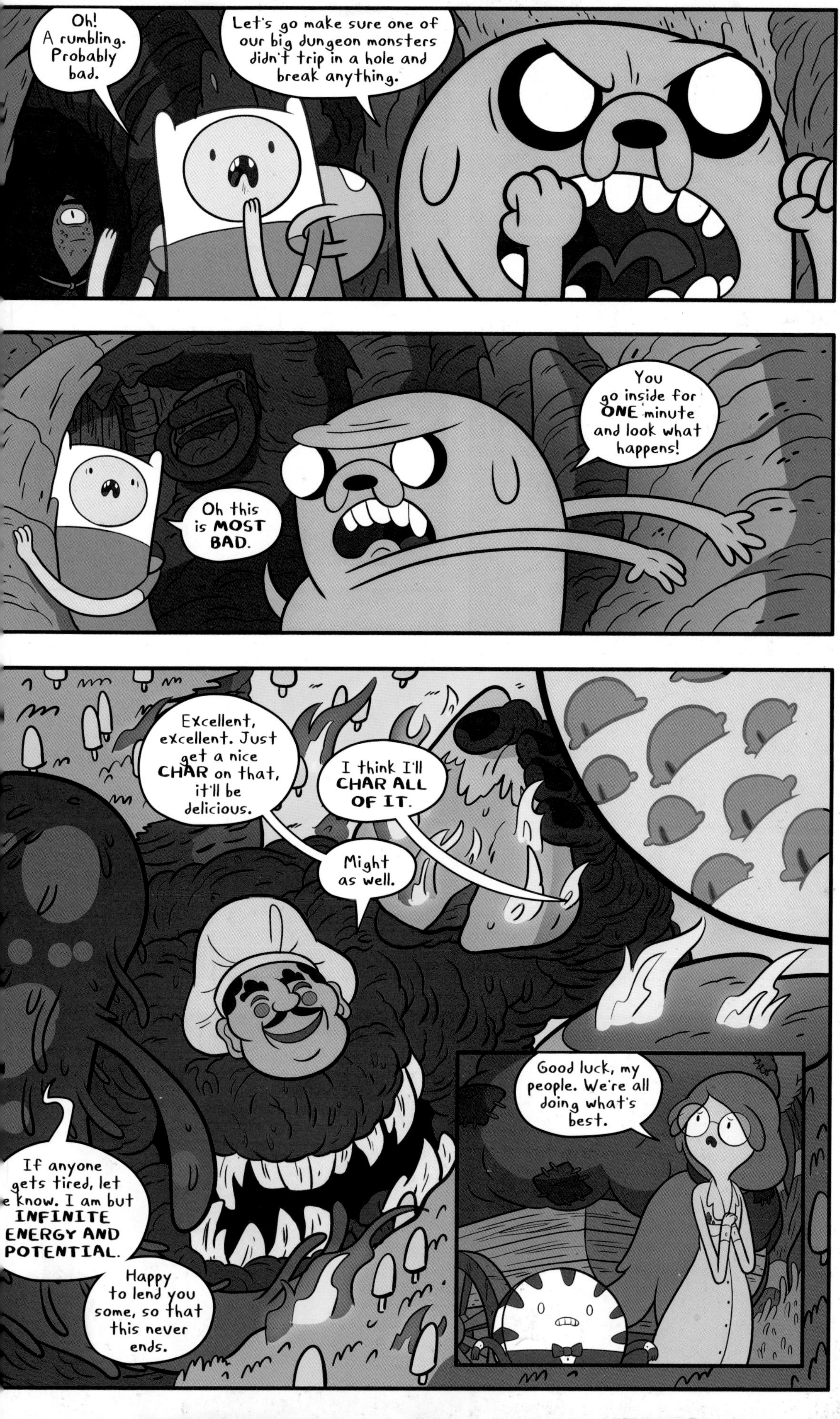

Oh! A rumbling. Probably bad.
Let's go make sure one of our big dungeon monsters didn't trip in a hole and break anything.
You go inside for ONE minute and look what happens!
Oh this is MOST BAD.
Excellent, excellent. Just get a nice CHAR on that, it'll be delicious.
I think I'll CHAR ALL OF IT.
Might as well.
Good luck, my people. We're all doing what's best.
If anyone gets tired, let e know. I am but INFINITE ENERGY AND POTENTIAL.
Happy to lend you some, so that this never ends.

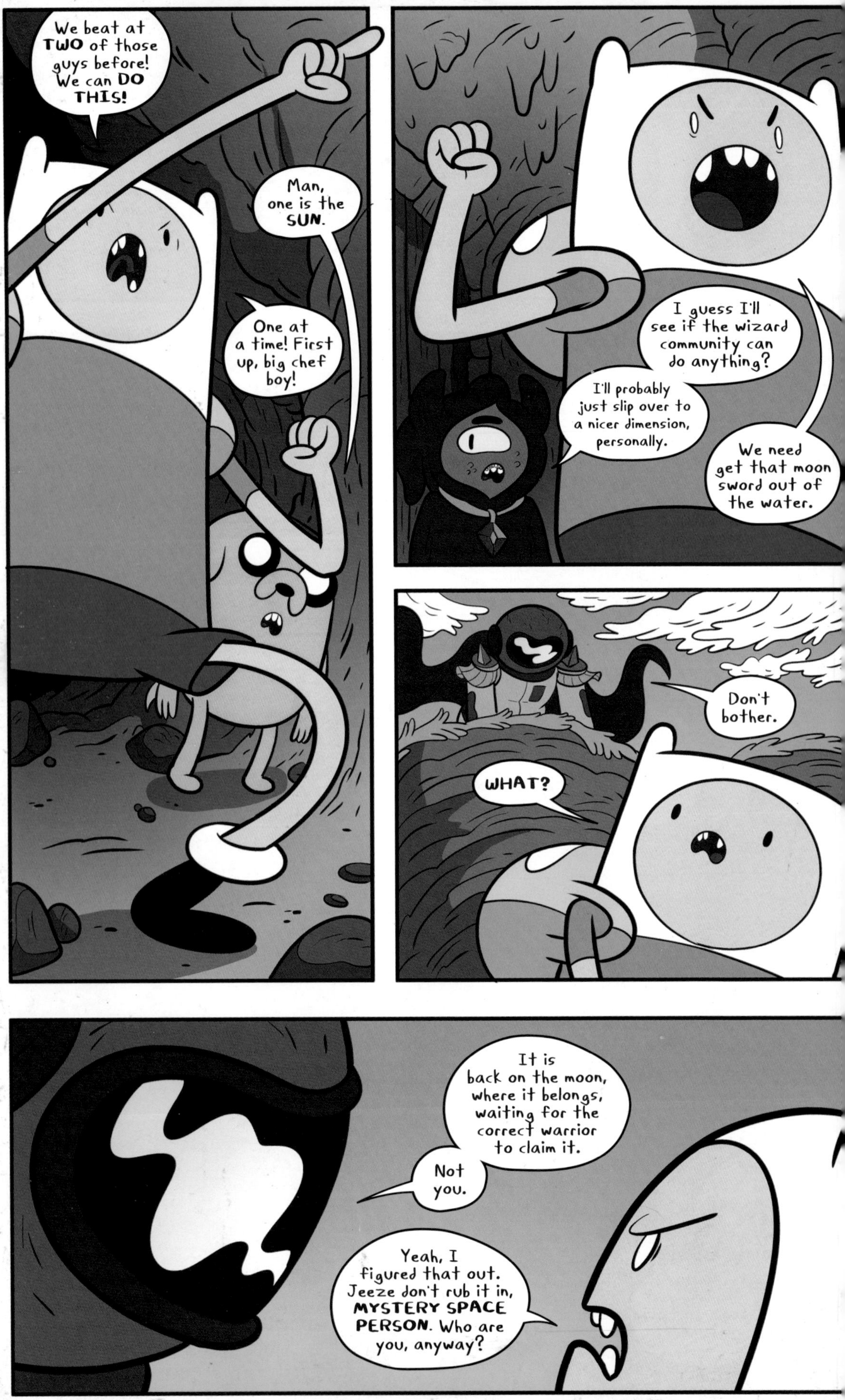
We beat at TWO of those guys before! We can DO THIS!
Man, one is the SUN.
One at a time! First up, big chef boy!
I guess I'll see if the wizard community can do anything?
I'll probably just slip over to a nicer dimension, personally.
We need get that moon sword out of the water.
Don't bother.
WHAT?
It is back on the moon, where it belongs, waiting for the correct warrior to claim it.
Not you.
Yeah, I figured that out. Jeeze don't rub it in, MYSTERY SPACE PERSON. Who are you, anyway?

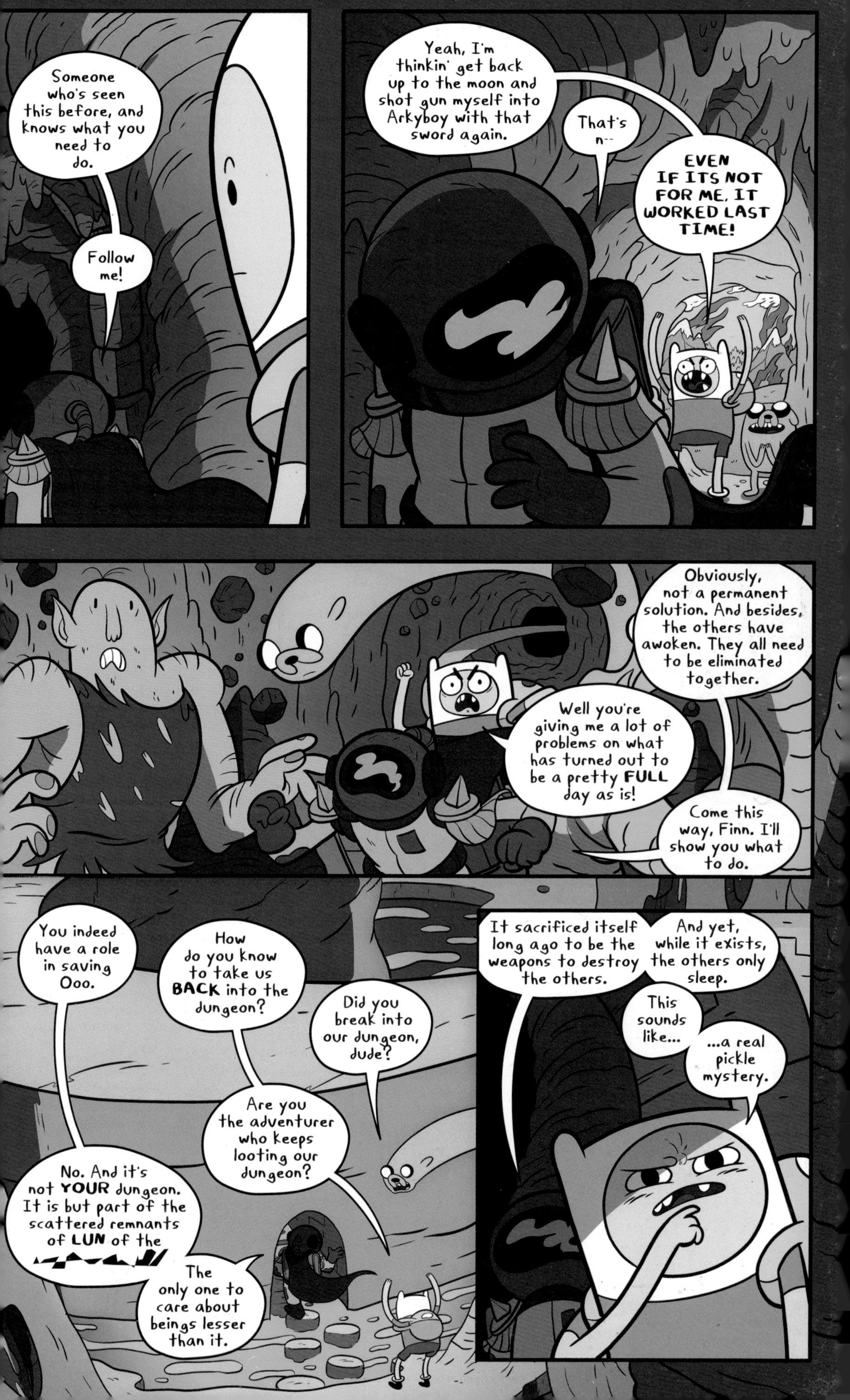
Someone who's seen this before, and knows what you need to do.
Follow me!
Yeah, I'm thinkin' get back up to the moon and shot gun myself into Arkyboy with that sword again.
That's n--
EVEN IF ITS NOT FOR ME, IT WORKED LAST TIME!
Obviously, not a permanent solution. And besides, the others have awoken. They all need to be eliminated together.
Well you're giving me a lot of problems on what has turned out to be a pretty FULL day as is!
Come this way, Finn. I'll show you what to do.
You indeed have a role in saving Ooo.
How do you know to take us BACK into the dungeon?
Did you break into our dungeon, dude?
Are you the adventurer who keeps looting our dungeon?
No. And it's not YOUR dungeon. It is but part of the scattered remnants of LUN of the
The only one to care about beings lesser than it.
It sacrificed itself long ago to be the weapons to destroy the others.
And yet, while it exists, the others only sleep.
This sounds like...
...a real pickle mystery.

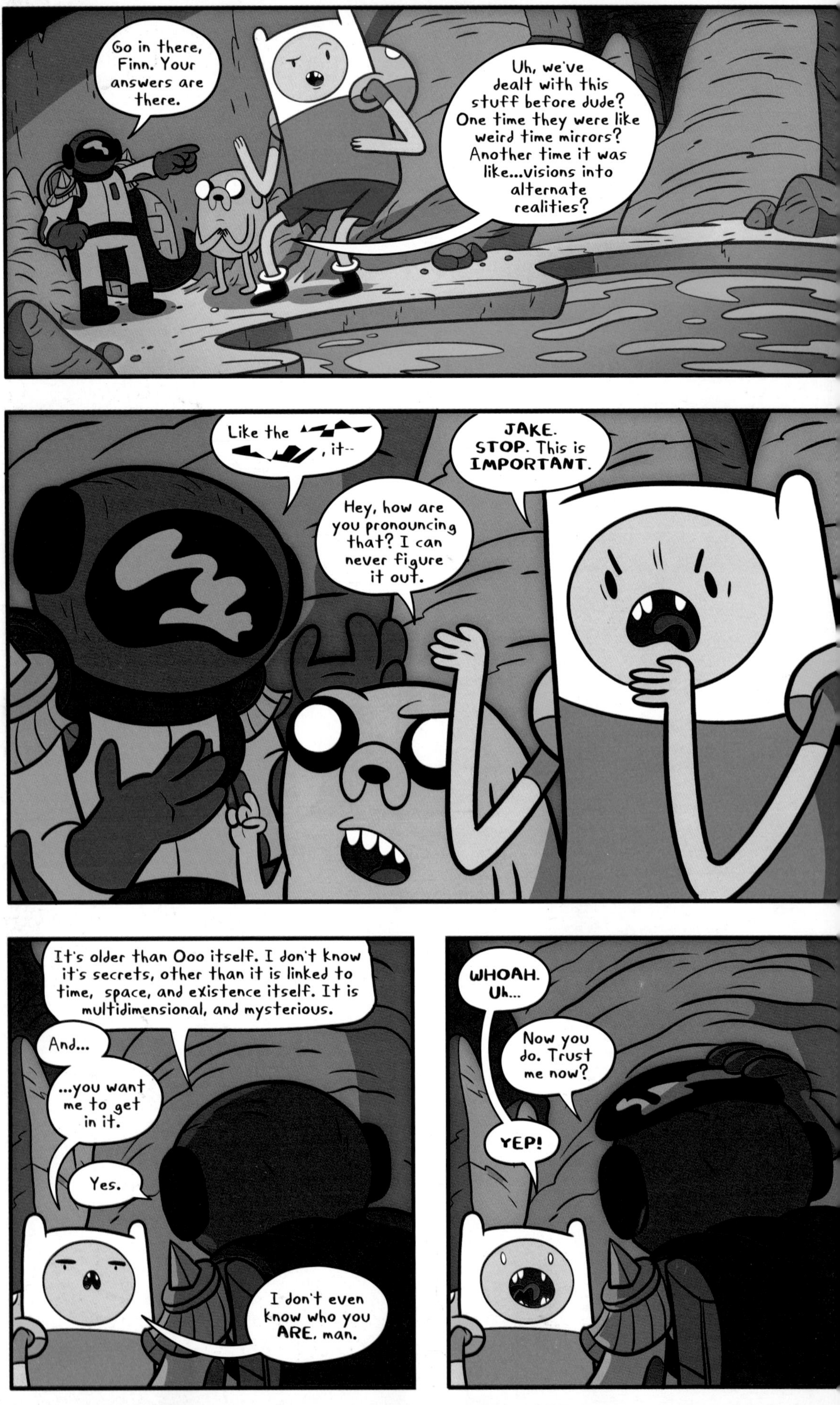
Go in there, Finn. Your answers are there.
Uh, we've dealt with this stuff before dude? One time they were like weird time mirrors? Another time it was like...visions into alternate realities?
Like the , it--
Hey, how are you pronouncing that? I can never figure it out.
JAKE. STOP. This is IMPORTANT.
It's older than Ooo itself. I don't know it's secrets, other than it is linked to time, space, and existence itself. It is multidimensional, and mysterious.
And...
...you want me to get in it.
Yes.
I don't even know who you ARE, man.
WHOAH. Uh...
Now you do. Trust me now?
YEP!

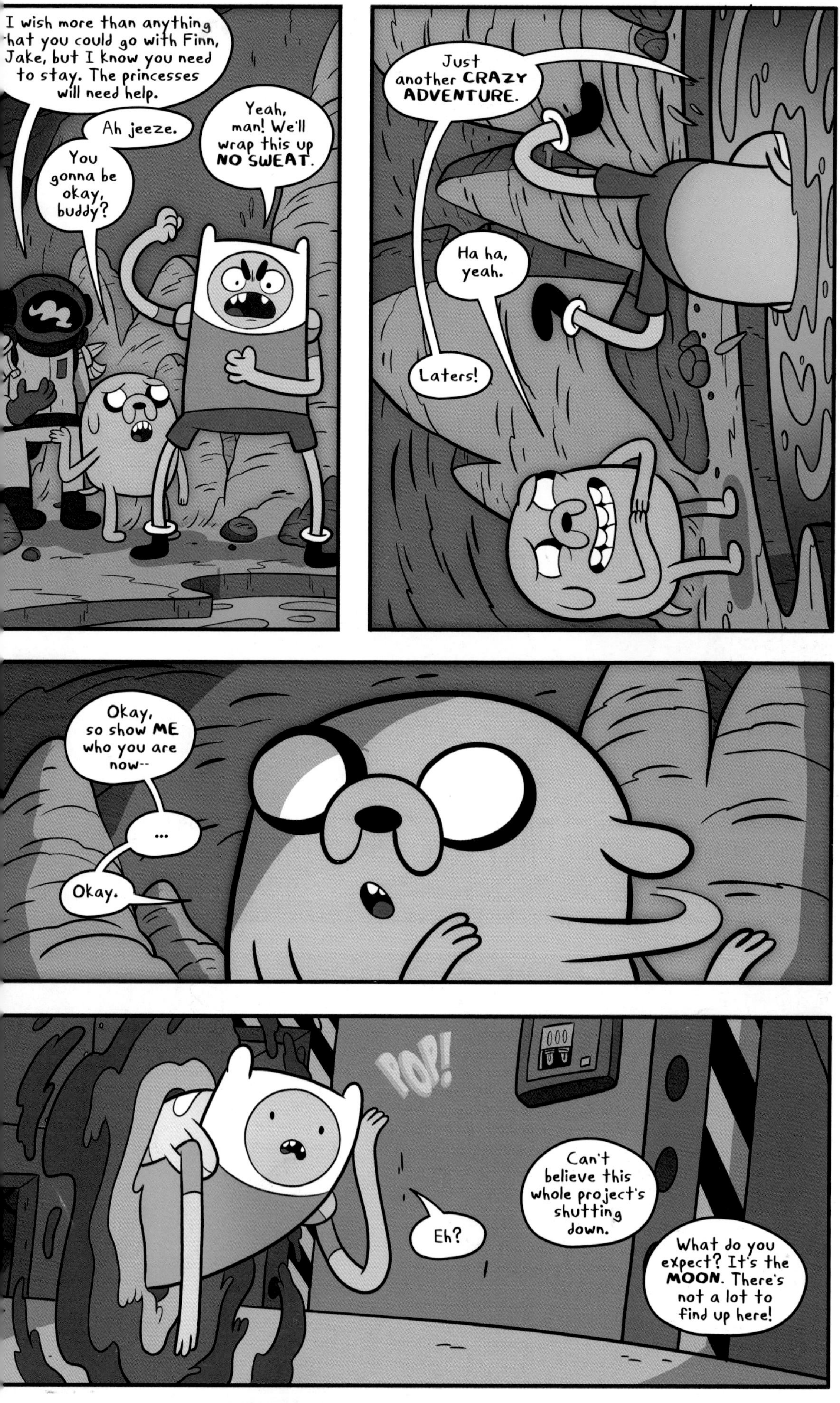
I wish more than anything that you could go with Finn, Jake, but I know you need to stay. The princesses will need help.
Ah jeeze.
You gonna be okay, buddy?
Yeah, man! We'll wrap this up NO SWEAT.
Just another CRAZY ADVENTURE.
Ha ha, yeah.
Laters!
Okay, so show ME who you are now--
...
Okay.
POP!
Eh?
Can't believe this whole project's shutting down.
What do you expect? It's the MOON. There's not a lot to find up here!

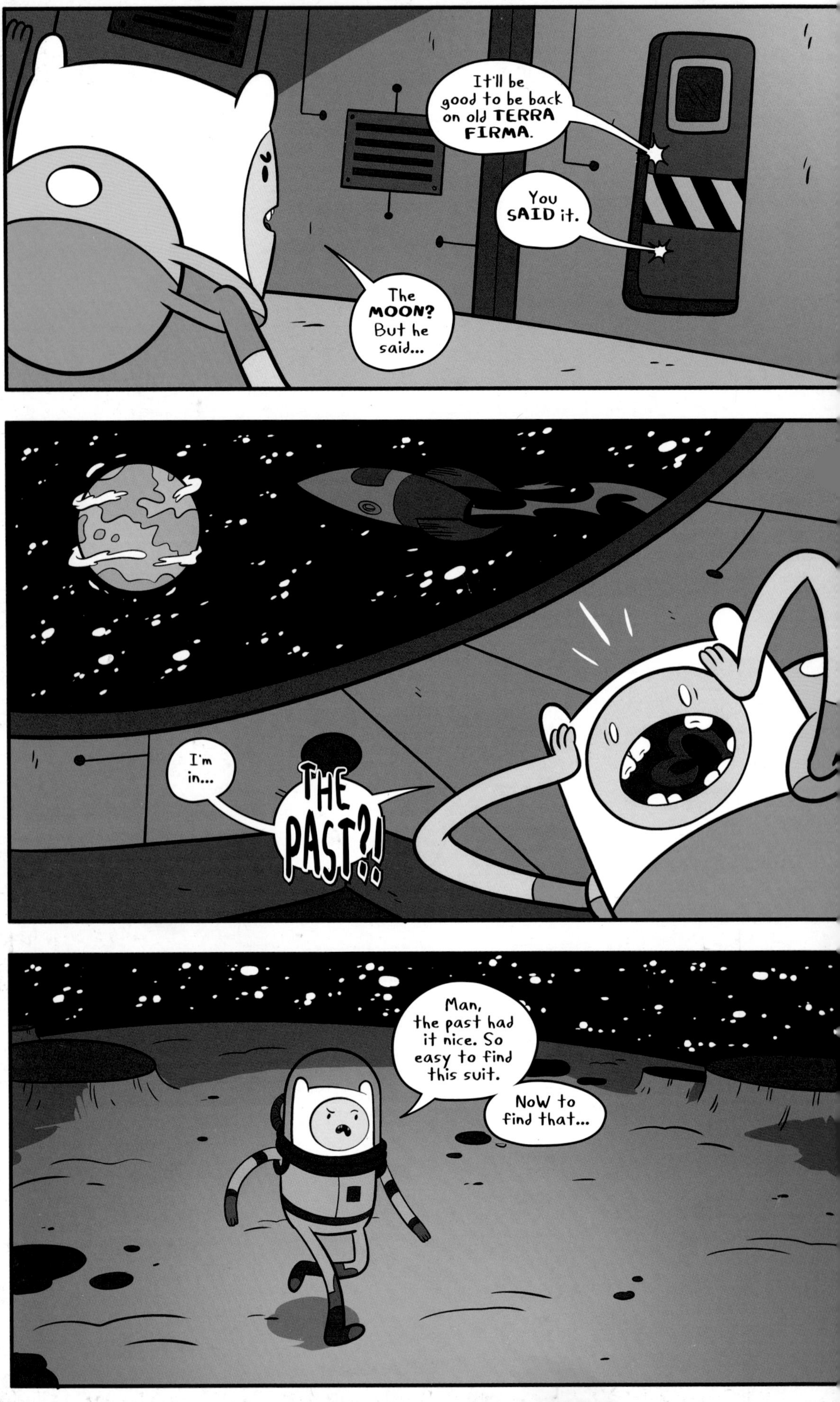

It'll be good to be back on old TERRA FIRMA.
You SAID it.
The MOON? But he said...
I'm in...
THE PAST?!
Man, the past had it nice. So easy to find this suit.
NoW to find that...

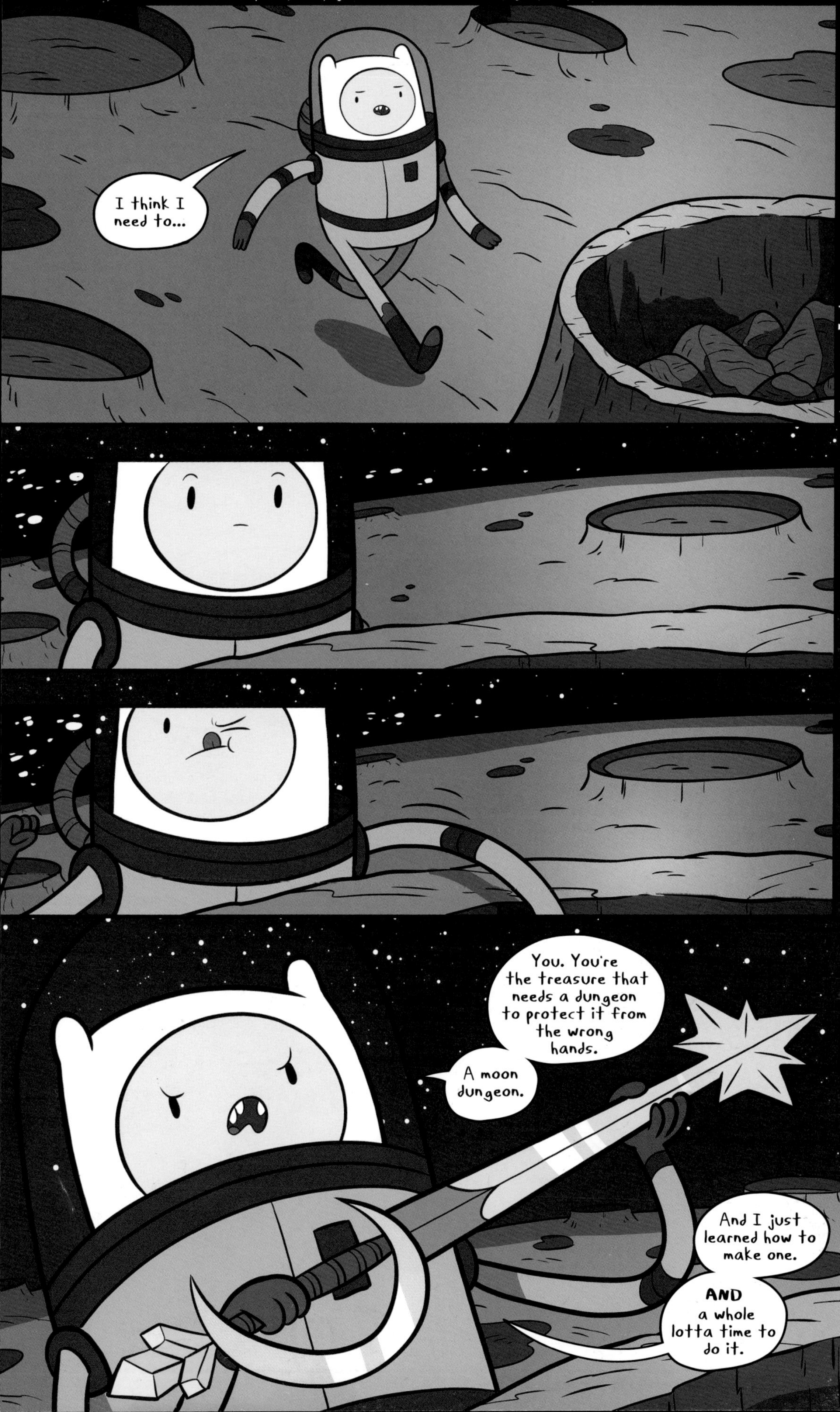
I think I need to...
You. You're the treasure that needs a dungeon to protect it from the wrong hands.
A moon dungeon.
And I just learned how to make one.
AND a whole lotta time to do it.

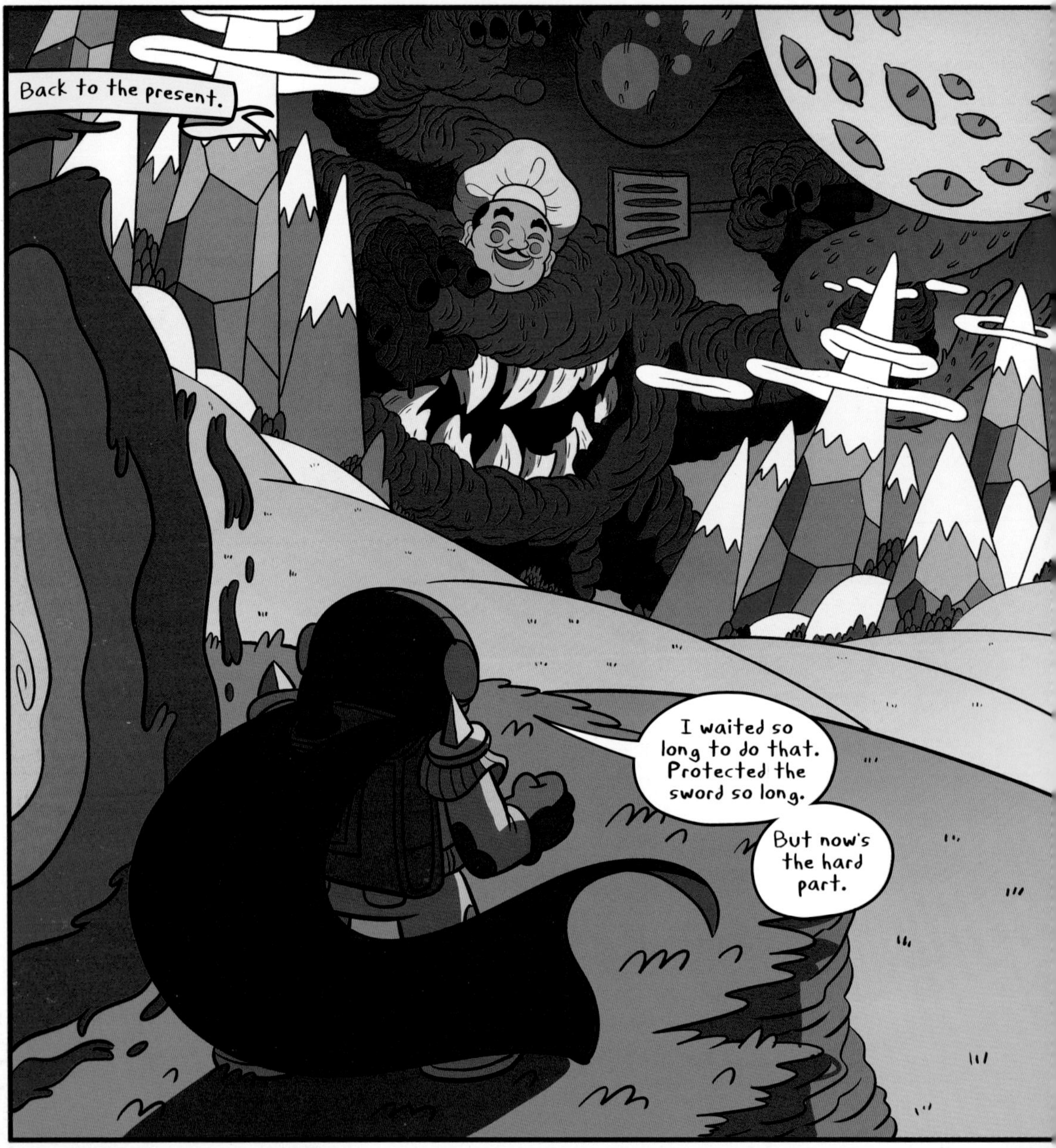
Back to the present.
I waited so long to do that. Protected the sword so long.
But now's the hard part.

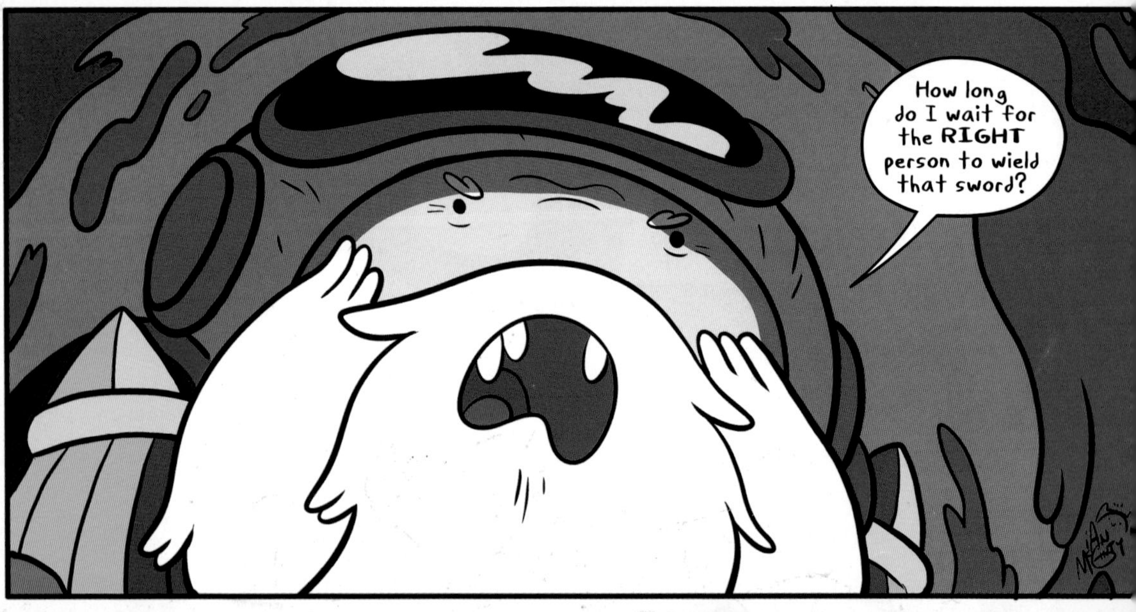
How long do I wait for the RIGHT person to wield that sword?

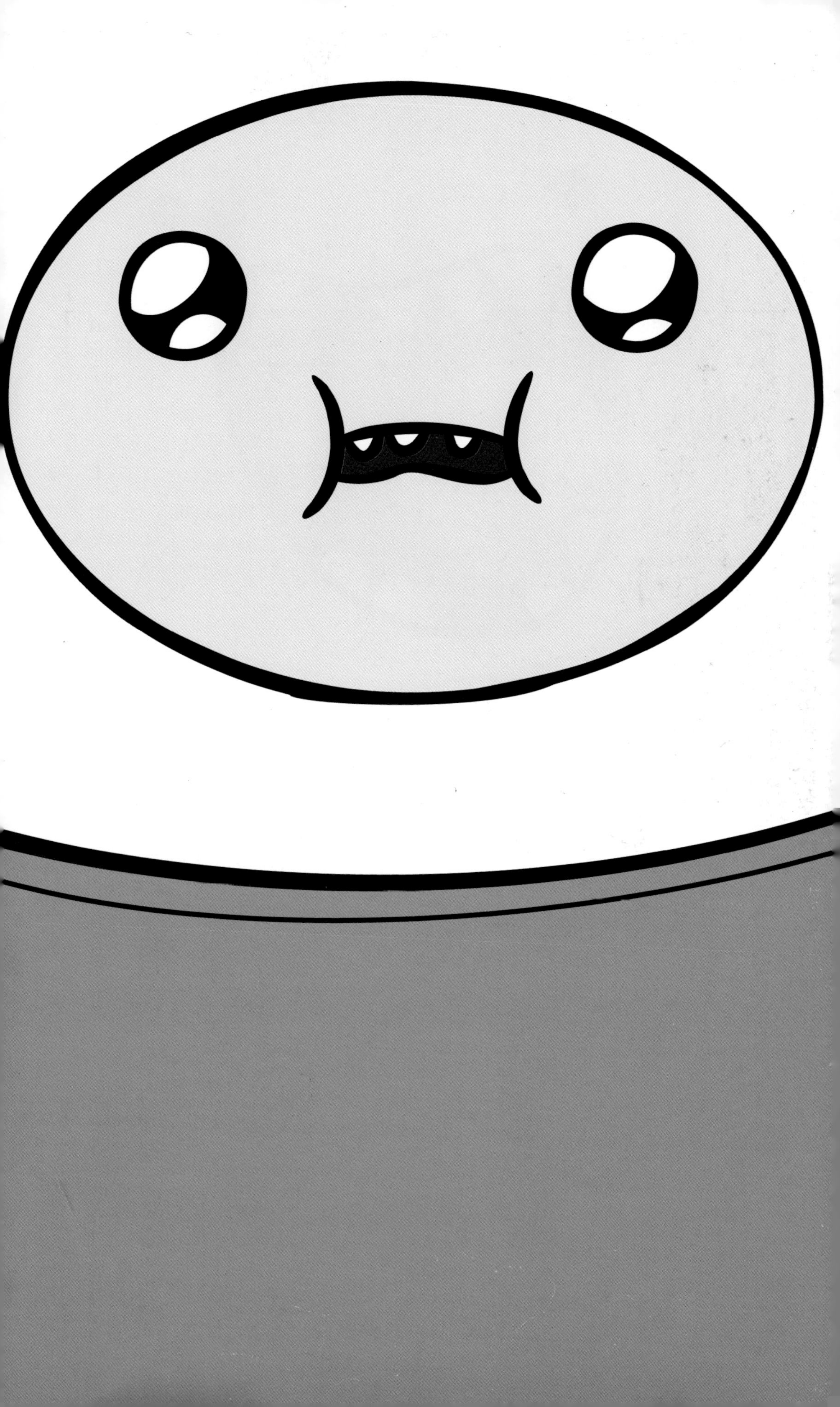

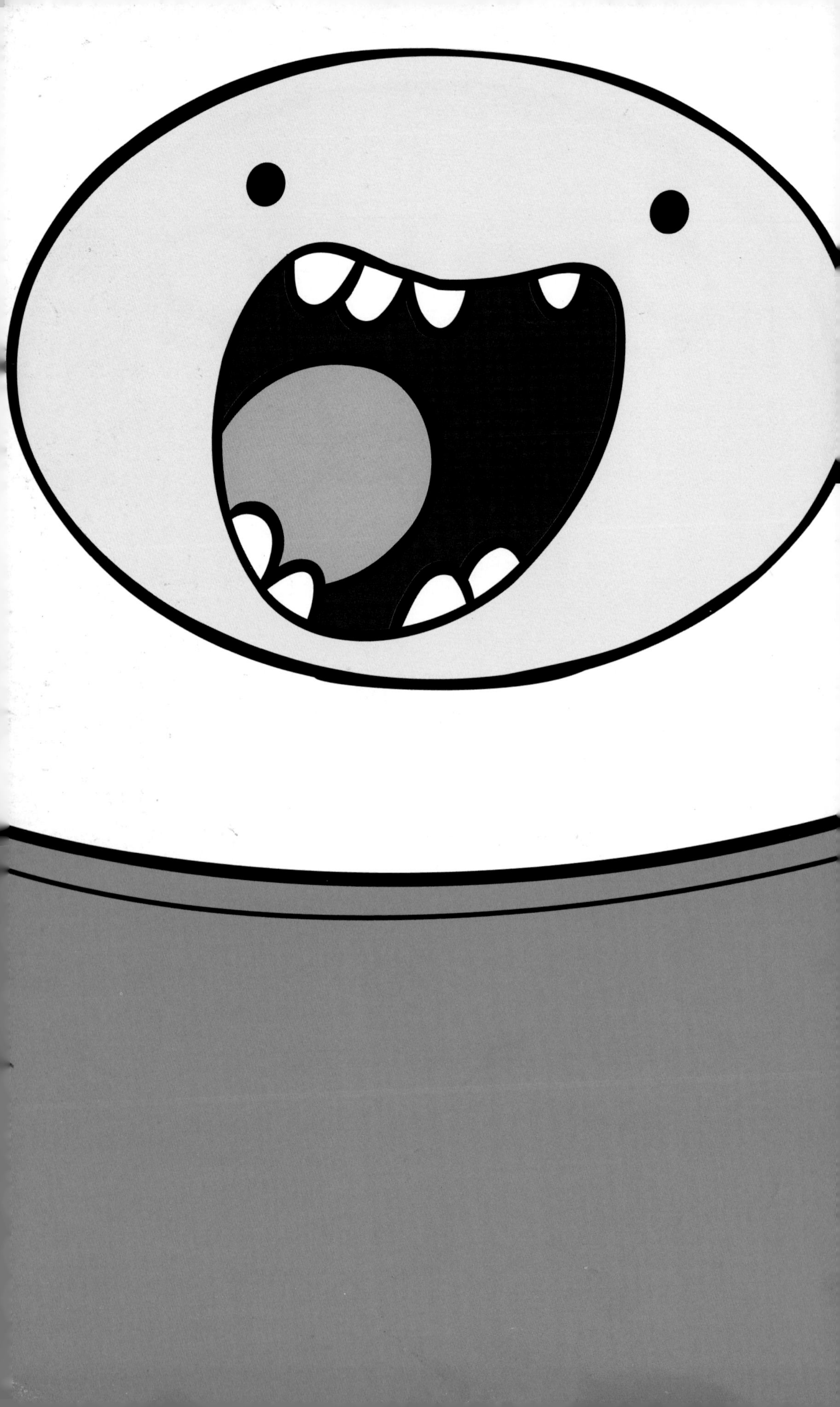

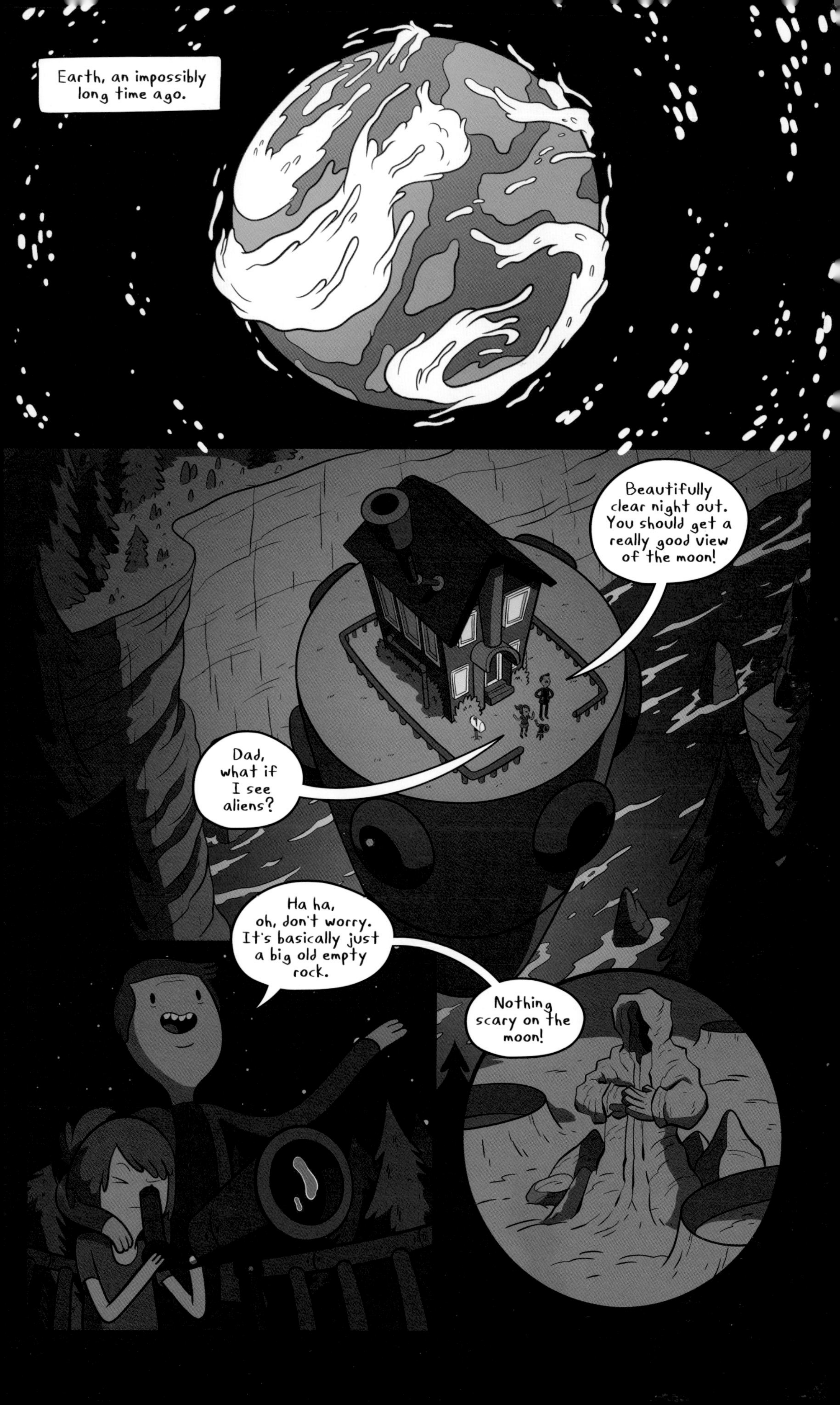
Earth, an impossibly long time ago.
Beautifully clear night out. You should get a really good view of the moon!
Dad, what if I see aliens?
Ha ha, oh, don't worry. It's basically just a big old empty rock.
Nothing scary on the moon!

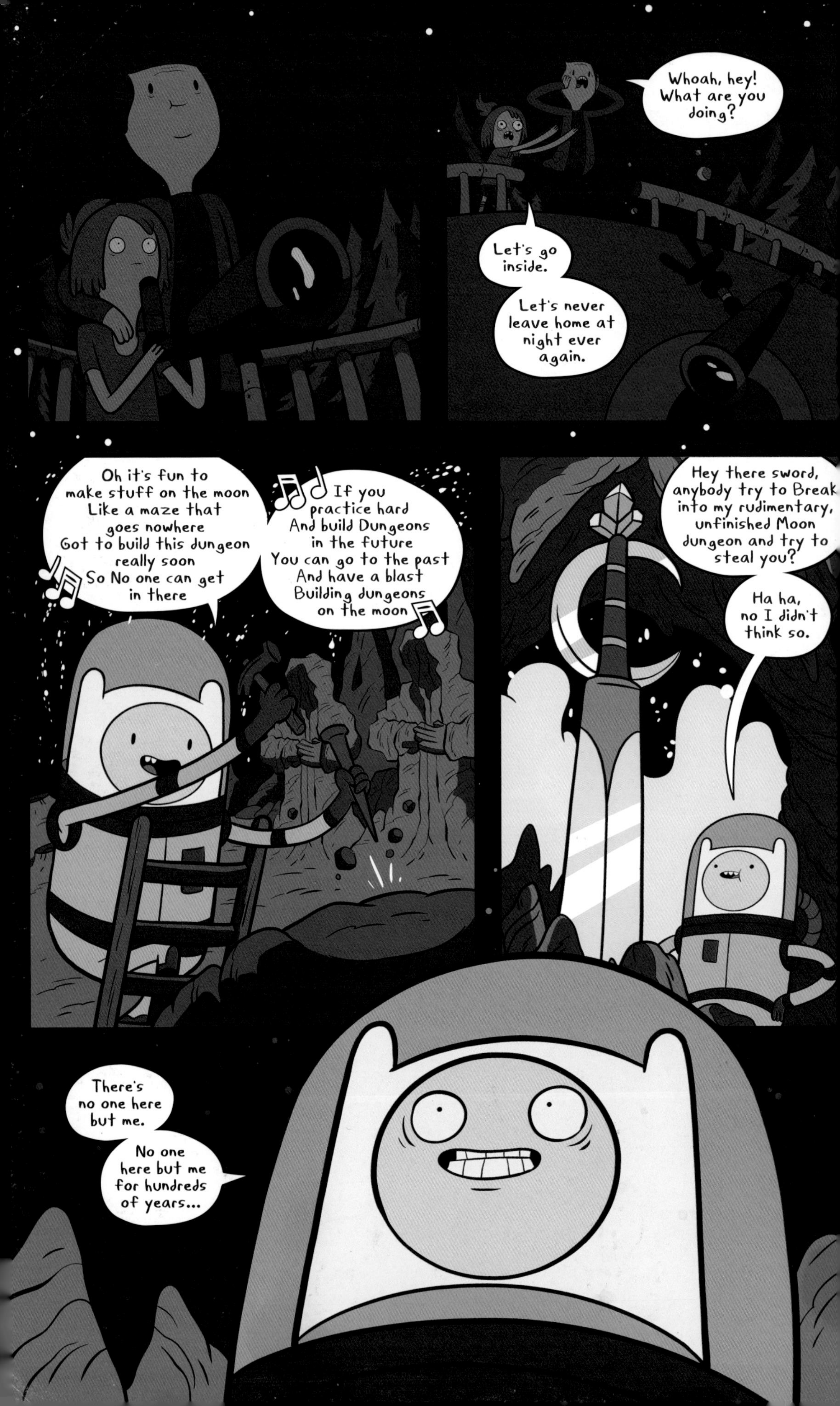

Whoah, hey! What are you doing?
Let's go inside.
Let's never leave home at night ever again.
Oh it's fun to make stuff on the moon Like a maze that goes nowhere Got to build this dungeon really soon So No one can get in there
If you practice hard And build Dungeons in the future You can go to the past And have a blast Building dungeons on the moon
Hey there sword, anybody try to Break into my rudimentary, unfinished Moon dungeon and try to steal you?
Ha ha, no I didn't think so.
There's no one here but me.
No one here but me for hundreds of years...

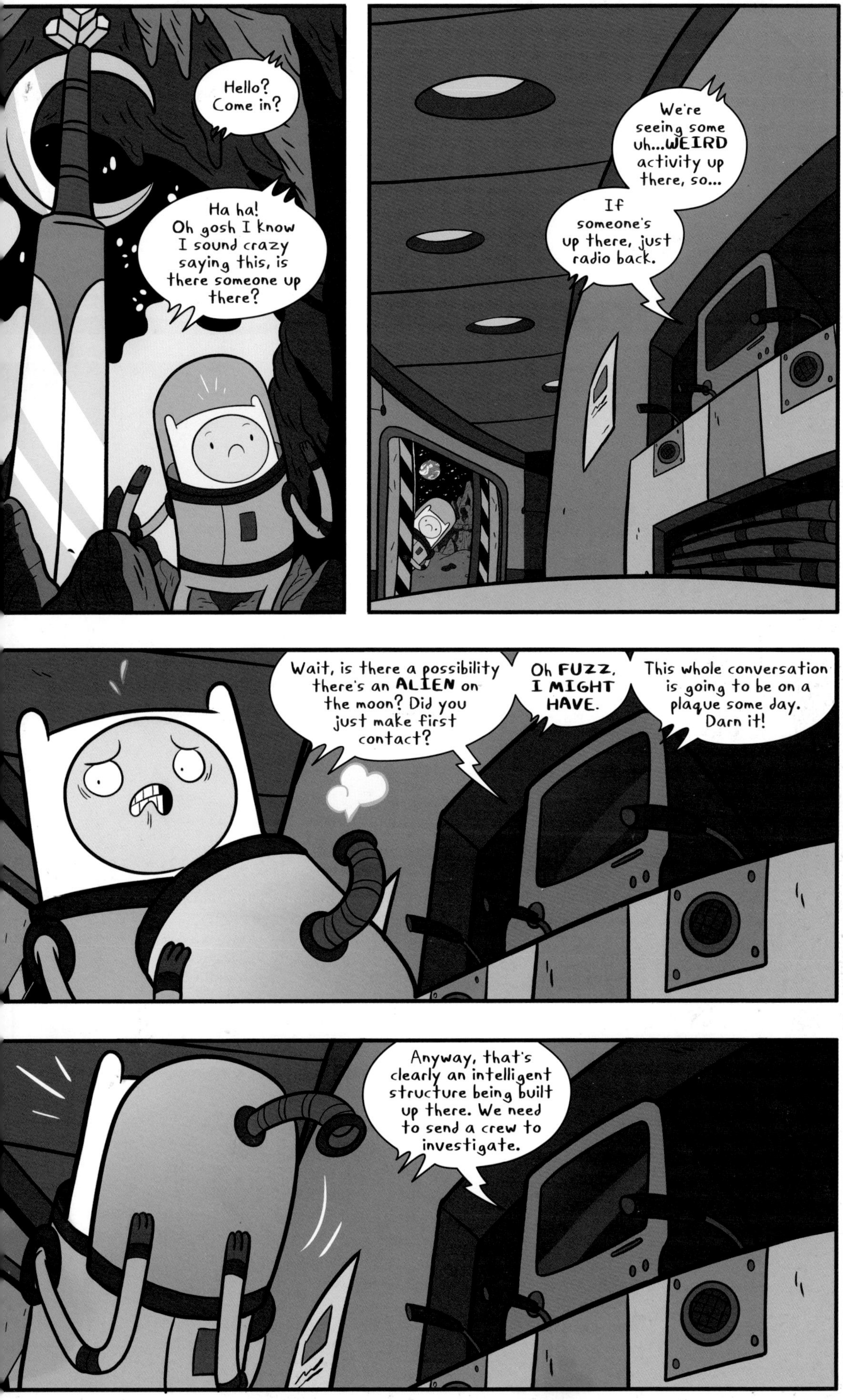
Hello? Come in?
Ha ha! Oh gosh I know I sound crazy saying this, is there someone up there?
We're seeing some uh...WEIRD activity up there, so...
If someone's up there, just radio back.
Wait, is there a possibility there's an ALIEN on the moon? Did you just make first contact?
Oh FUZZ, I MIGHT HAVE.
This whole conversation is going to be on a plaque some day. Darn it!
Anyway, that's clearly an intelligent structure being built up there. We need to send a crew to investigate.

Hello.

aah! HELLO?!

Hello, who's there?

This is...

Computer.

Computer was left on.

Uh... stand by.

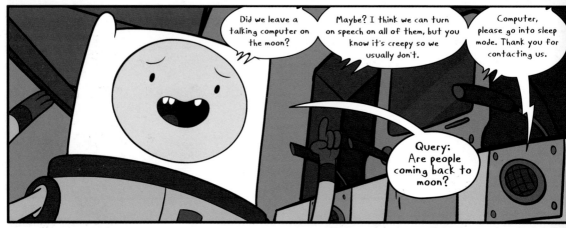

Did we leave a talking computer on the moon?

Maybe? I think we can turn on speech on all of them, but you know it's creepy so we usually don't.

Computer, please go into sleep mode. Thank you for contacting us.

Query: Are people coming back to moon?

Uh, yes, we think so, computer.

When?

Uh probably YEARS from now. Lotta hoops. Don't really have the budget at the moment...

THANK.

YOU.

Going to sleep now!

Okay, bye?

That wasn't a computer.

Yeah there's someone on the moon.

Much **MUCH** later...

Alright, team, solid approach. Once you're docked with the base, you can maybe unpack your stuff, get a lunch in, and relax.

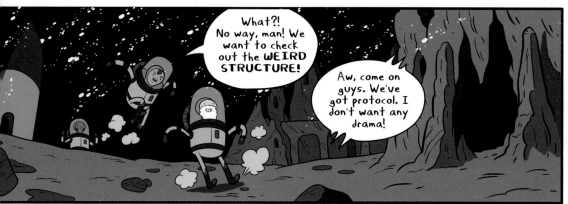

What?! No way, man! We want to check out the **WEIRD STRUCTURE!**

Aw, come on guys. We've got protocol. I don't want any drama!

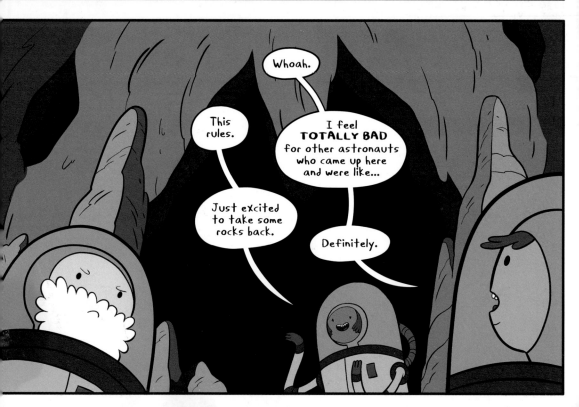

Whoah.

This rules.

I feel **TOTALLY BAD** for other astronauts who came up here and were like...

Just excited to take some rocks back.

Definitely.

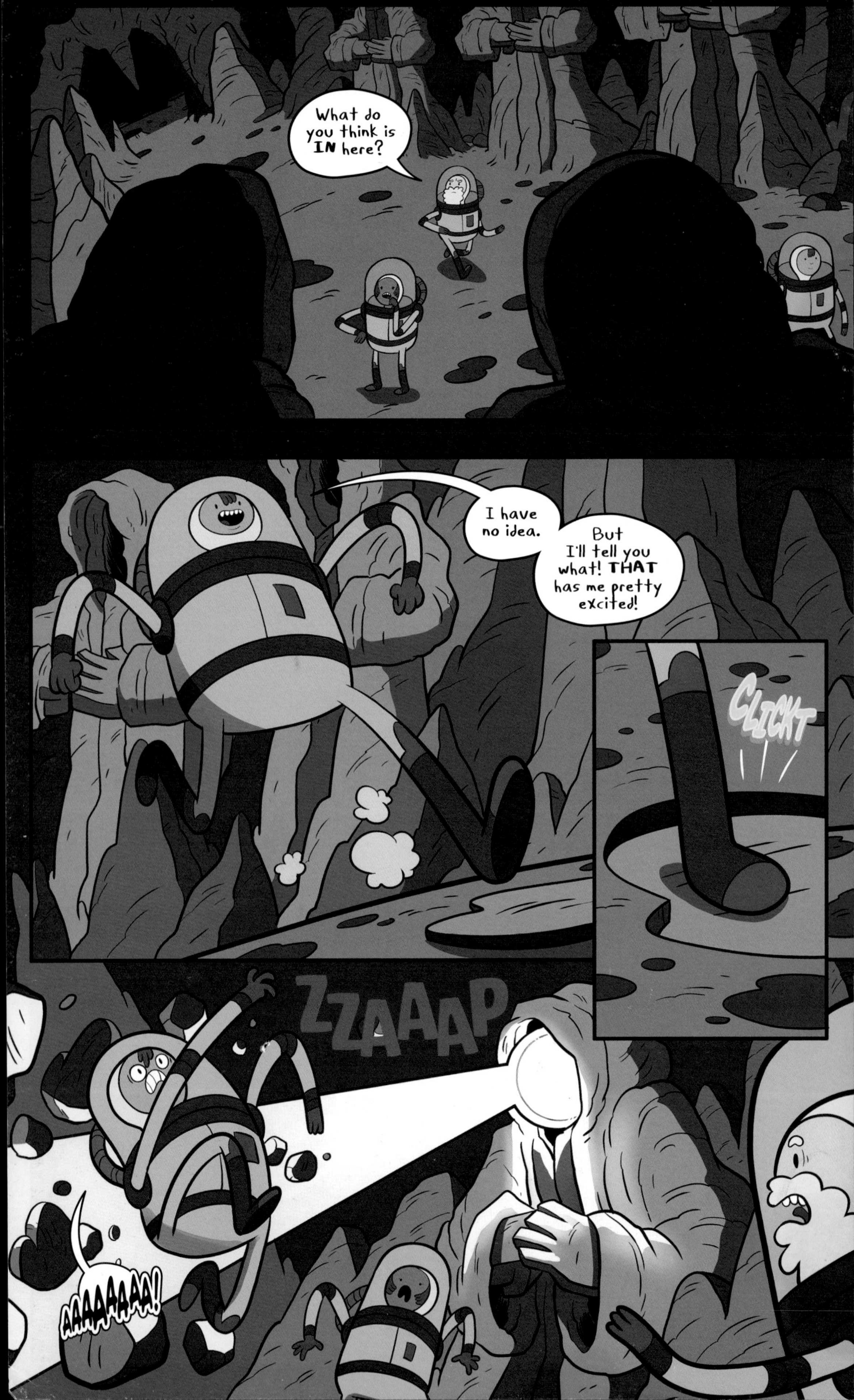
What do you think is IN here?
I have no idea.
But I'll tell you what! THAT has me pretty excited!
CLICKT
ZZAAAP
AAAAAAAA!

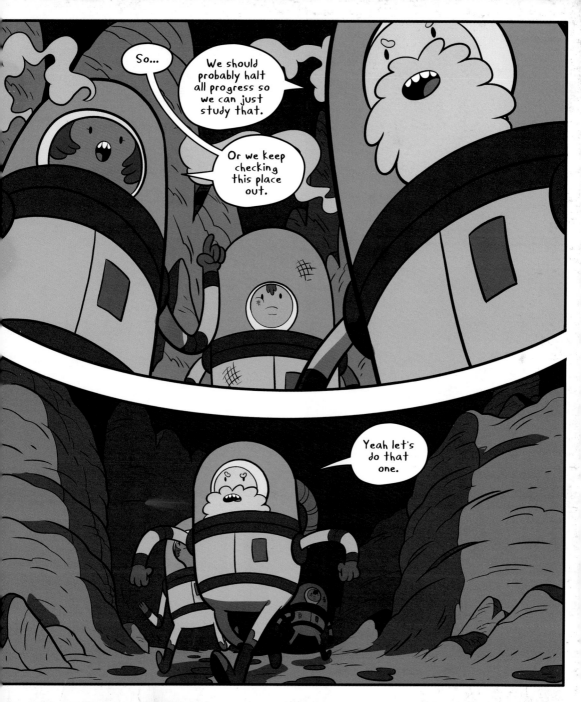

So...

We should probably halt all progress so we can just study that.

Or we keep checking this place out.

Yeah let's do that one.

Yo, is that a SWORD?

What IS this place?

I'm gonna check out that SWORD.

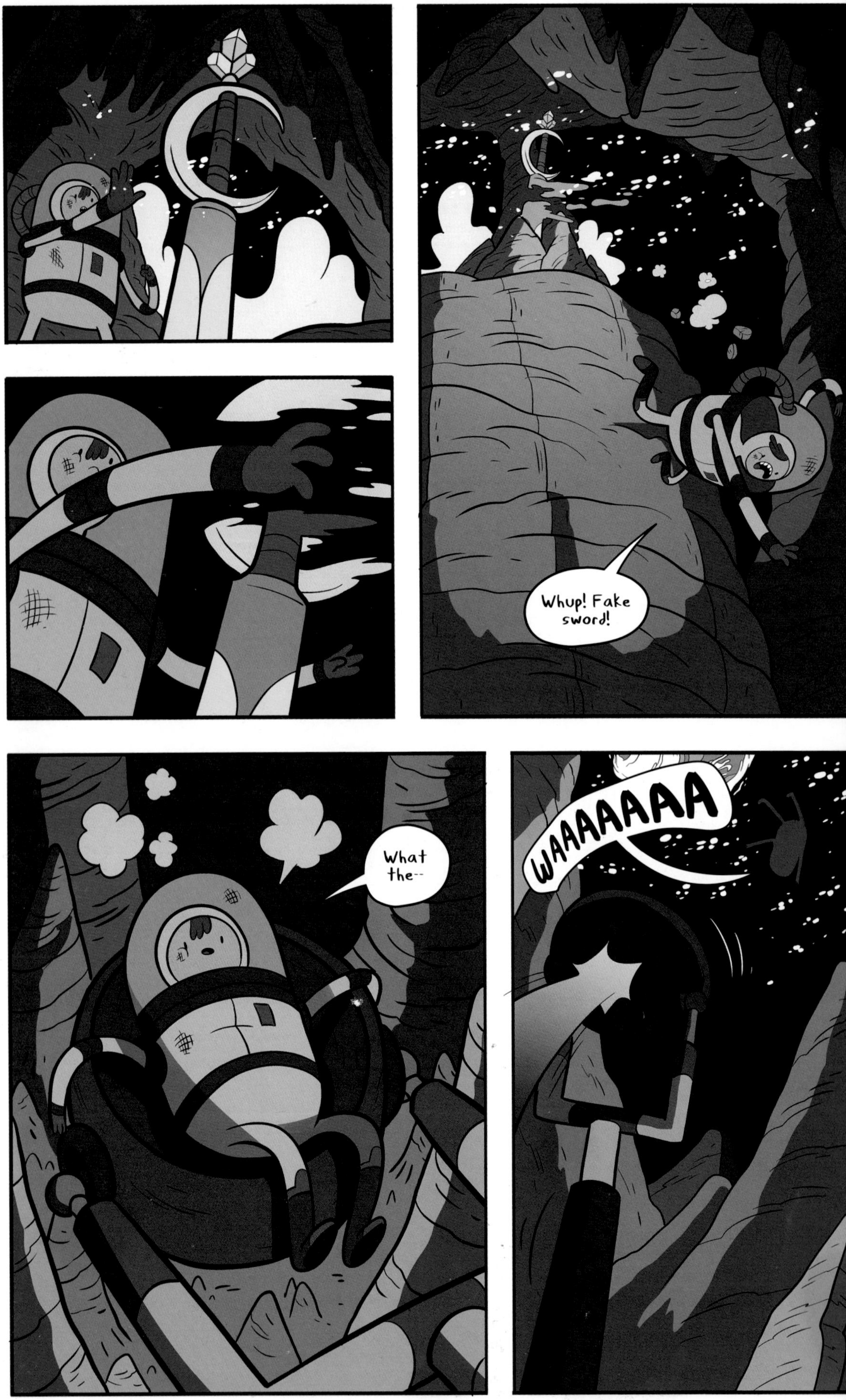
Whup! Fake sword!
What the--
WAAAAAAA

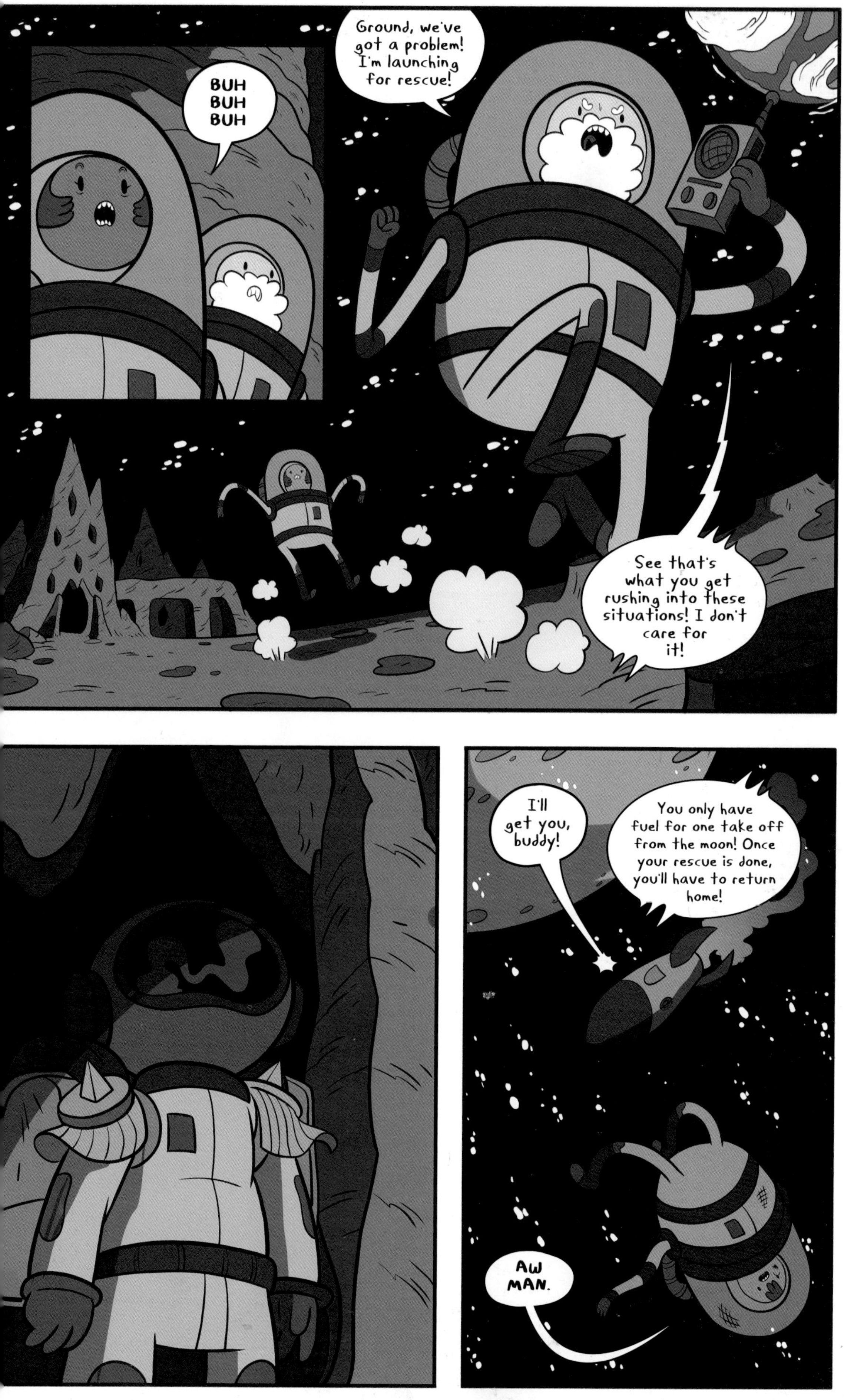
BUH
BUH
BUH
Ground, we've got a problem! I'm launching for rescue!
See that's what you get rushing into these situations! I don't care for it!
I'll get you, buddy!
You only have fuel for one take off from the moon! Once your rescue is done, you'll have to return home!
AW MAN.

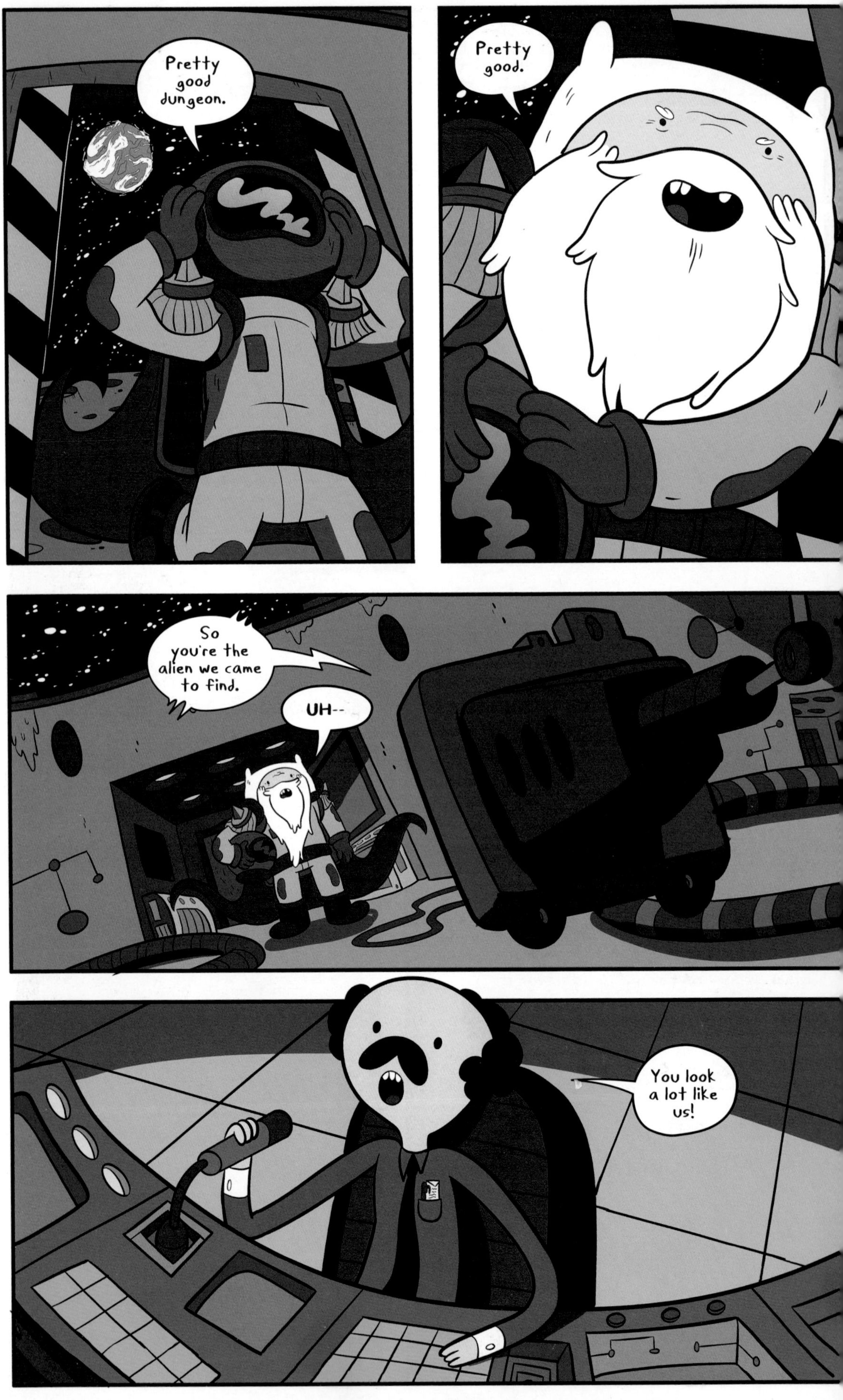
Pretty good dungeon.
Pretty good.
So you're the alien we came to find.
UH--
You look a lot like us!

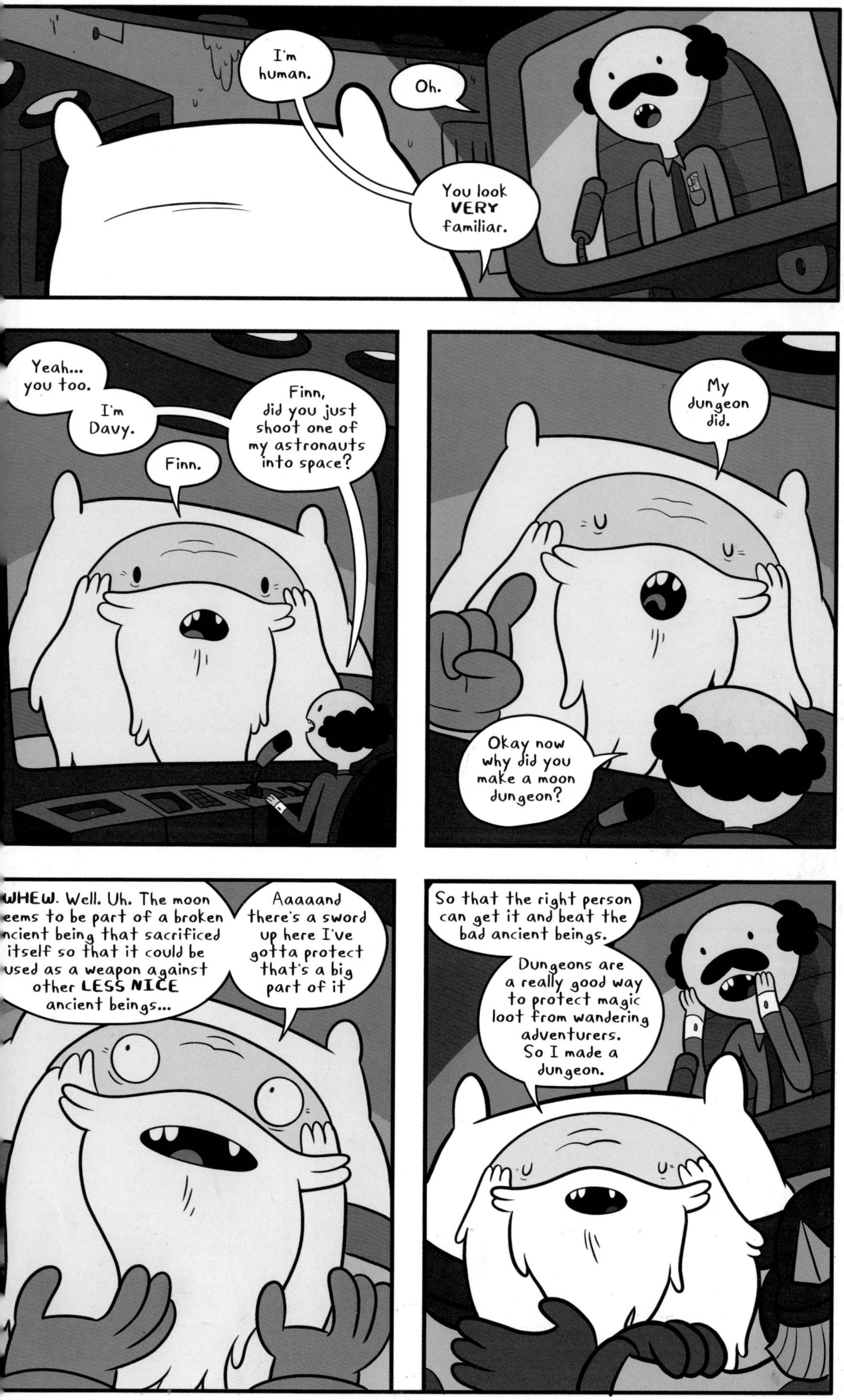
I'm human.
Oh.
You look VERY familiar.
Yeah... you too.
I'm Davy.
Finn.
Finn, did you just shoot one of my astronauts into space?
My dungeon did.
Okay now why did you make a moon dungeon?
WHEW. Well. Uh. The moon eems to be part of a broken ncient being that sacrificed itself so that it could be used as a weapon against other LESS NICE ancient beings...
Aaaaand there's a sword up here I've gotta protect that's a big part of it
So that the right person can get it and beat the bad ancient beings.
Dungeons are a really good way to protect magic loot from wandering adventurers. So I made a dungeon.

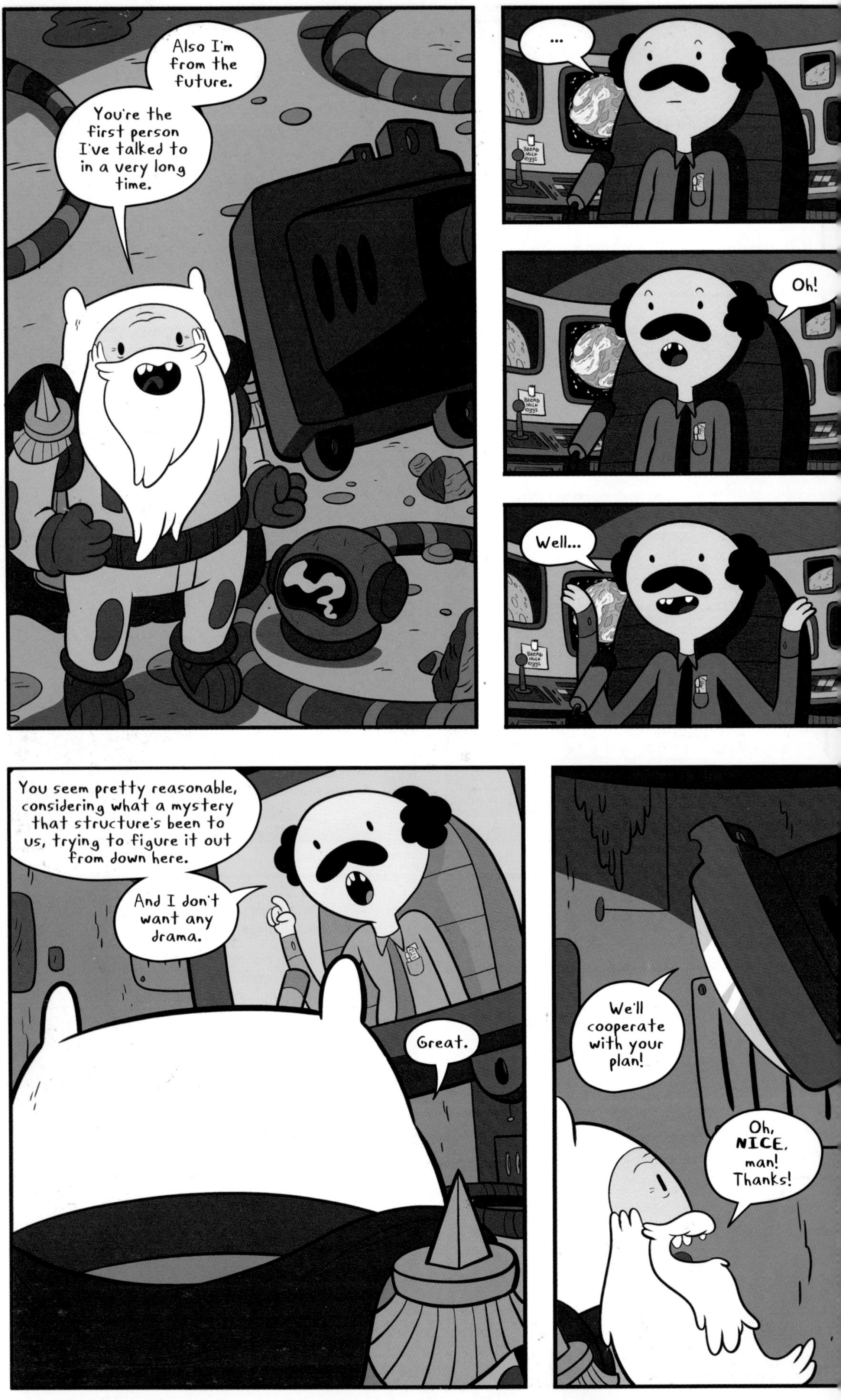
Also I'm from the future.
You're the first person I've talked to in a very long time.
...
BREAD MILK eggs
Oh!
Well...
You seem pretty reasonable, considering what a mystery that structure's been to us, trying to figure it out from down here.
And I don't want any drama.
Great.
We'll cooperate with your plan!
Oh, **NICE**, man! Thanks!

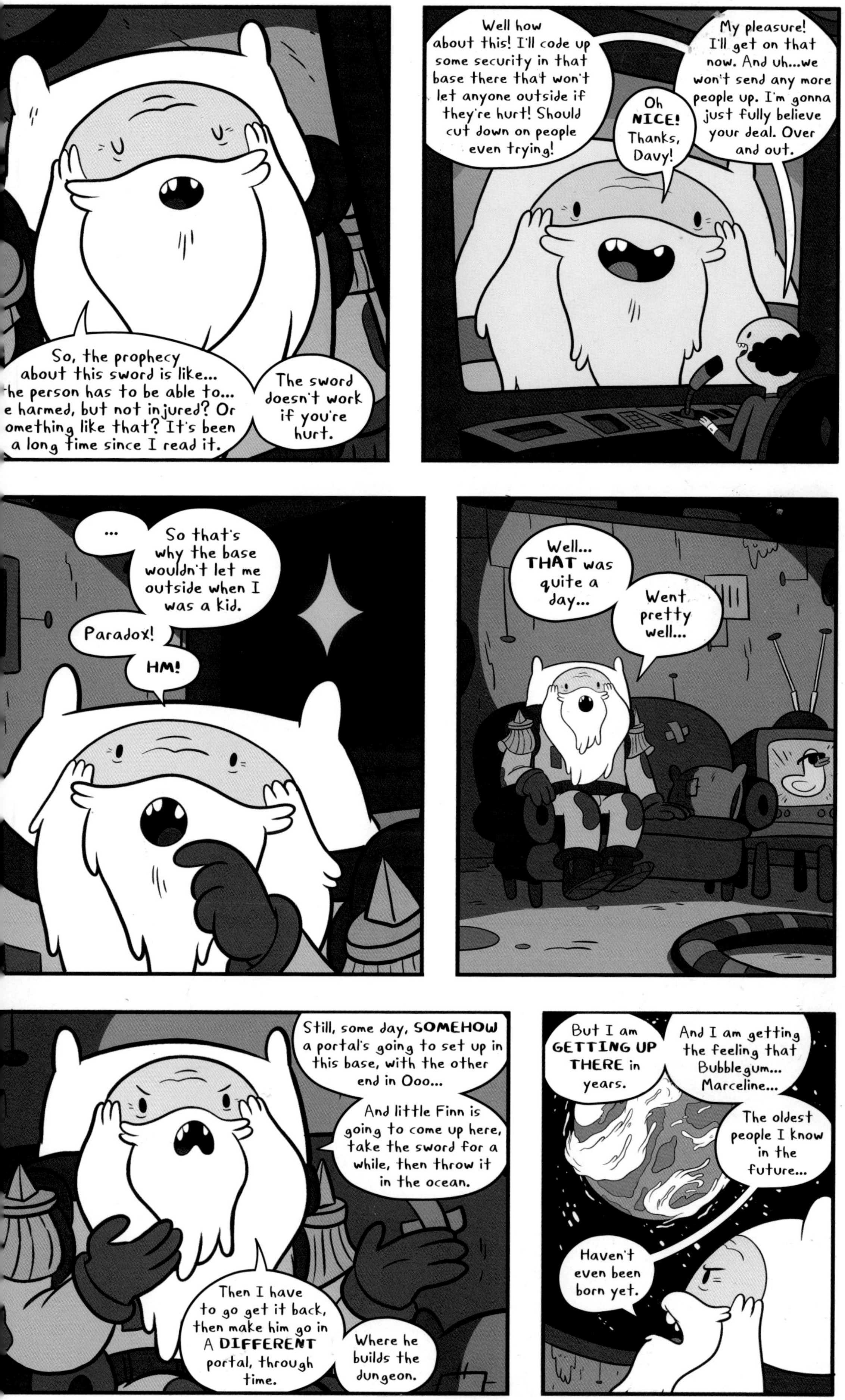

So, the prophecy about this sword is like... the person has to be able to... e harmed, but not injured? Or omething like that? It's been a long time since I read it.
The sword doesn't work if you're hurt.
Well how about this! I'll code up some security in that base there that won't let anyone outside if they're hurt! Should cut down on people even trying!
Oh NICE! Thanks, Davy!
My pleasure! I'll get on that now. And uh...we won't send any more people up. I'm gonna just fully believe your deal. Over and out.
...
So that's why the base wouldn't let me outside when I was a kid.
Paradox!
HM!
Well... THAT was quite a day...
Went pretty well...
Still, some day, SOMEHOW a portal's going to set up in this base, with the other end in Ooo...
And little Finn is going to come up here, take the sword for a while, then throw it in the ocean.
Then I have to go get it back, then make him go in A DIFFERENT portal, through time.
Where he builds the dungeon.
But I am GETTING UP THERE in years.
And I am getting the feeling that Bubblegum... Marceline...
The oldest people I know in the future...
Haven't even been born yet.

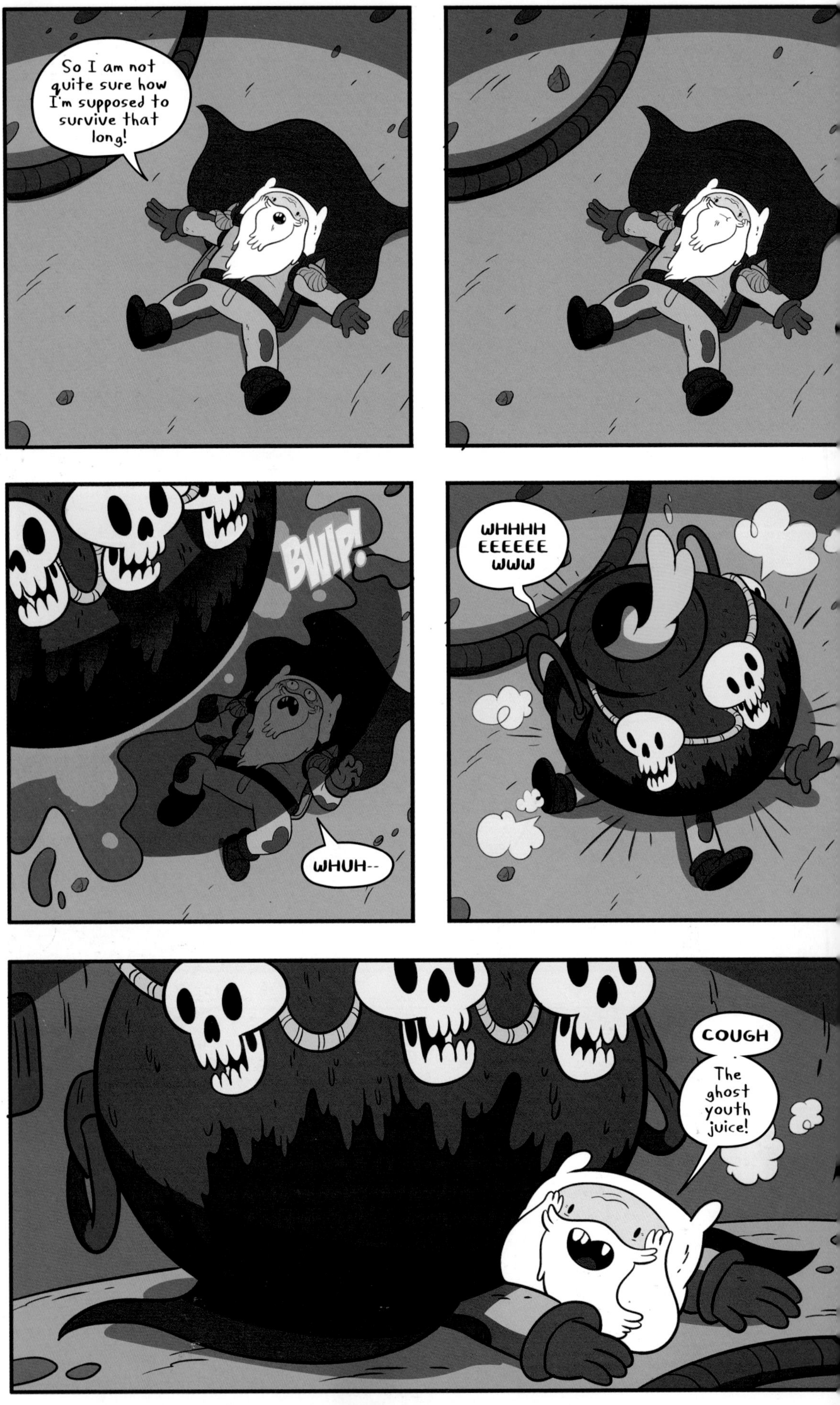
So I am not quite sure how I'm supposed to survive that long!
BWIP!
WHUH--
WHHHH EEEEEE WWW
COUGH
The ghost youth juice!

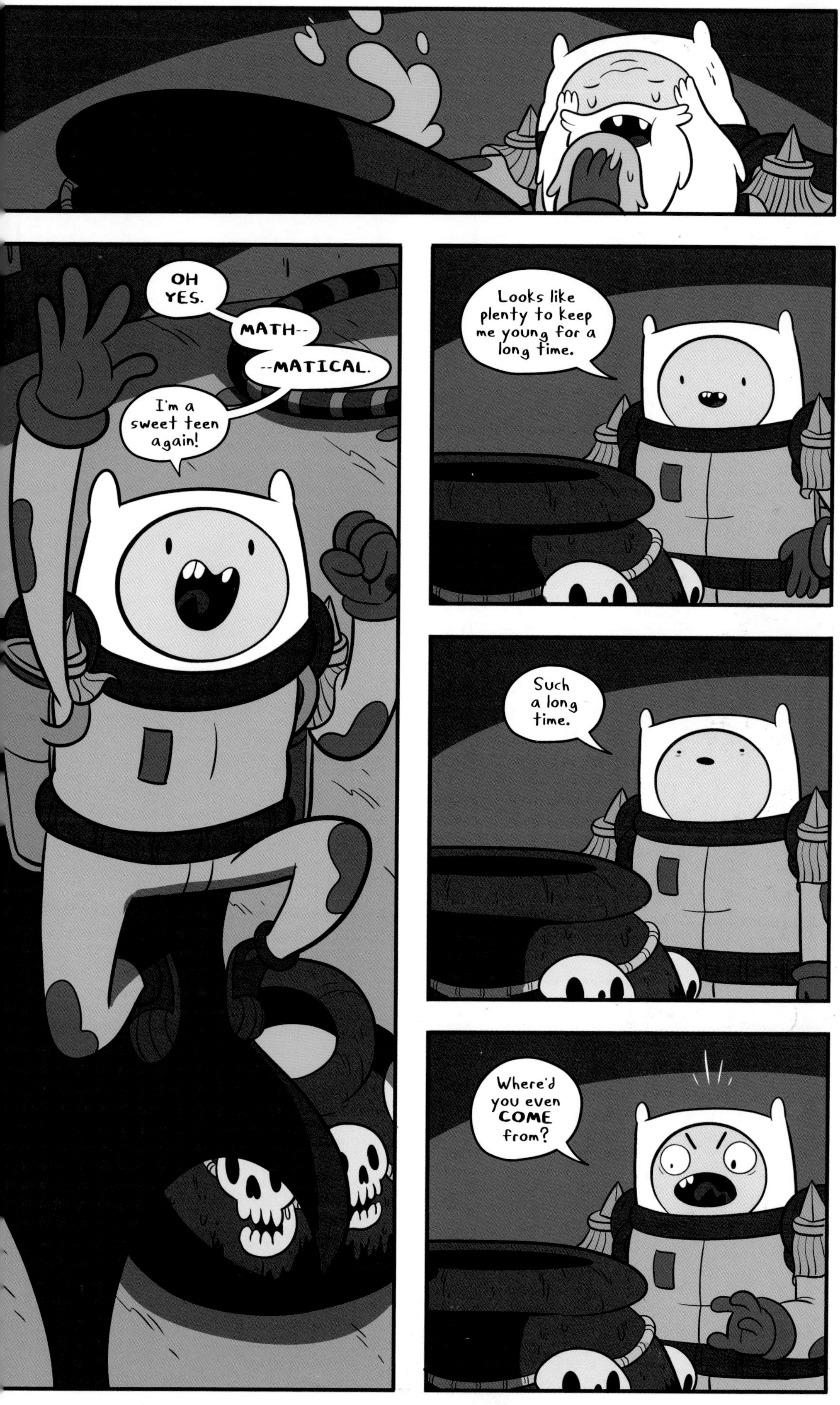

OH YES.
MATH--
--MATICAL.
I'm a sweet teen again!
Looks like plenty to keep me young for a long time.
Such a long time.
Where'd you even COME from?

The future.

Or the present?

Depends on your perspective, I guess.

DUNGEON

Thank you, Jake.

Hey I just hope Jake's better years in liquid form **GET** to the little guy.

It will. It is **HAS BEEN FORETOLD.**

Yeah, by **WHO?**

I don't know, man. Crazy magic told me here.

Crazy magic's always right.

Wherever he is, I wish I could be there with him.

Well, I suppose...

There's no reason why you can't. You helped us find the time portal that sent him to his long guardianship.

A buddy would probably be nice.

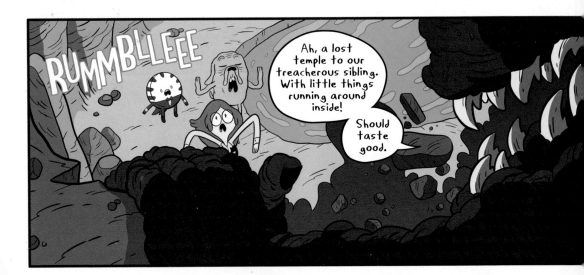

RUMMBLLEEE

Ah, a lost temple to our treacherous sibling. With little things running around inside!

Should taste good.

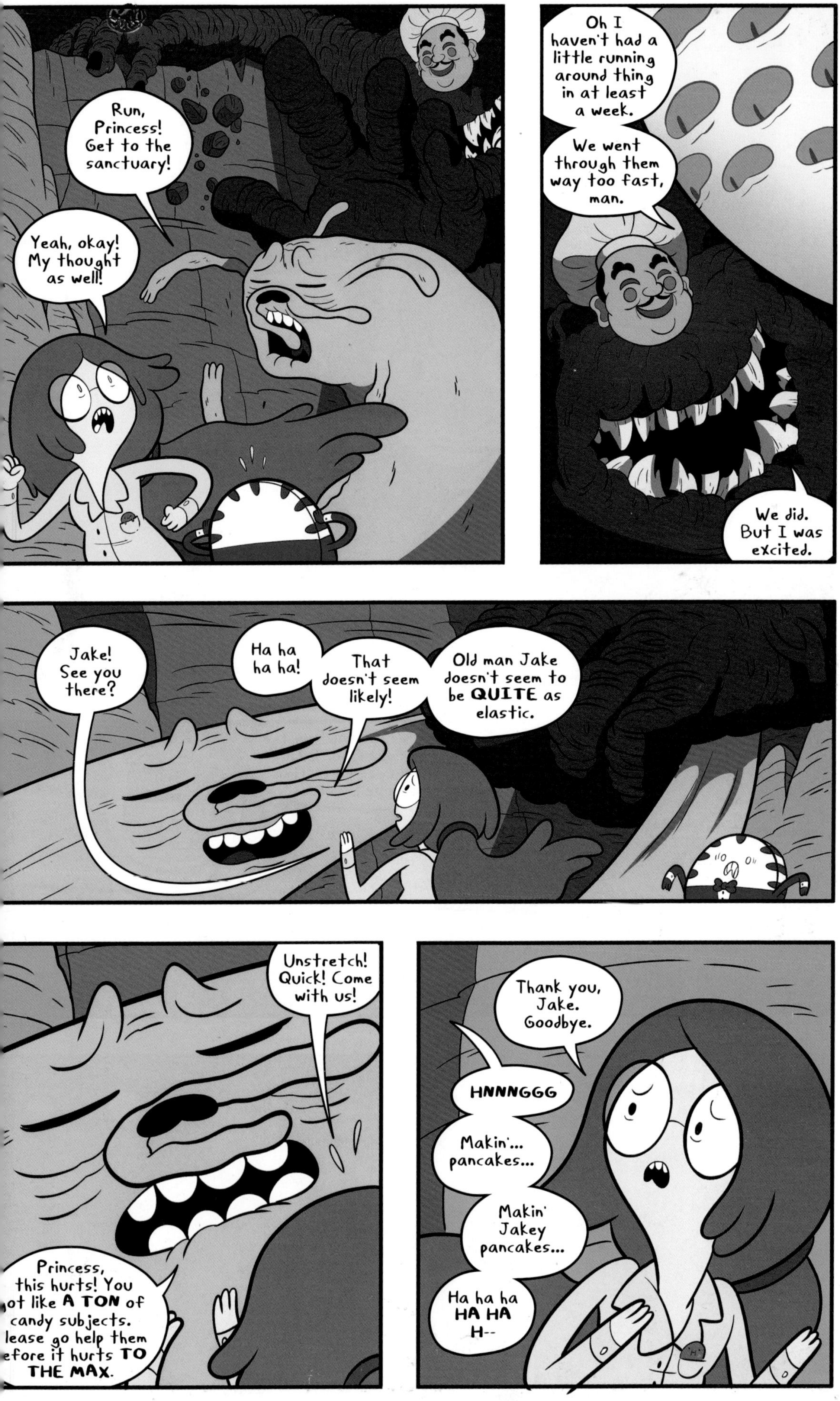
Run, Princess! Get to the sanctuary!
Yeah, okay! My thought as well!
Oh I haven't had a little running around thing in at least a week.
We went through them way too fast, man.
We did. But I was excited.
Jake! See you there?
Ha ha ha ha!
That doesn't seem likely!
Old man Jake doesn't seem to be **QUITE** as elastic.
Unstretch! Quick! Come with us!
Princess, this hurts! You ot like **A TON** of candy subjects. lease go help them efore it hurts **TO THE MAX**.
Thank you, Jake. Goodbye.
HNNNGGG
Makin'... pancakes...
Makin' Jakey pancakes...
Ha ha ha **HA HA** H--

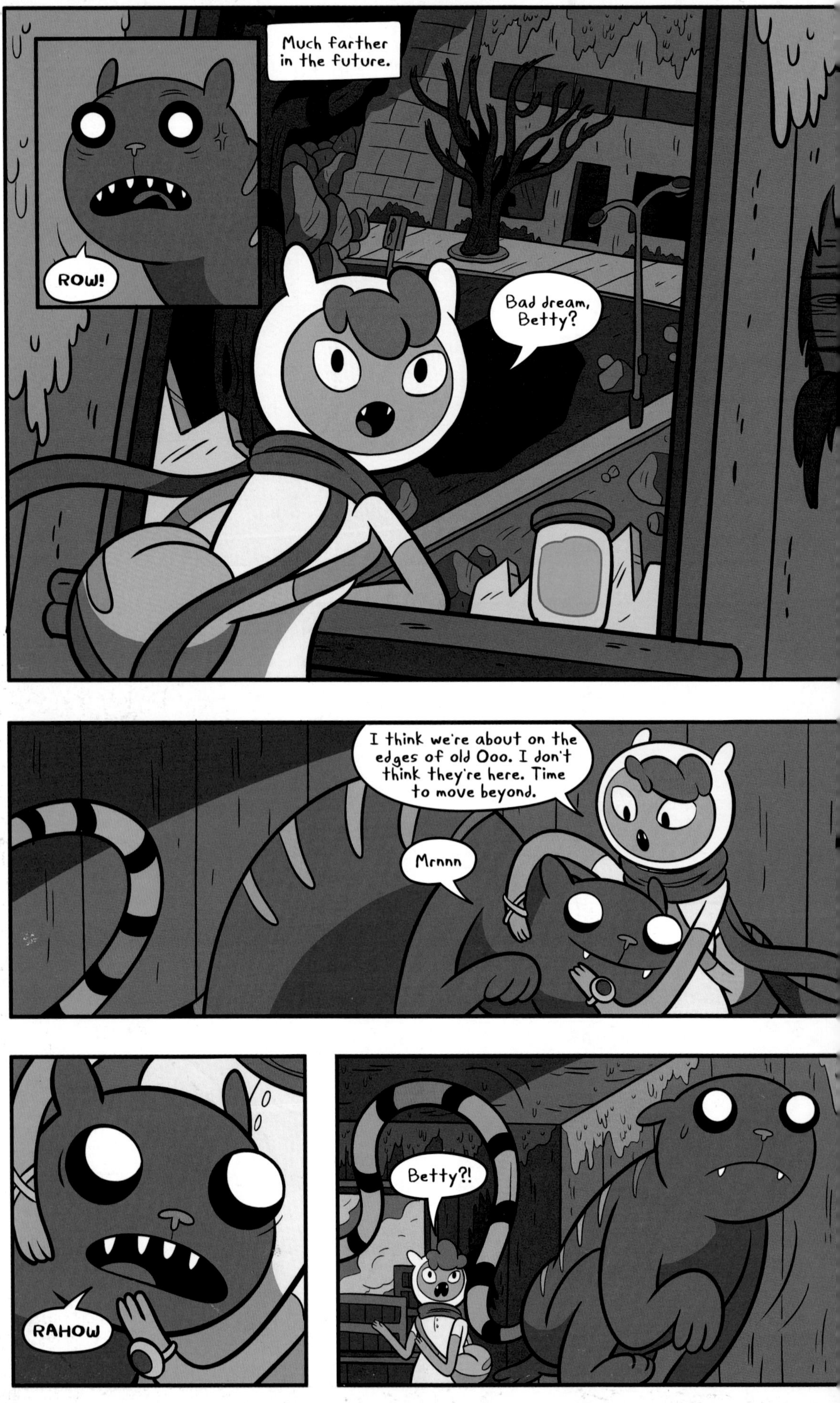
Much farther in the future.
ROW!
Bad dream, Betty?
I think we're about on the edges of old Ooo. I don't think they're here. Time to move beyond.
Mrnnn
RAHOW
Betty?!

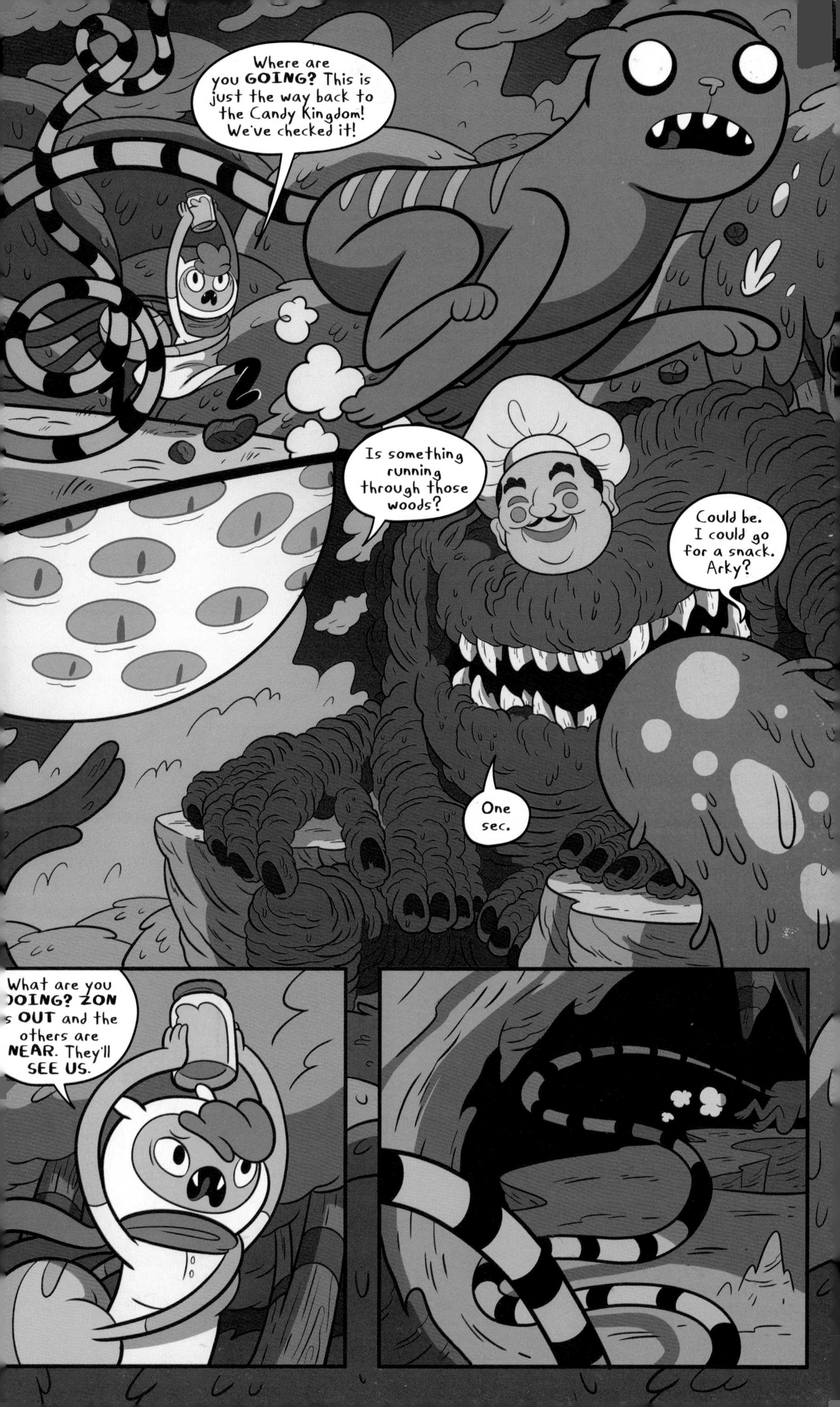
Where are you **GOING?** This is just the way back to the Candy Kingdom! We've checked it!
Is something running through those woods?
Could be. I could go for a snack. Arky?
One sec.
What are you **DOING? ZON** is **OUT** and the others are **NEAR**. They'll **SEE US.**

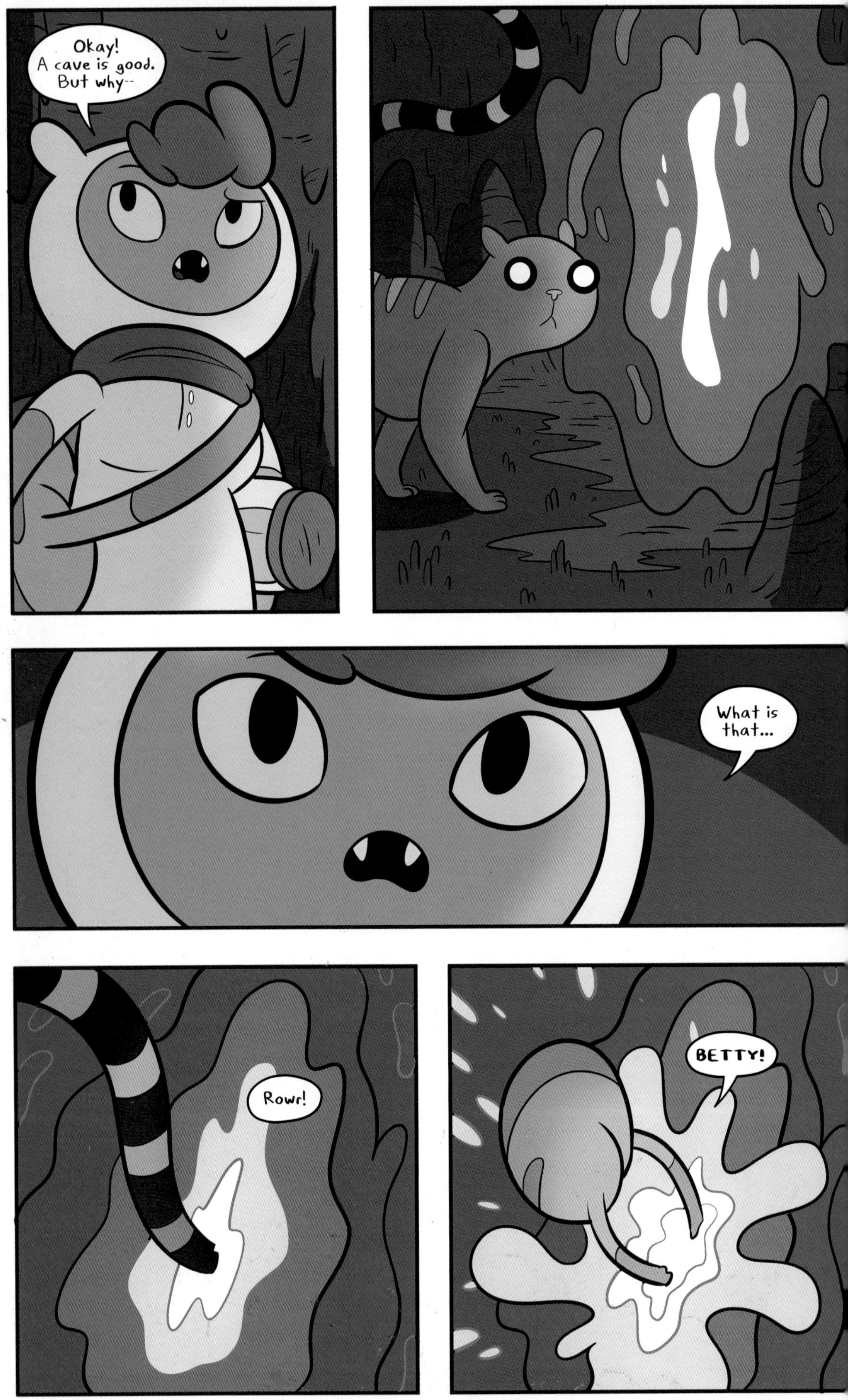

Okay! A cave is good. But why--
What is that...
Rowr!
BETTY!

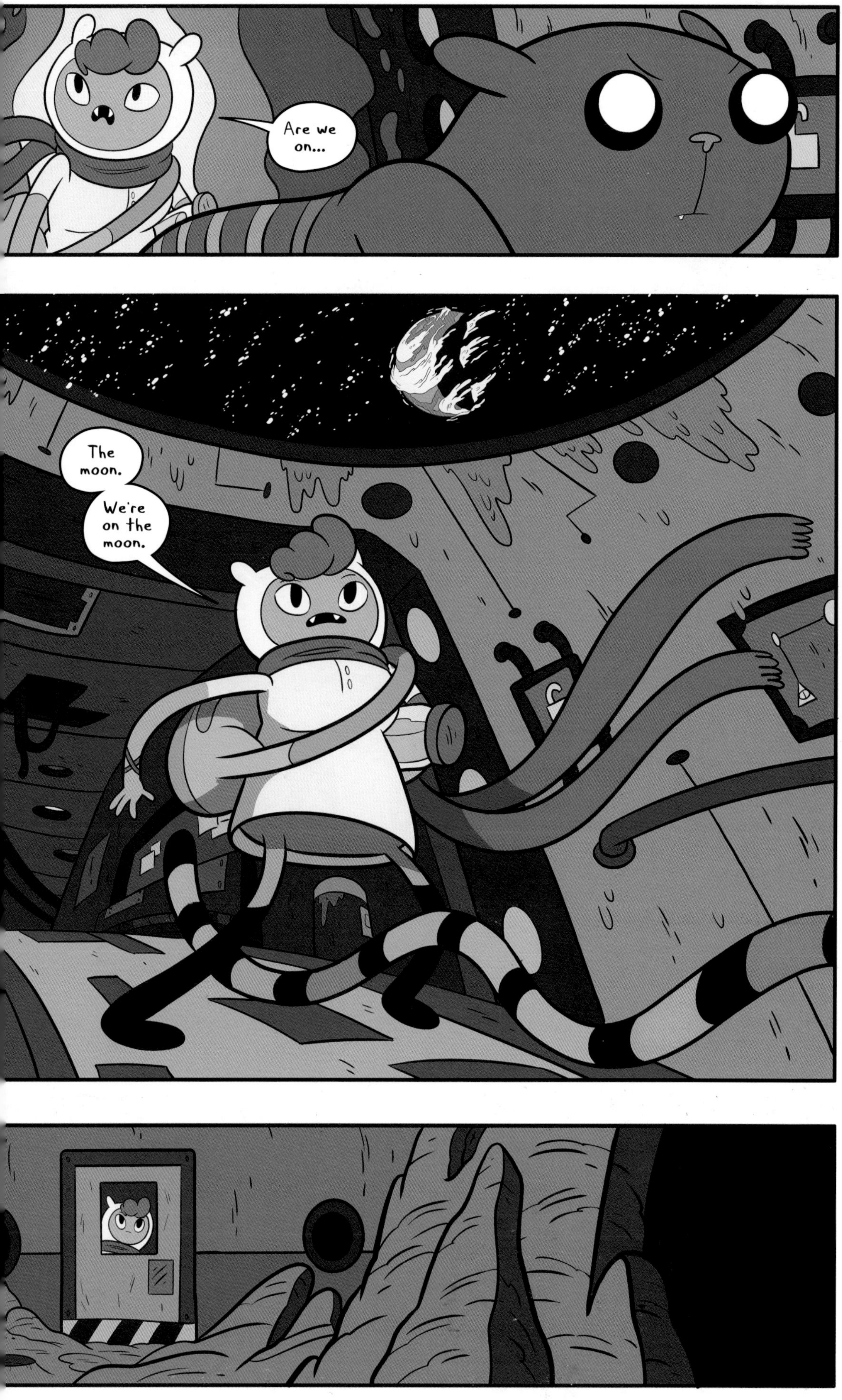
Are we on...
The moon.
We're on the moon.

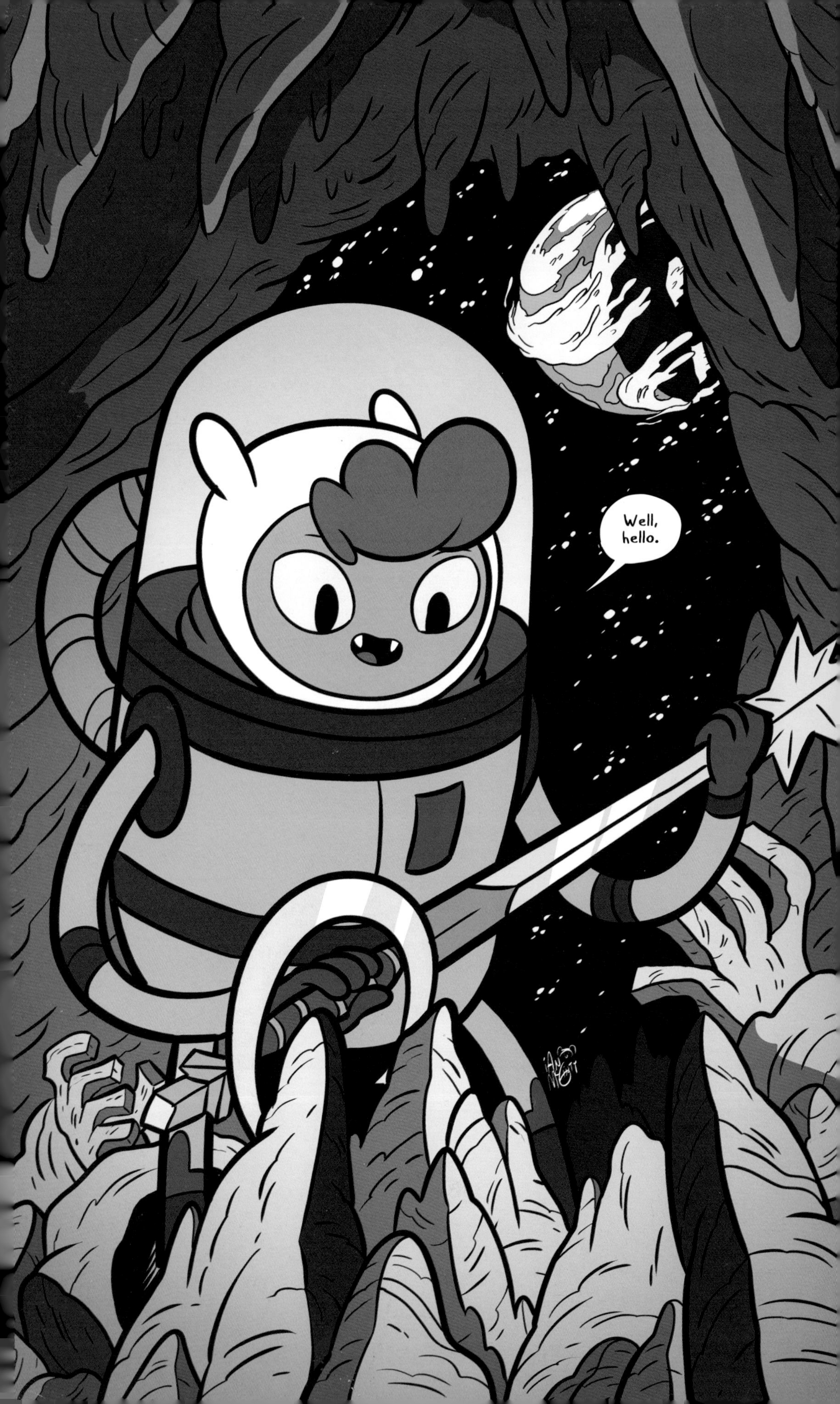
Well, hello.

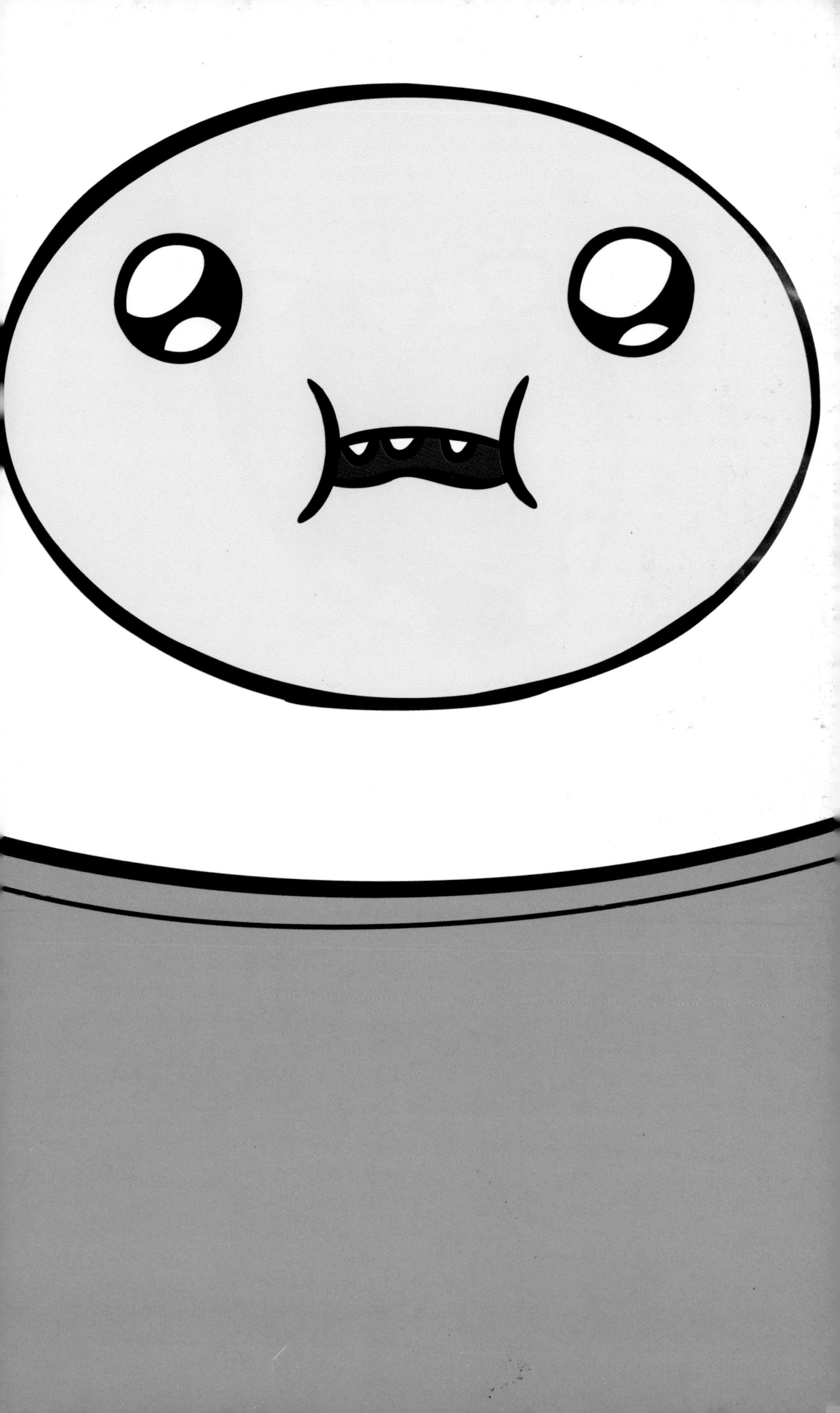

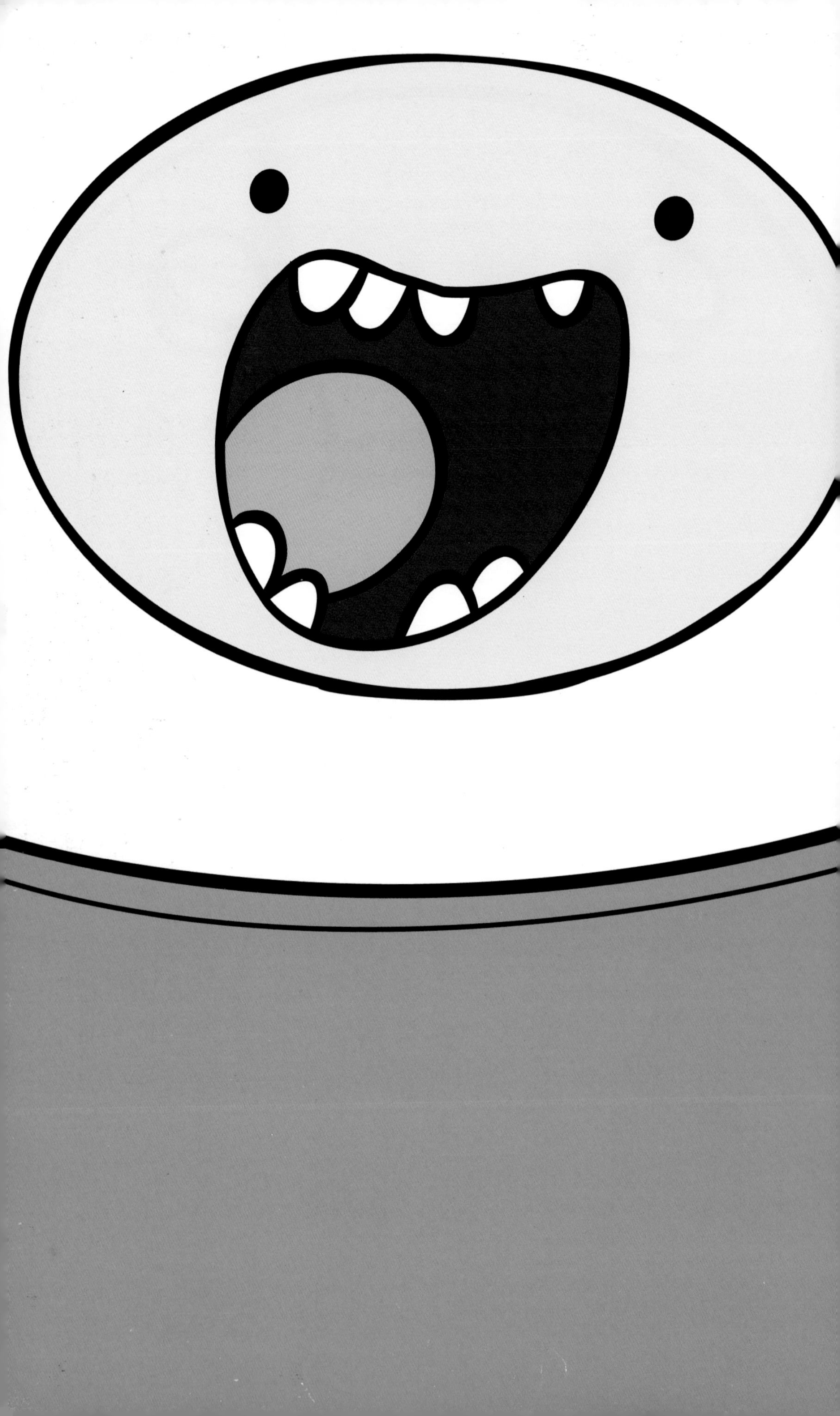

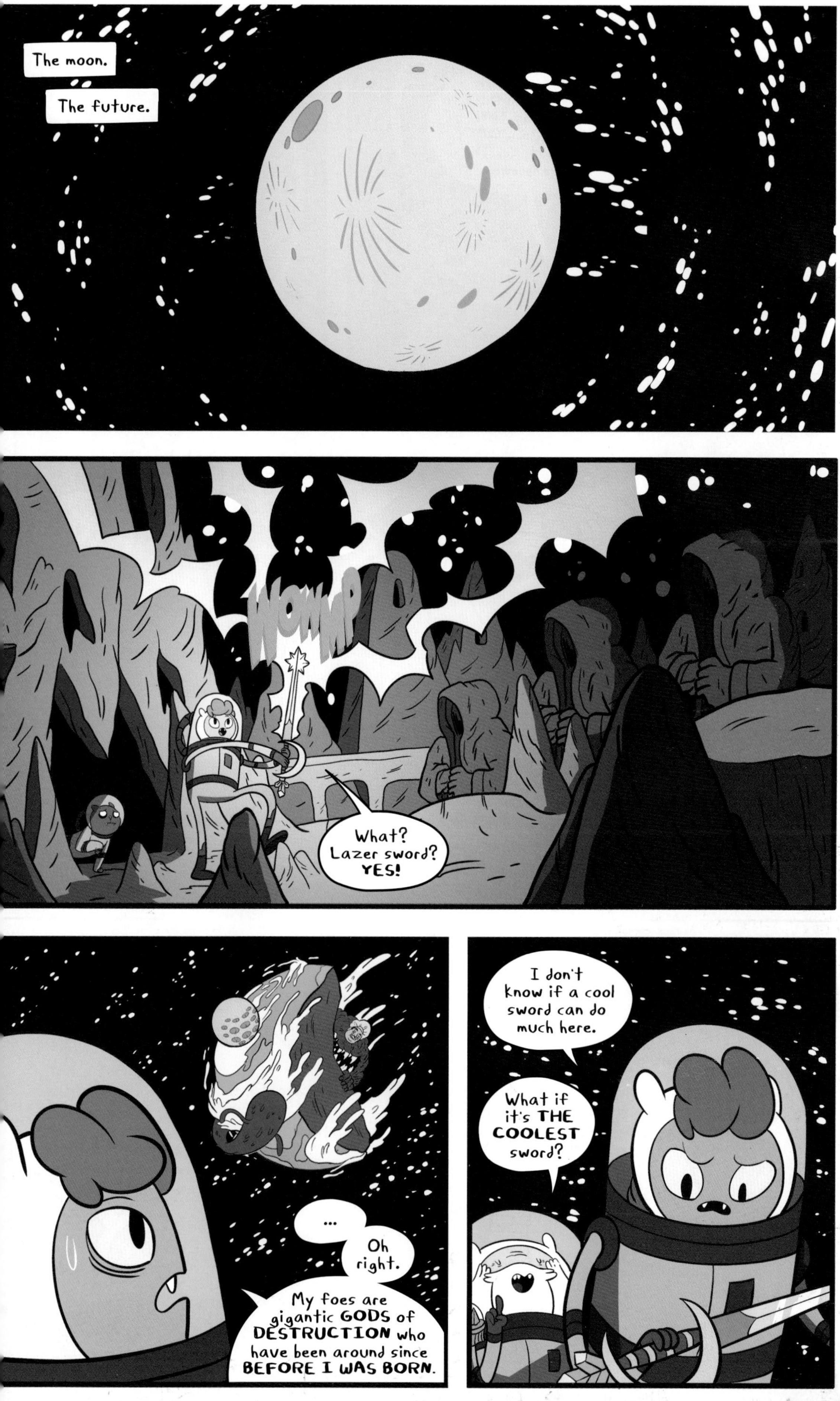
The moon.
The future.
What? Lazer sword? YES!
...
Oh right.
My foes are gigantic GODS of DESTRUCTION who have been around since BEFORE I WAS BORN.
I don't know if a cool sword can do much here.
What if it's THE COOLEST sword?

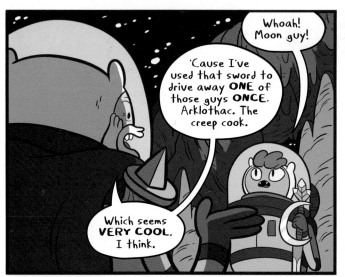

Whoah! Moon guy!

'Cause I've used that sword to drive away **ONE** of those guys **ONCE**. Arklothac. The creep cook.

Which seems **VERY COOL**, I think.

THIS works on **THEM?**

Wait, then why are they still here? If you used it successfully...

Well given that Arklothac still came back and cooked up Ooo, I wouldn't say it was **TOTALLY** successful?

I'm Finn, by the way.

Penelope. And this is my tigercorn.

I'm **MY OWN** Tigercorn. But hi.

I think you're about to do something pretty mathematical, Penelope.

Mathematical?

Eh, old saying.

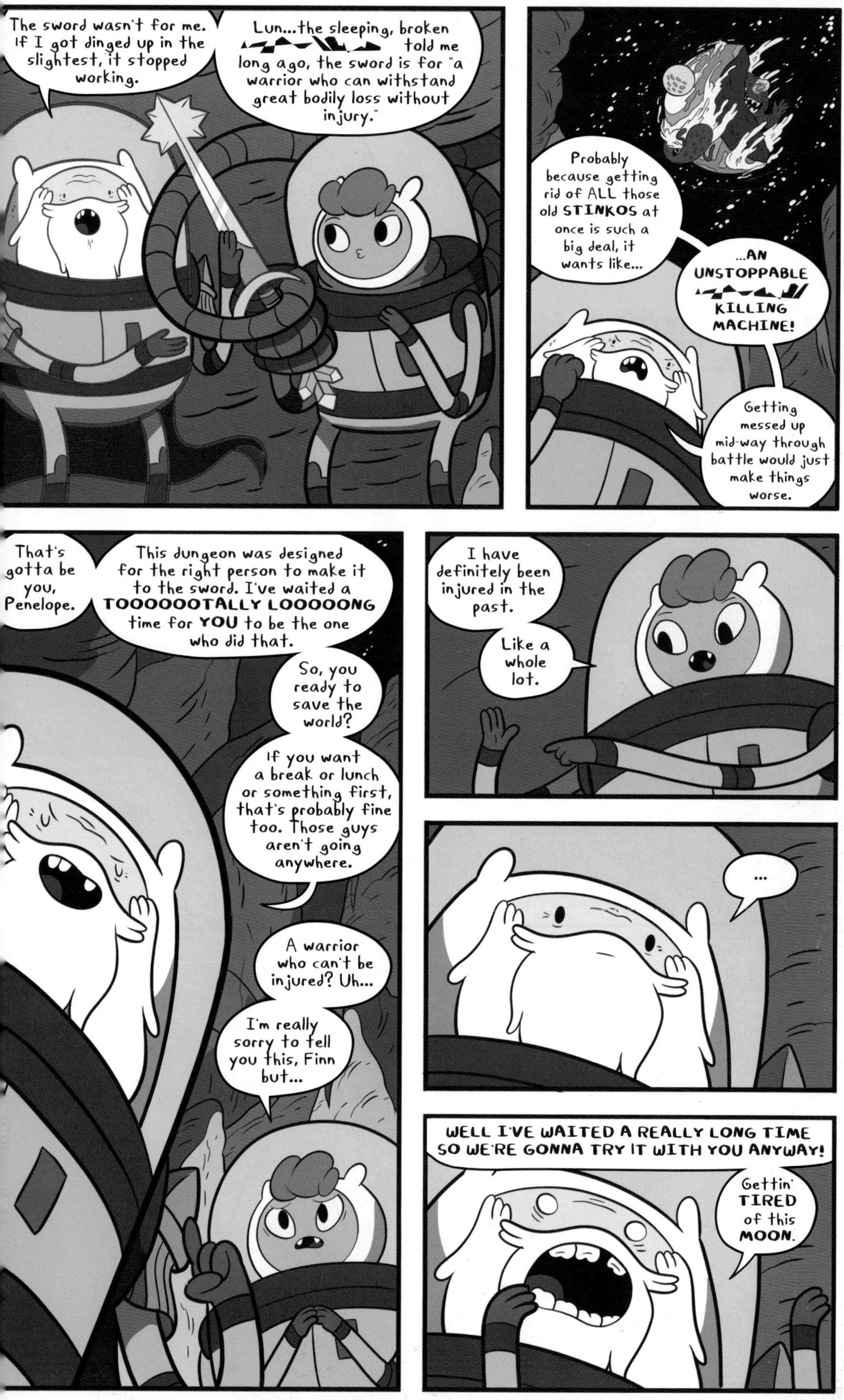
The sword wasn't for me. If I got dinged up in the slightest, it stopped working.
Lun...the sleeping, broken told me long ago, the sword is for "a warrior who can withstand great bodily loss without injury."
Probably because getting rid of ALL those old STINKOS at once is such a big deal, it wants like...
...AN UNSTOPPABLE KILLING MACHINE!
Getting messed up mid-way through battle would just make things worse.
That's gotta be you, Penelope.
This dungeon was designed for the right person to make it to the sword. I've waited a TOOOOOOTALLY LOOOOONG time for YOU to be the one who did that.
So, you ready to save the world?
If you want a break or lunch or something first, that's probably fine too. Those guys aren't going anywhere.
A warrior who can't be injured? Uh...
I'm really sorry to tell you this, Finn but...
I have definitely been injured in the past.
Like a whole lot.
...
WELL I'VE WAITED A REALLY LONG TIME SO WE'RE GONNA TRY IT WITH YOU ANYWAY!
Gettin' TIRED of this MOON.

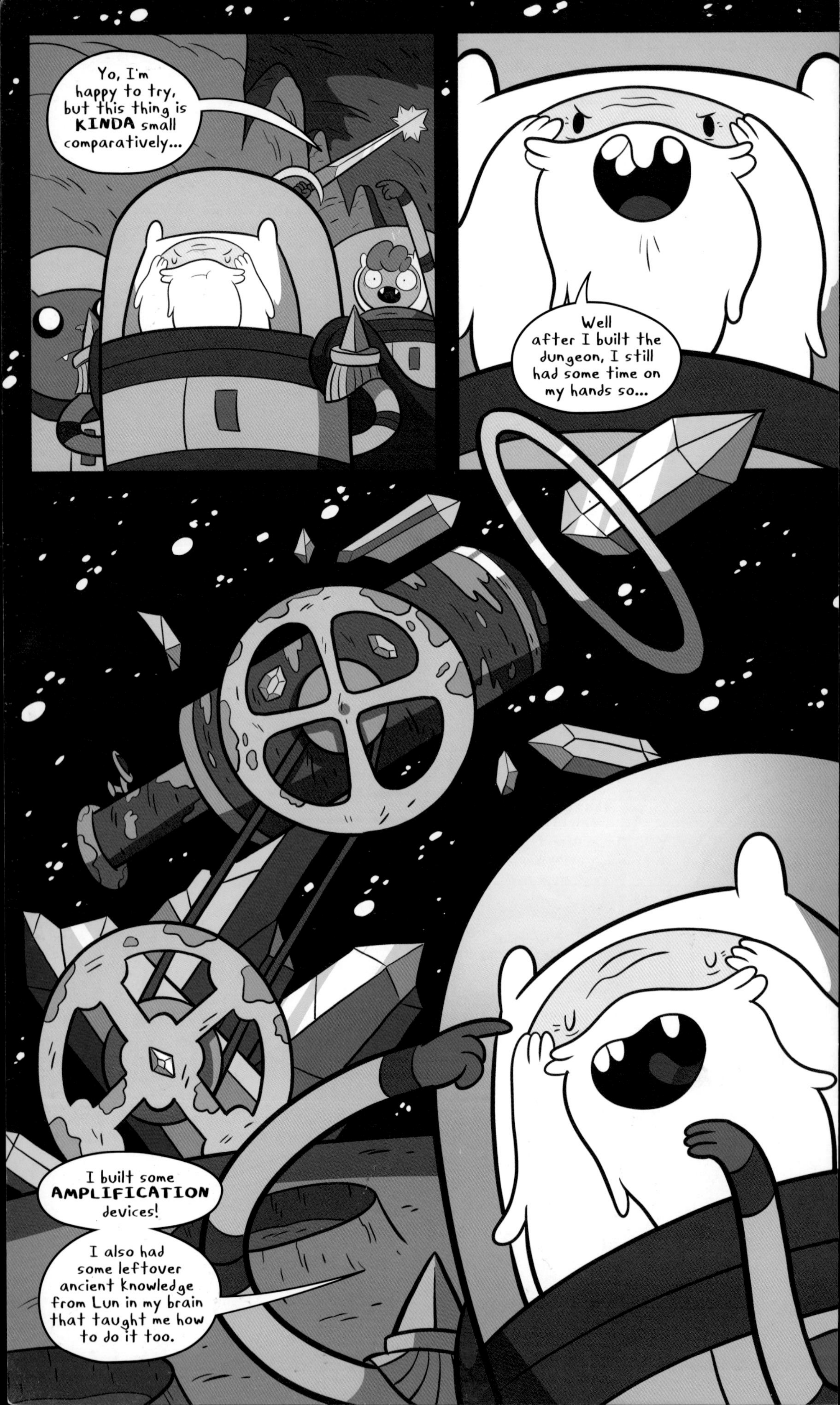
Yo, I'm happy to try, but this thing is KINDA small comparatively...
Well after I built the dungeon, I still had some time on my hands so...
I built some AMPLIFICATION devices!
I also had some leftover ancient knowledge from Lun in my brain that taught me how to do it too.

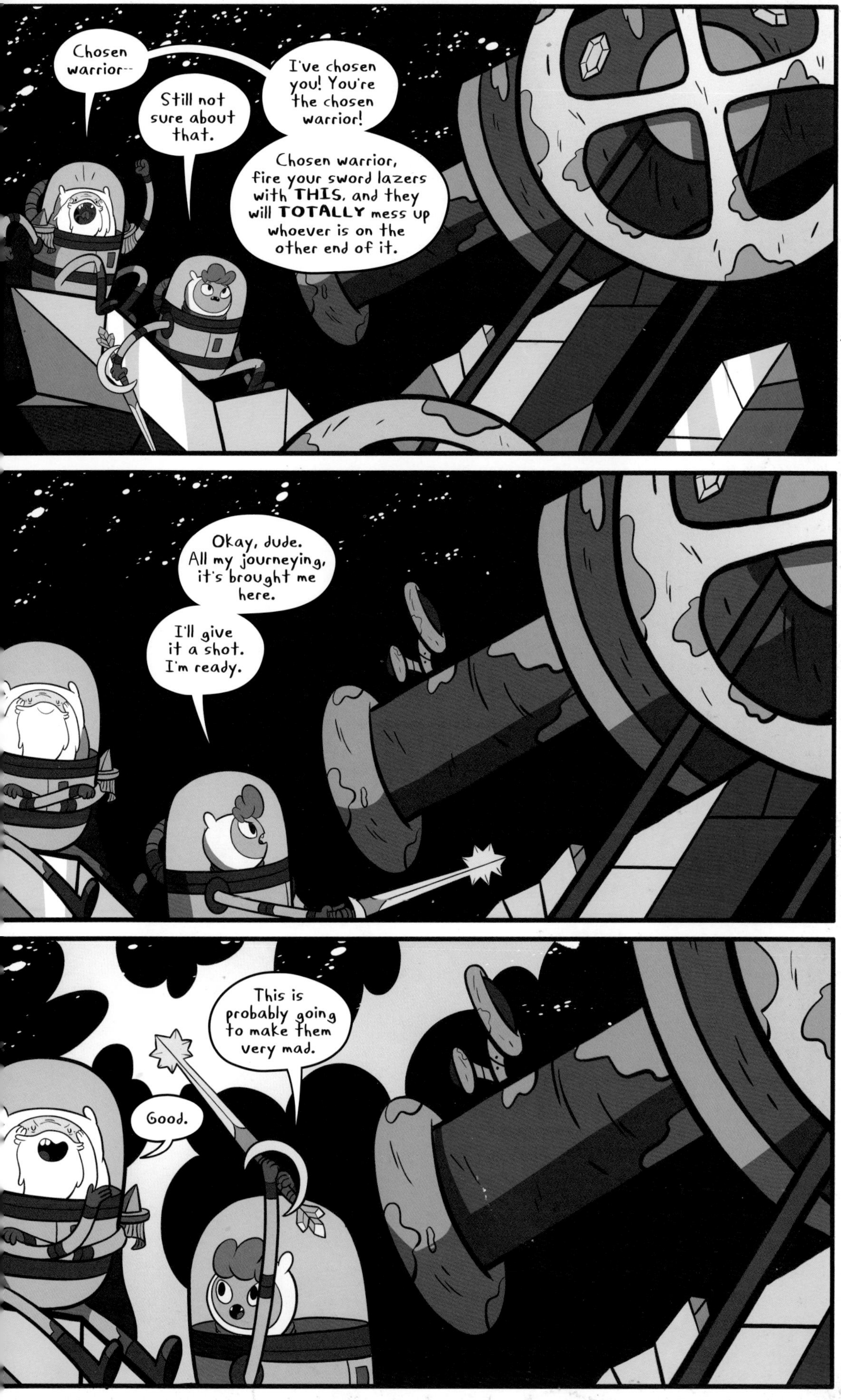
Chosen warrior--
Still not sure about that.
I've chosen you! You're the chosen warrior!
Chosen warrior, fire your sword lazers with THIS, and they will TOTALLY mess up whoever is on the other end of it.
Okay, dude. All my journeying, it's brought me here.
I'll give it a shot. I'm ready.
This is probably going to make them very mad.
Good.

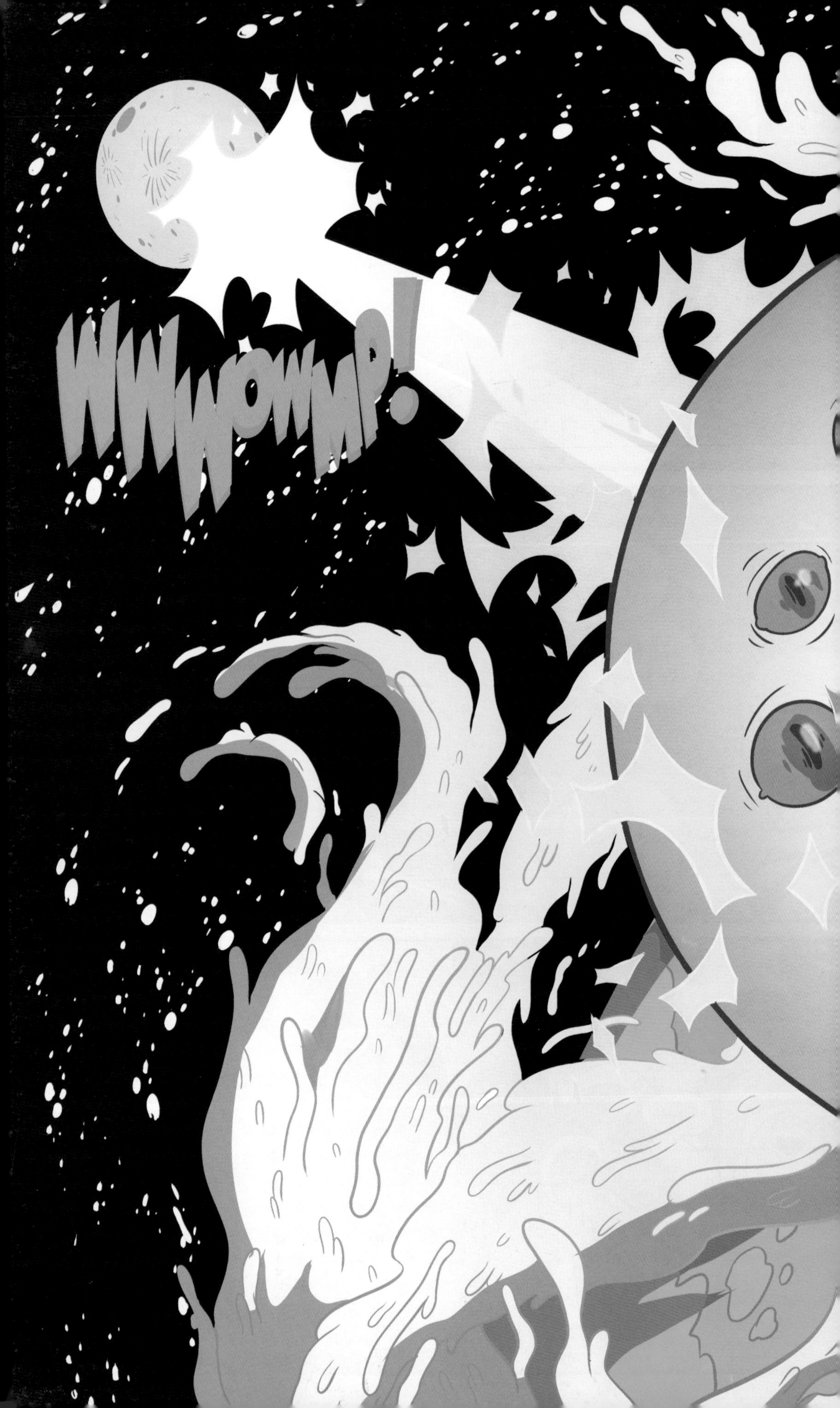
WWWOWMP!

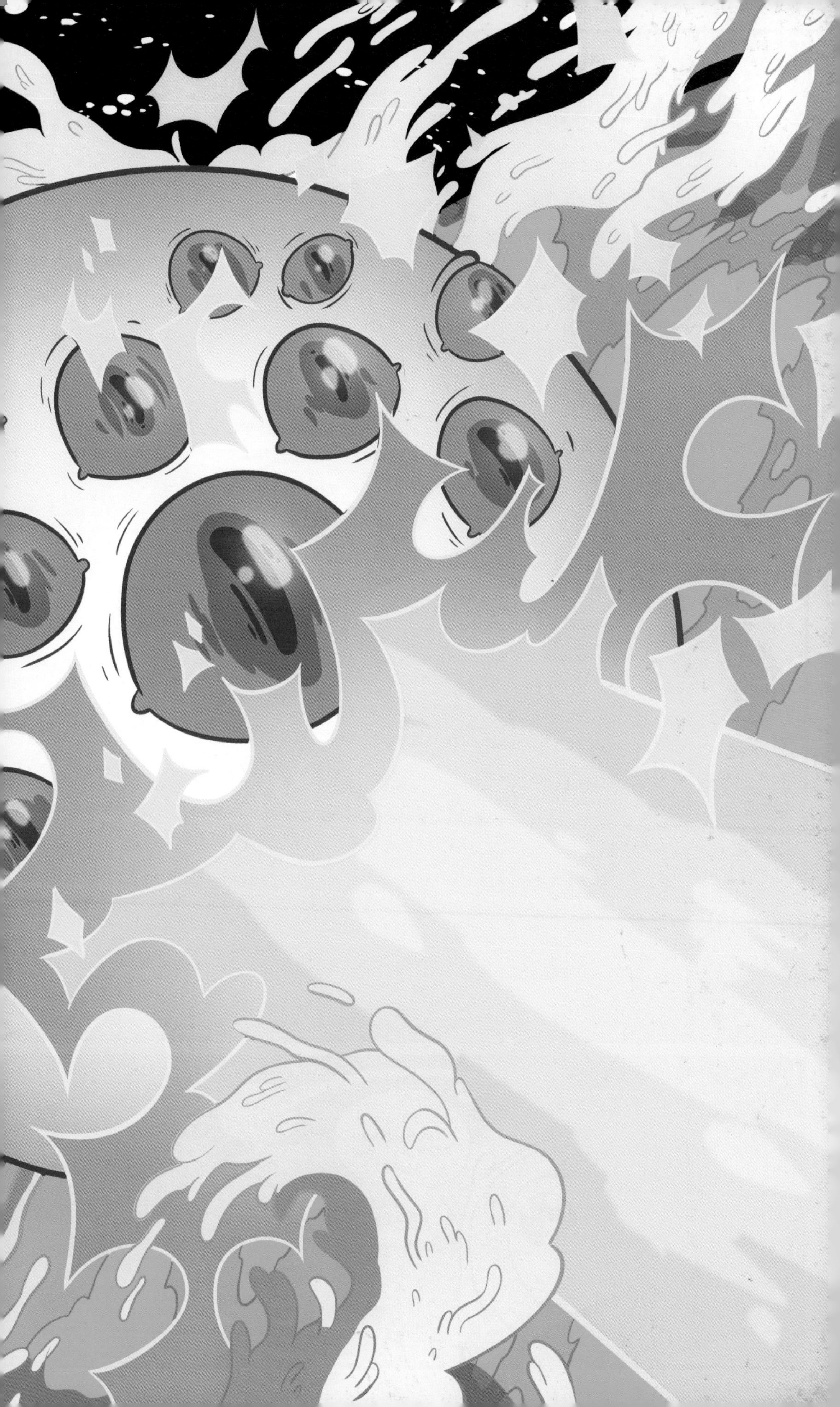

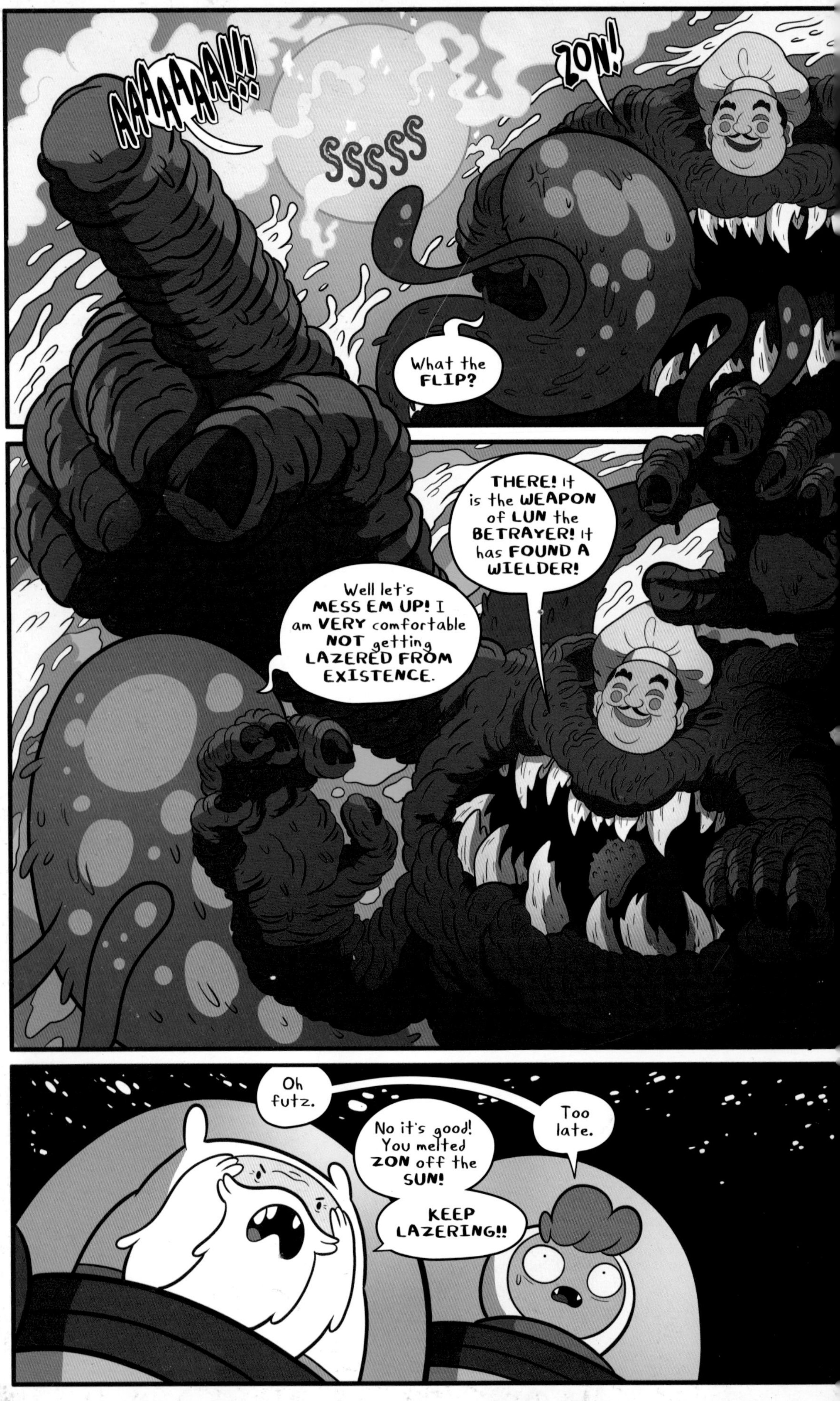
AAAAAAA!!!
SSSSS
ZON!
What the FLIP?
THERE! It is the WEAPON of LUN the BETRAYER! It has FOUND A WIELDER!
Well let's MESS EM UP! I am VERY comfortable NOT getting LAZERED FROM EXISTENCE.
Oh futz.
Too late.
No it's good! You melted ZON off the SUN!
KEEP LAZERING!!

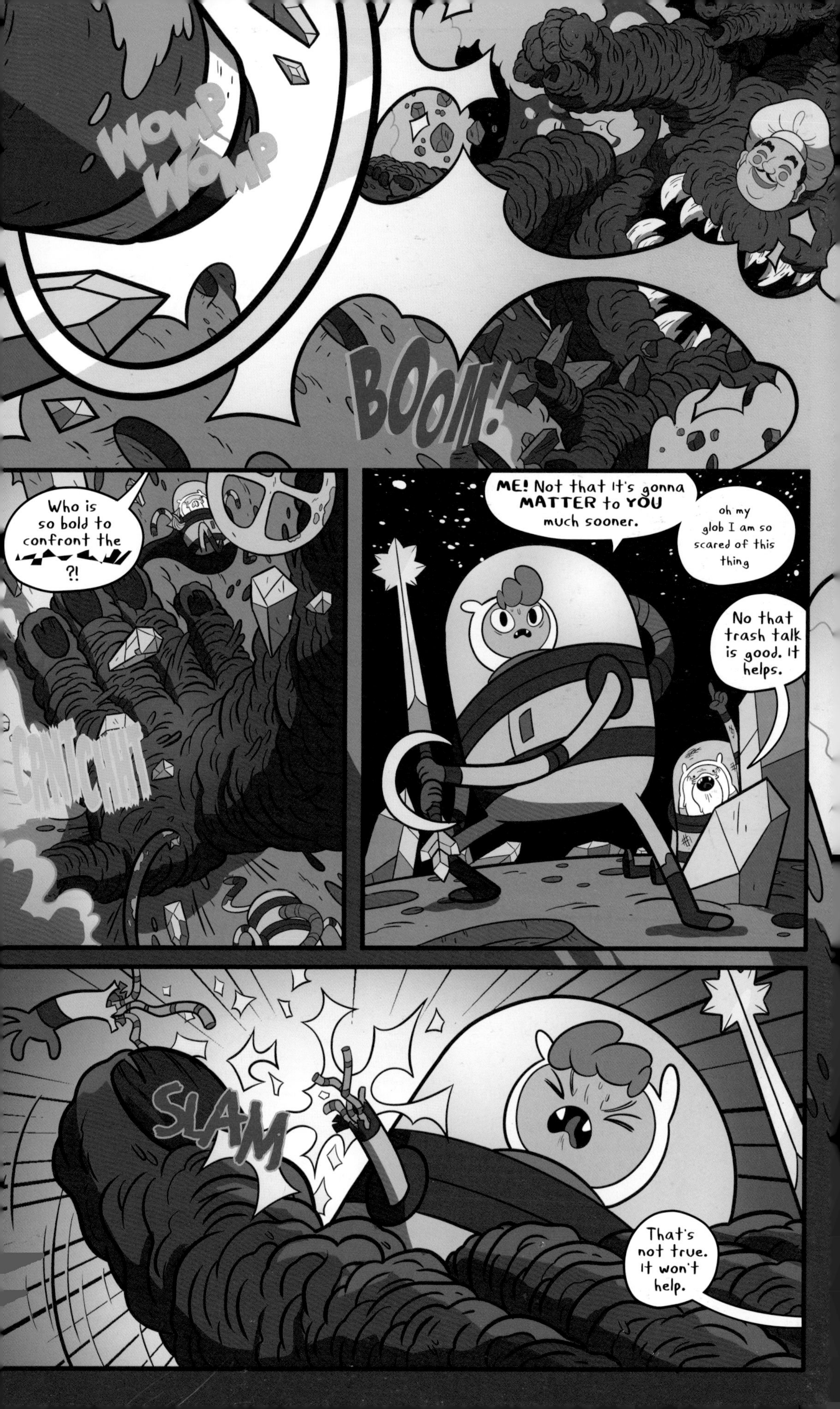
WOMP
WOMP
BOOM!
Who is so bold to confront the
?!
CRNTCHHT
ME! Not that It's gonna MATTER to YOU much sooner.
oh my glob I am so scared of this thing
No that trash talk is good. It helps.
SLAM
That's not true. It won't help.

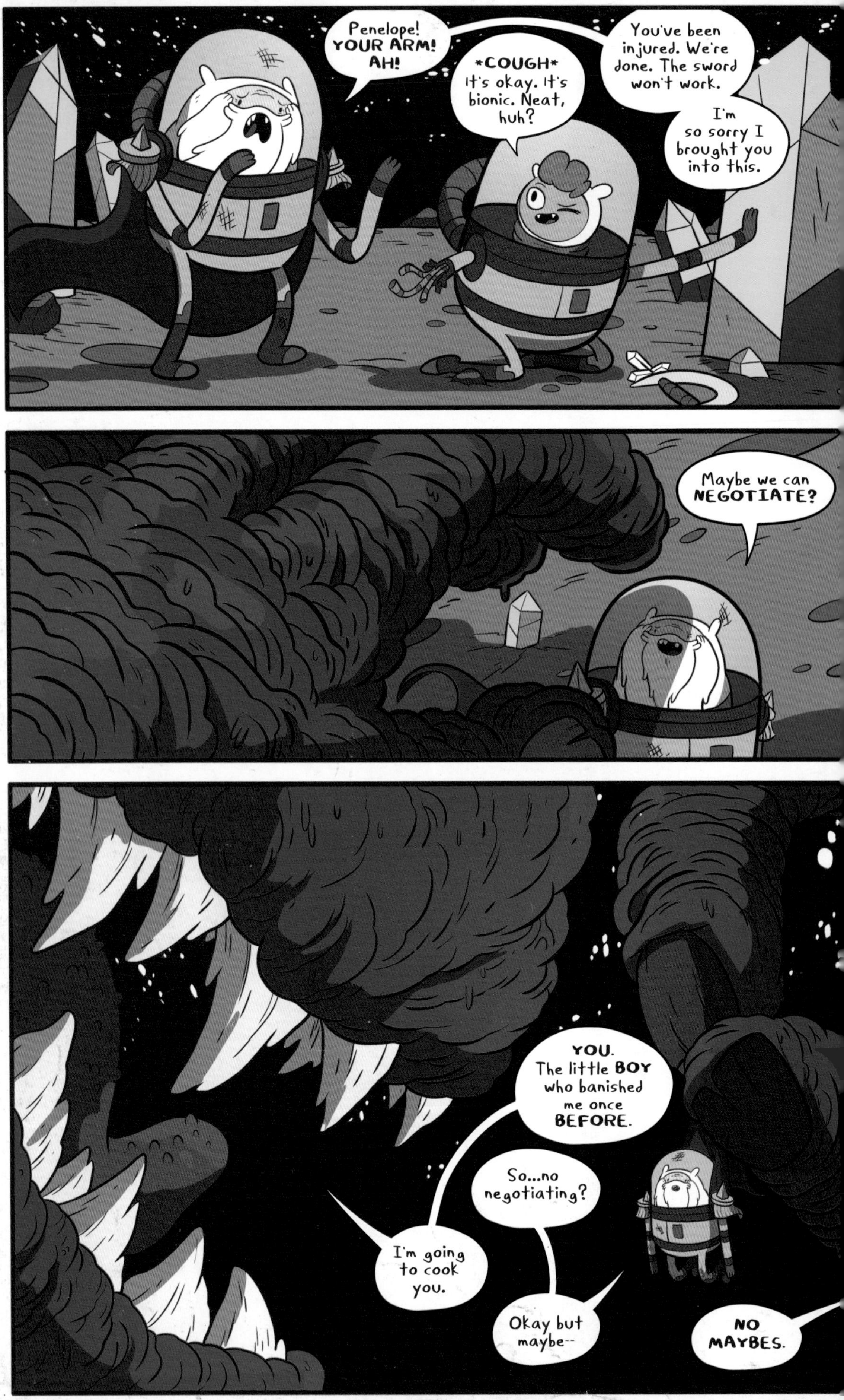
Penelope! YOUR ARM! AH!
COUGH It's okay. It's bionic. Neat, huh?
You've been injured. We're done. The sword won't work.
I'm so sorry I brought you into this.
Maybe we can NEGOTIATE?
YOU. The little BOY who banished me once BEFORE.
I'm going to cook you.
So...no negotiating?
Okay but maybe--
NO MAYBES.

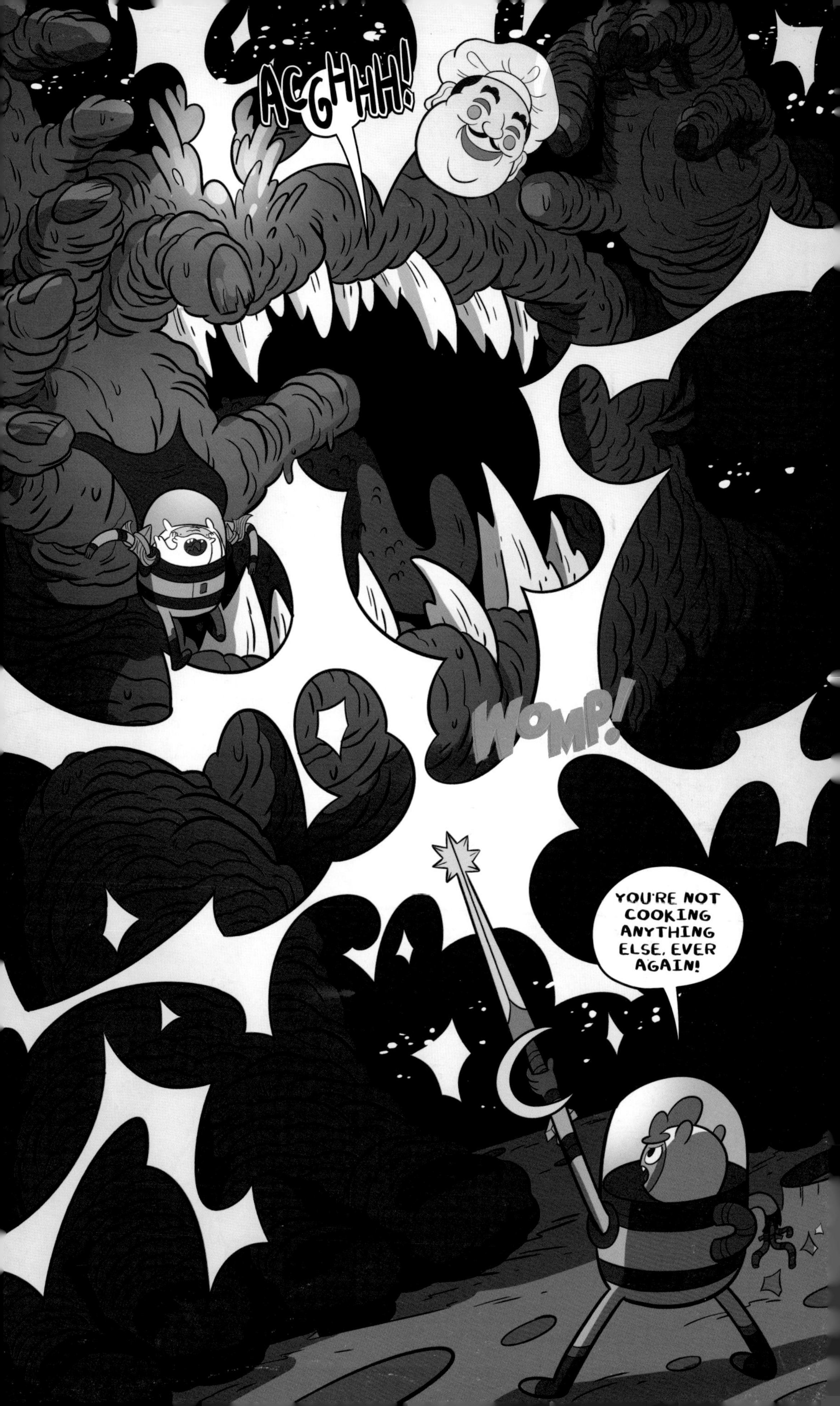
ACGHHH!
WOMP!
YOU'RE NOT COOKING ANYTHING ELSE, EVER AGAIN!

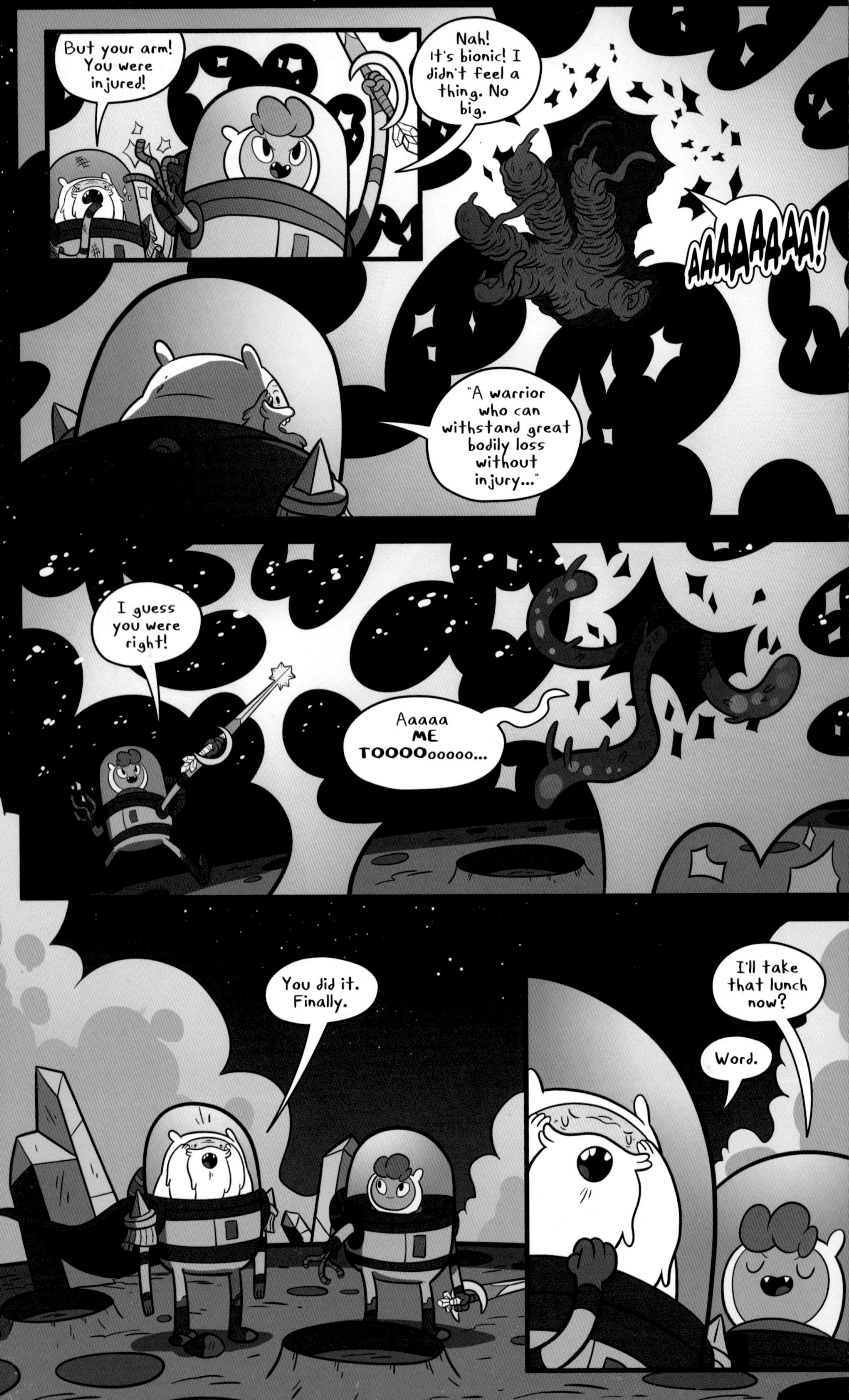

But your arm! You were injured!
Nah! It's bionic! I didn't feel a thing. No big.
AAAAAAAA!
"A warrior who can withstand great bodily loss without injury..."
I guess you were right!
Aaaaa ME TOOOOooooo...
You did it. Finally.
I'll take that lunch now?
Word.

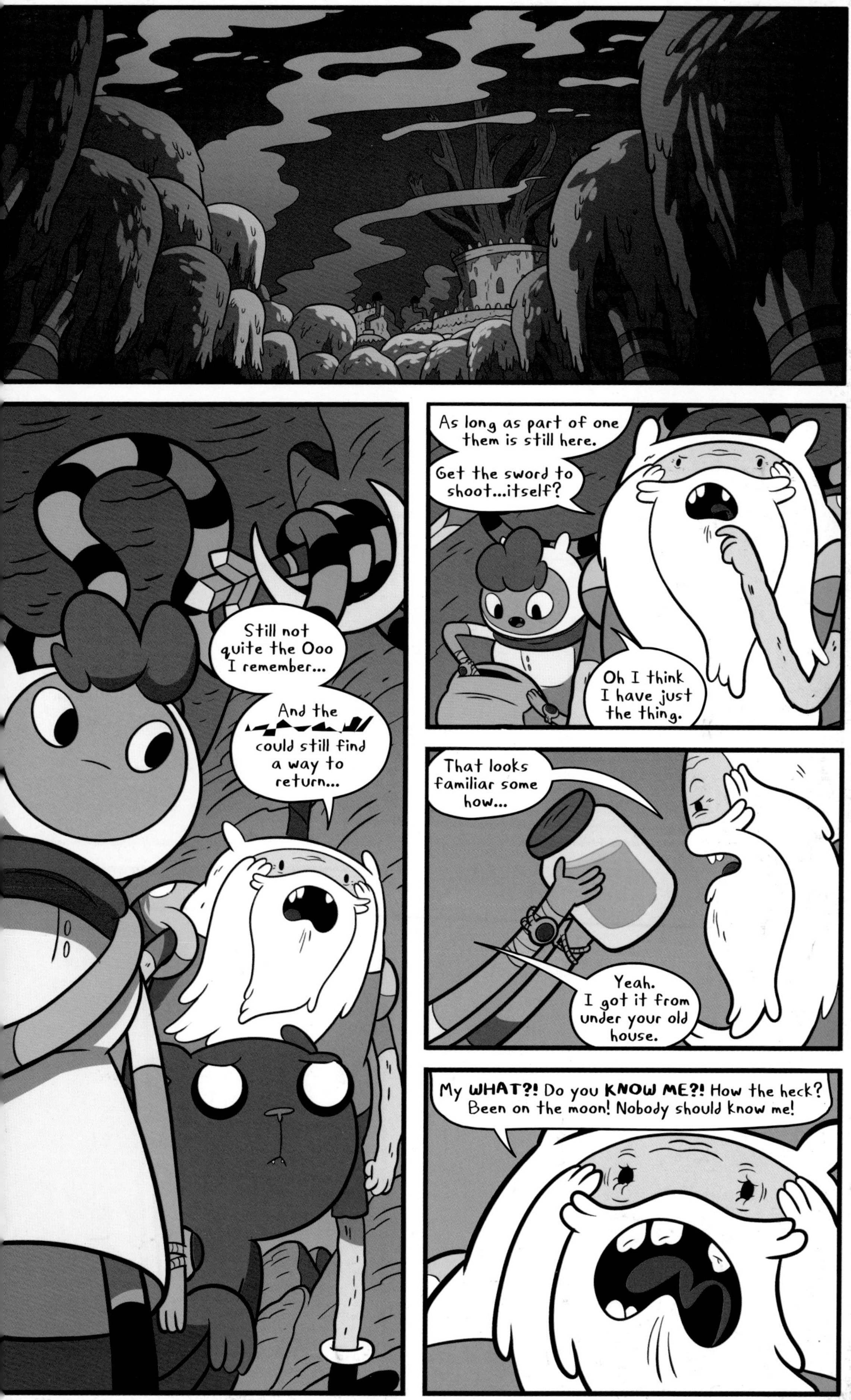

Still not quite the Ooo I remember...
And the
could still find a way to return...
As long as part of one them is still here.
Get the sword to shoot...itself?
Oh I think I have just the thing.
That looks familiar some how...
Yeah. I got it from under your old house.
My **WHAT?!** Do you **KNOW ME?!** How the heck? Been on the moon! Nobody should know me!

I'm **YOU**, dude. And you become **ME**.

"I found the book of all our prior incarnations. I lived in them, the same way you did. Your life gave me the clues I needed to defeat the...

Whatever you call them."

⚡⚡⚡. It does take practice to nail that pronunciation.

So you saw all of it too... The comet. The butterfly. Shoko. Davy.

The weird crystal goo thing in another dimension?

Yeah what was up with **THAT?**

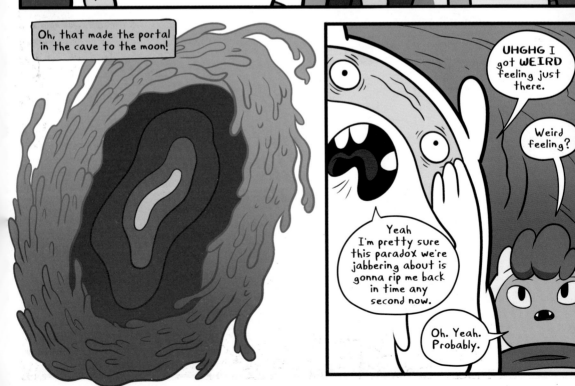

Oh, that made the portal in the cave to the moon!

UHGHG I got **WEIRD** feeling just there.

Weird feeling?

Yeah I'm pretty sure this paradox we're jabbering about is gonna rip me back in time any second now.

Oh. Yeah. Probably.

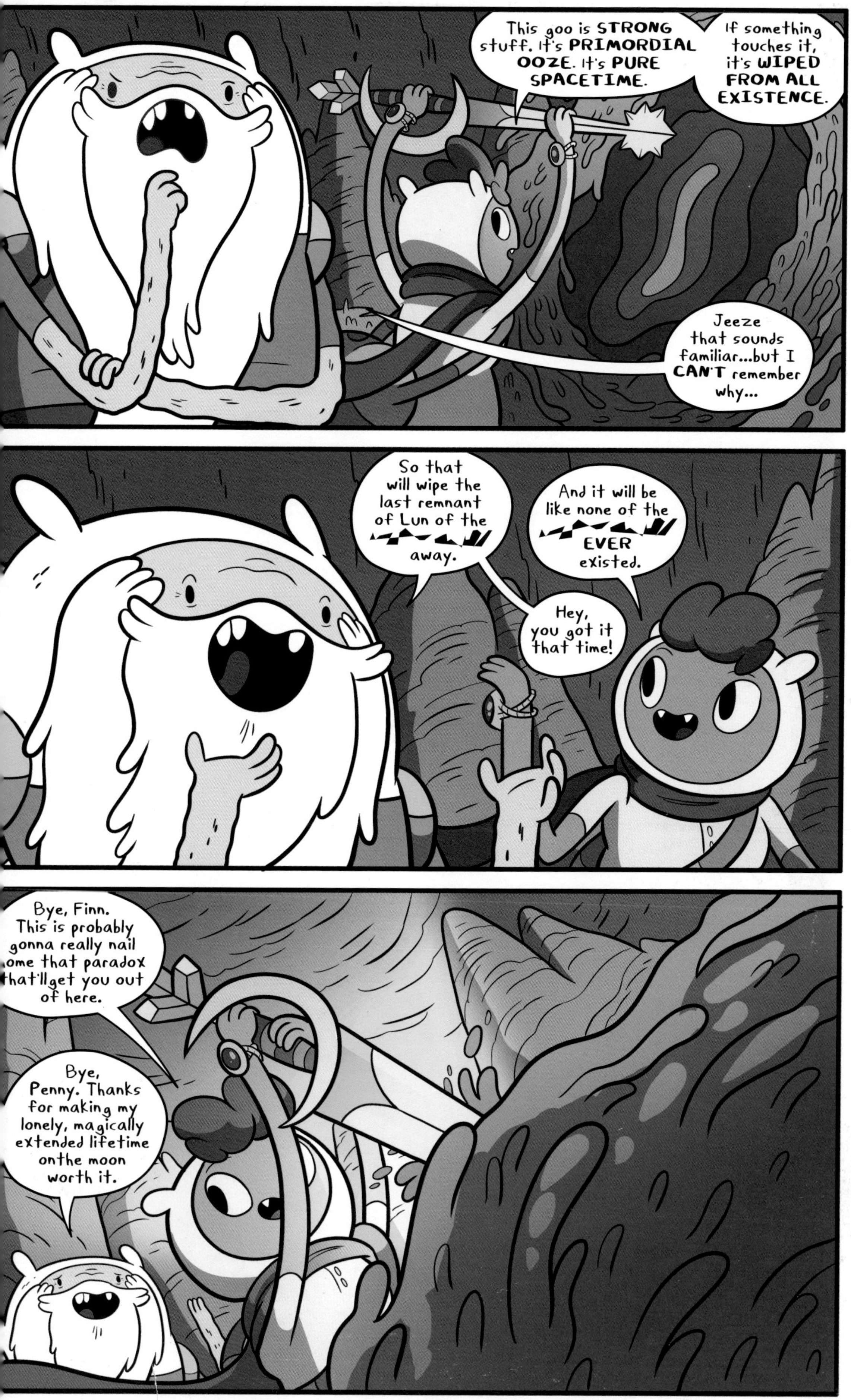

This goo is **STRONG** stuff. It's **PRIMORDIAL OOZE.** It's **PURE SPACETIME.**
If something touches it, it's **WIPED FROM ALL EXISTENCE.**
Jeeze that sounds familiar...but I **CAN'T** remember why...
So that will wipe the last remnant of Lun of the away.
And it will be like none of the **EVER** existed.
Hey, you got it that time!
Bye, Finn. This is probably gonna really nail ome that paradox that'll get you out of here.
Bye, Penny. Thanks for making my lonely, magically extended lifetime on the moon worth it.

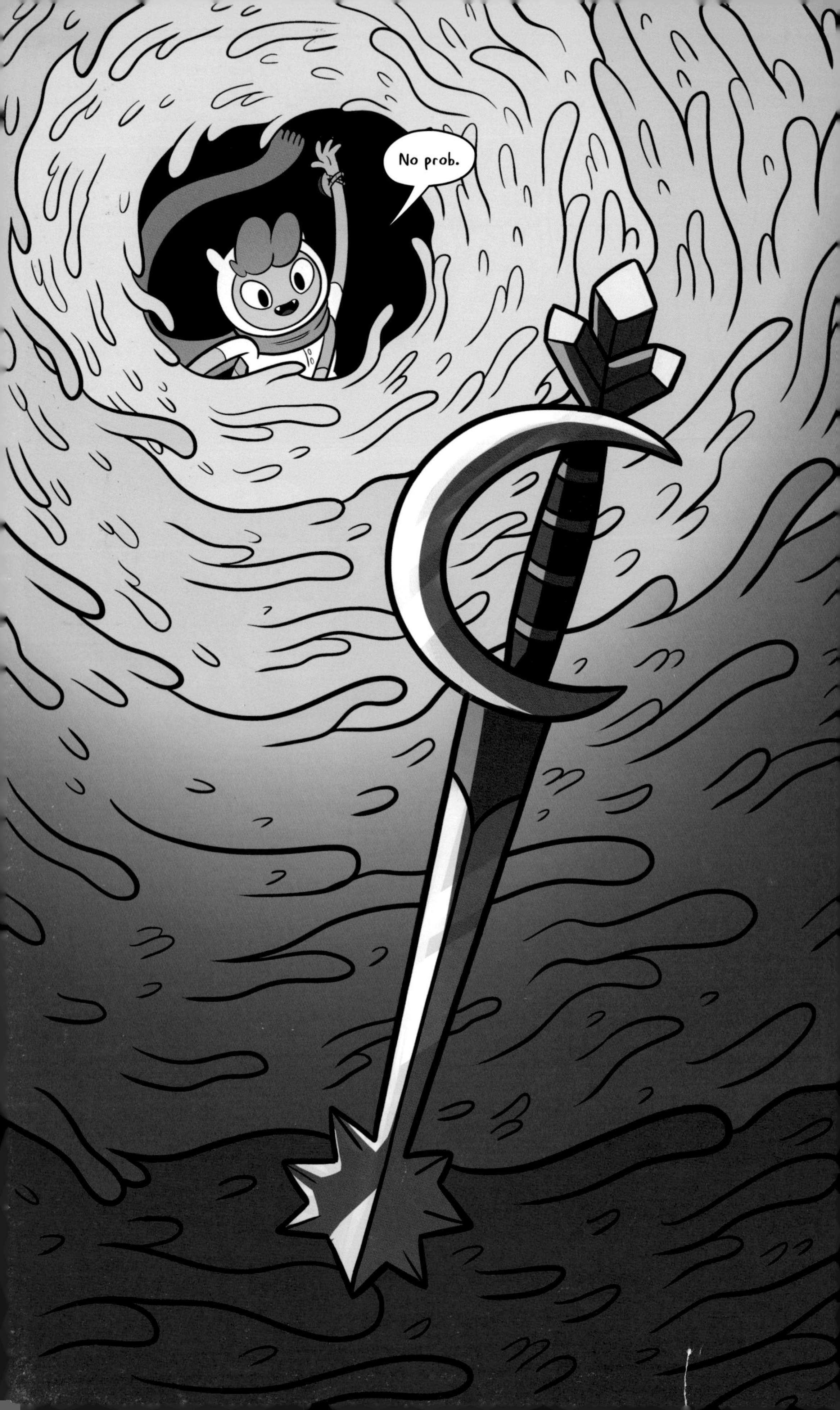
No prob.

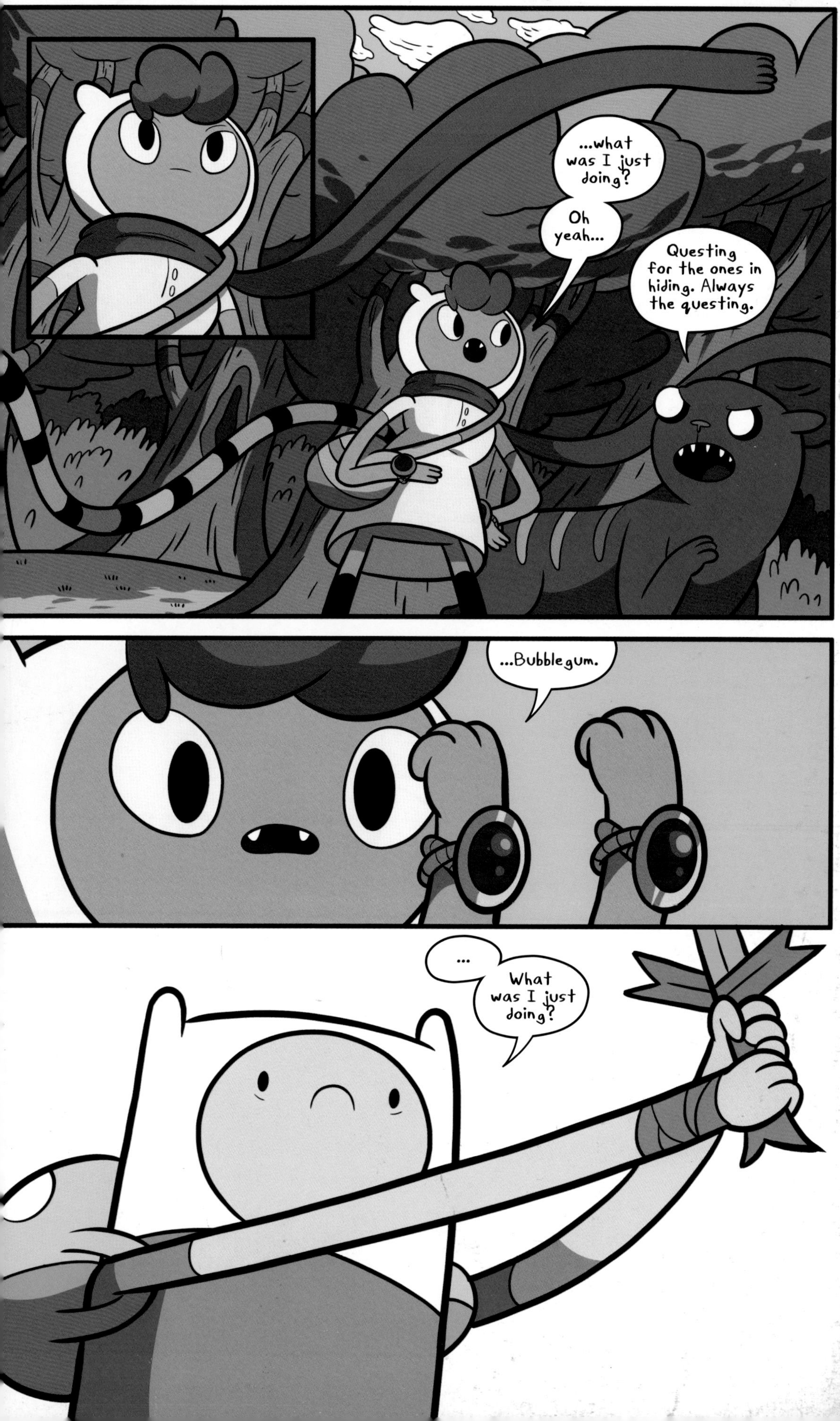
...what was I just doing?
Oh yeah...
Questing for the ones in hiding. Always the questing.
...Bubblegum.
...
What was I just doing?

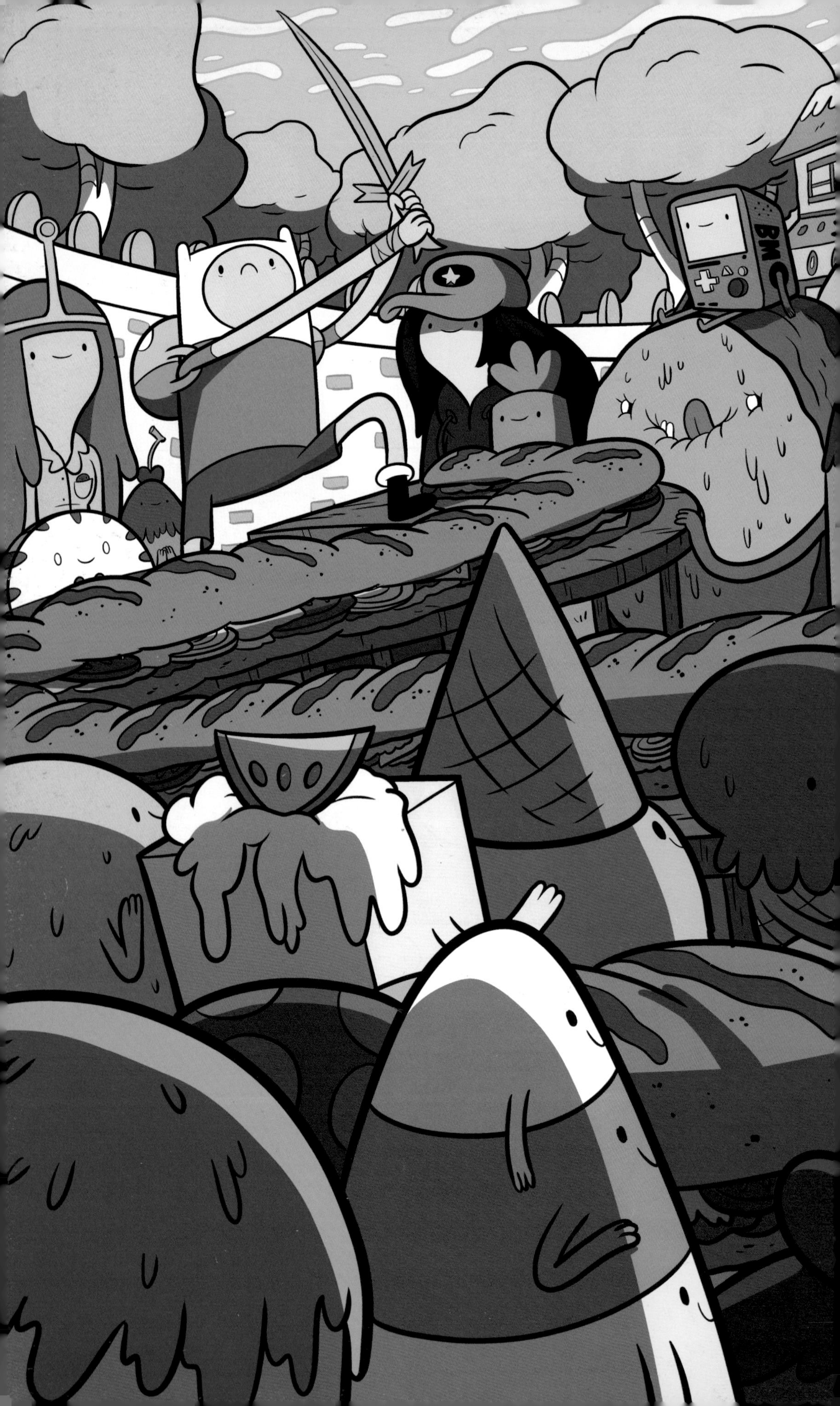

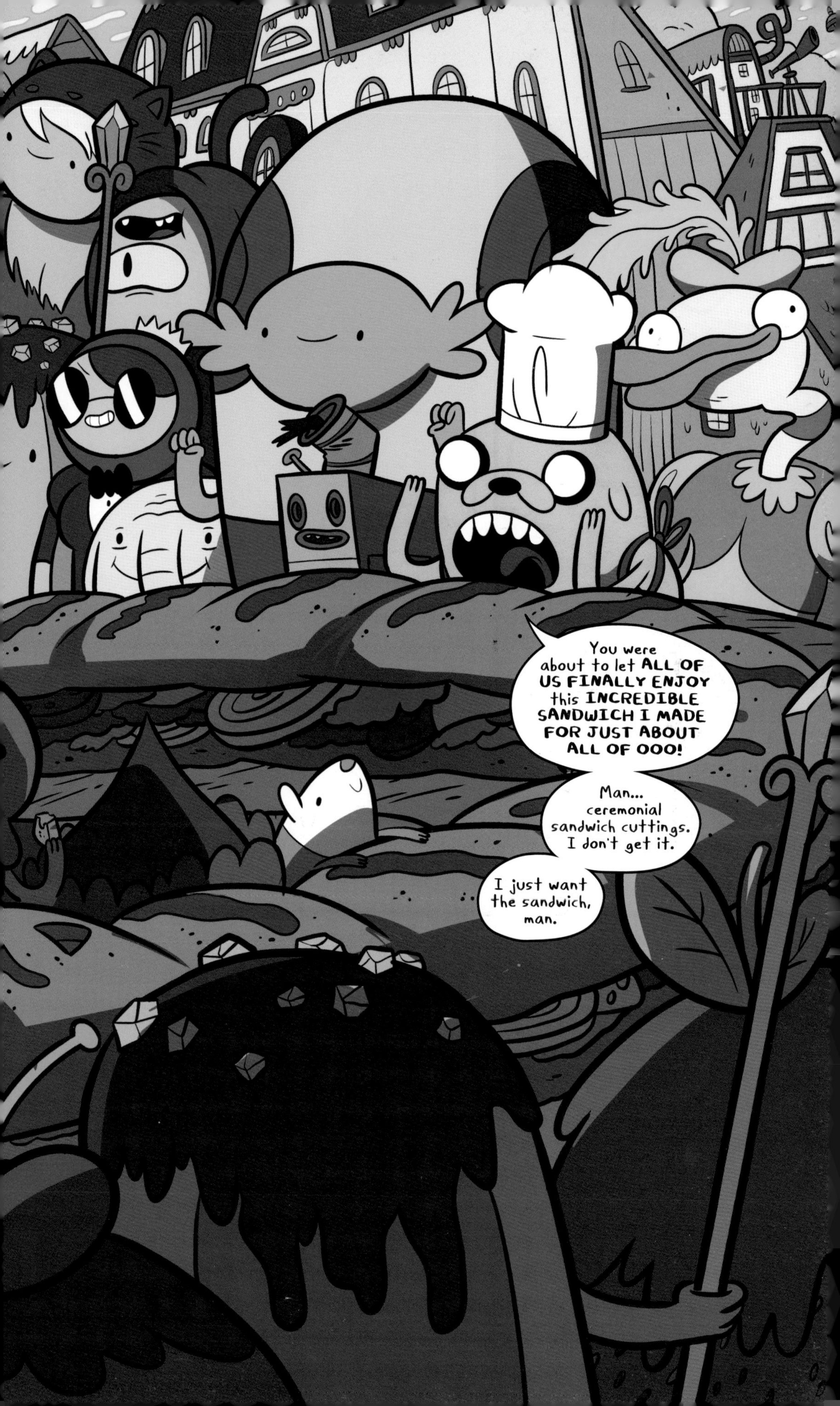
You were about to let ALL OF US FINALLY ENJOY this INCREDIBLE SANDWICH I MADE FOR JUST ABOUT ALL OF OOO!
Man... ceremonial sandwich cuttings. I don't get it.
I just want the sandwich, man.

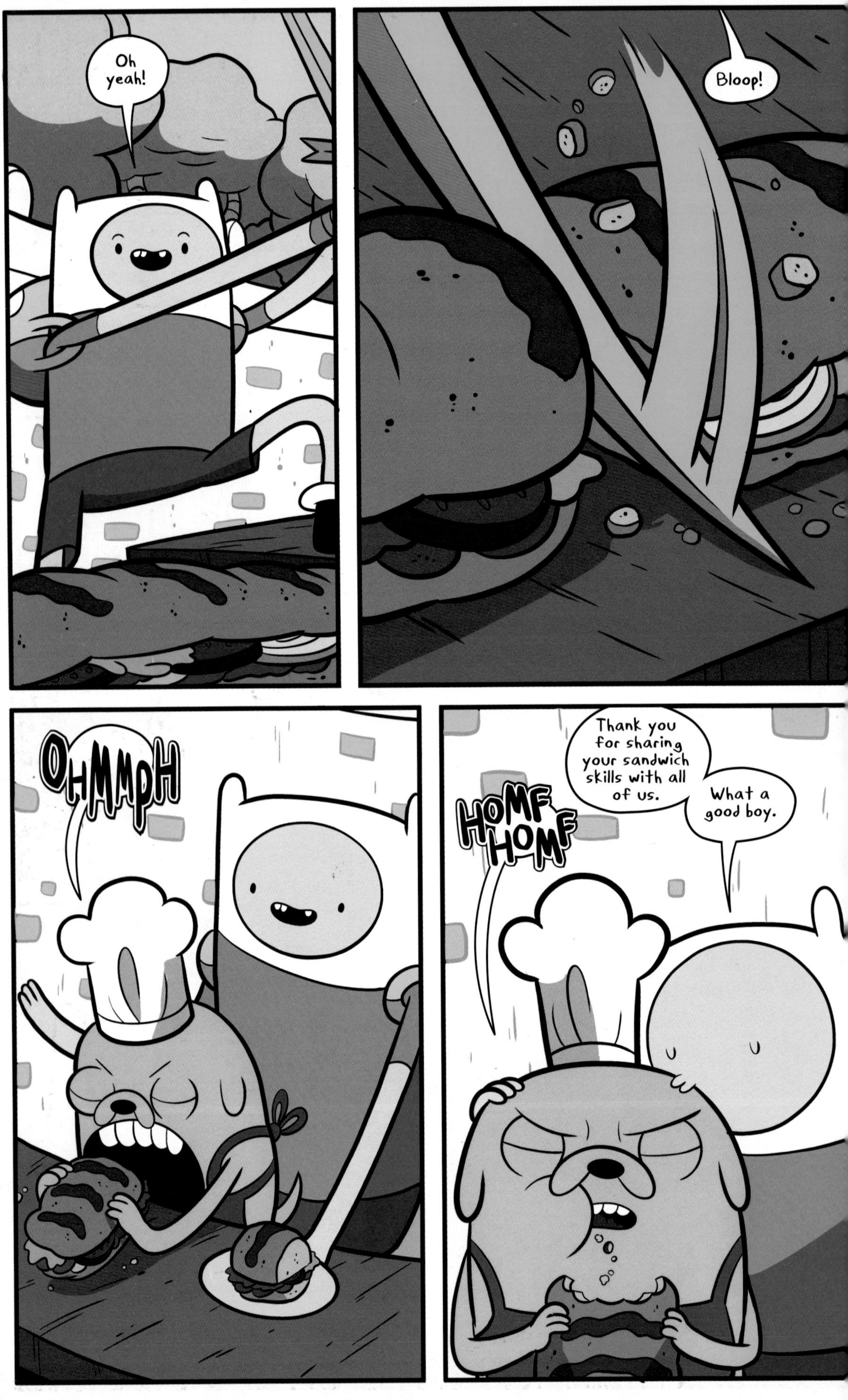

Oh yeah!
Bloop!
OHMMPH
HOMF HOMF
Thank you for sharing your sandwich skills with all of us.
What a good boy.

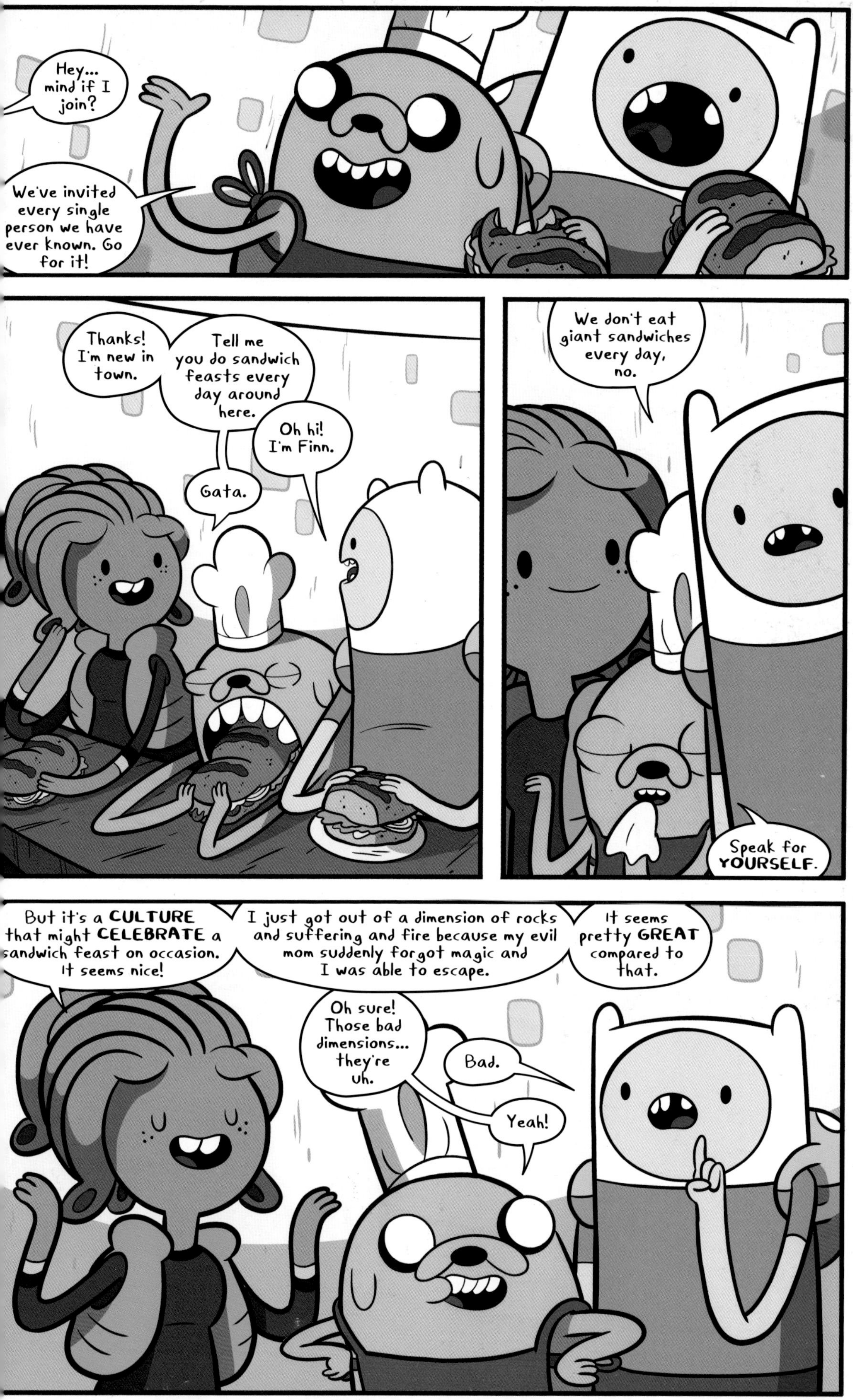
Hey... mind if I join?
We've invited every single person we have ever known. Go for it!
Thanks! I'm new in town.
Tell me you do sandwich feasts every day around here.
Gata.
Oh hi! I'm Finn.
We don't eat giant sandwiches every day, no.
Speak for YOURSELF.
But it's a CULTURE that might CELEBRATE a sandwich feast on occasion. It seems nice!
I just got out of a dimension of rocks and suffering and fire because my evil mom suddenly forgot magic and I was able to escape.
It seems pretty GREAT compared to that.
Oh sure! Those bad dimensions... they're uh.
Bad.
Yeah!

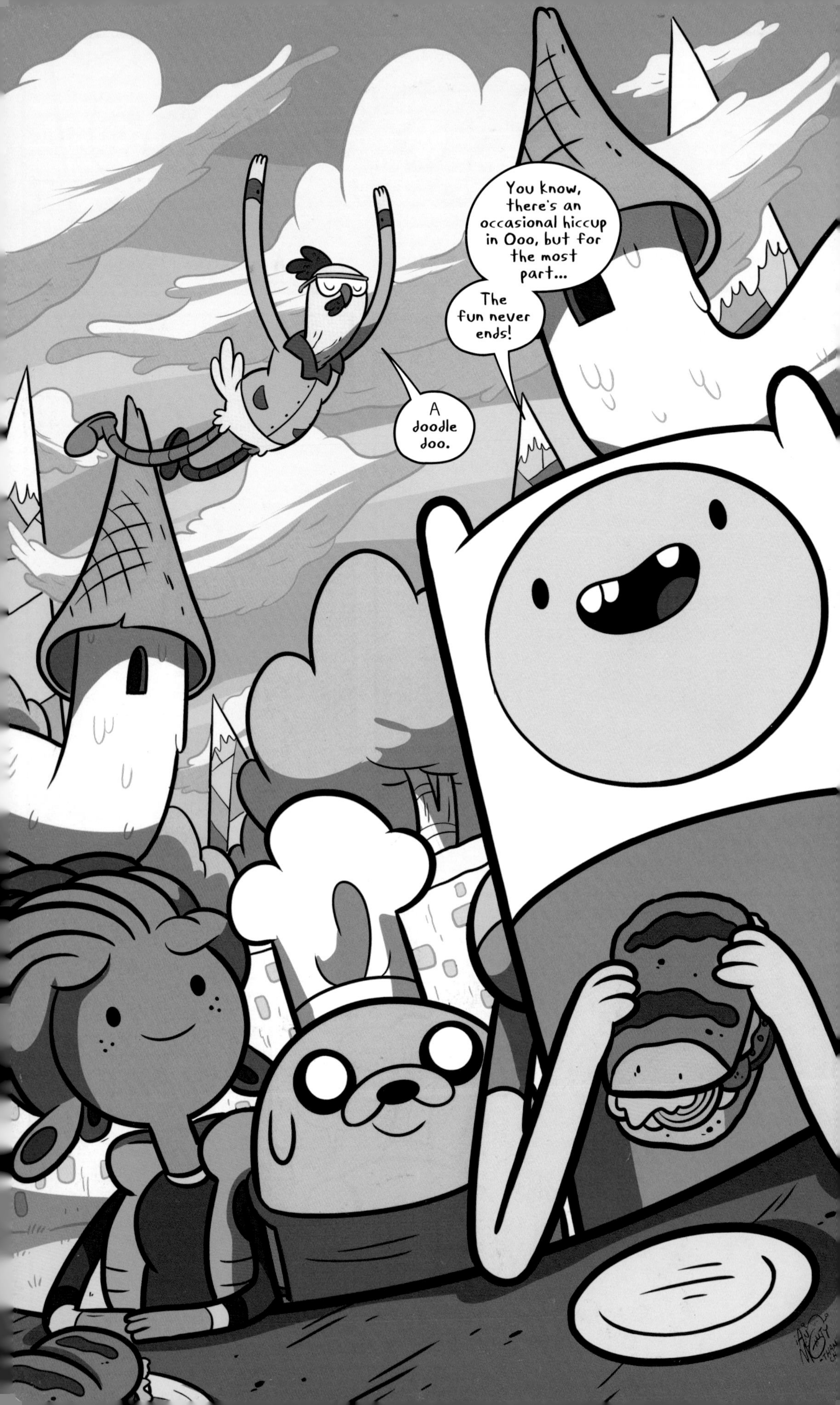
You know, there's an occasional hiccup in Ooo, but for the most part...
The fun never ends!
A doodle doo.

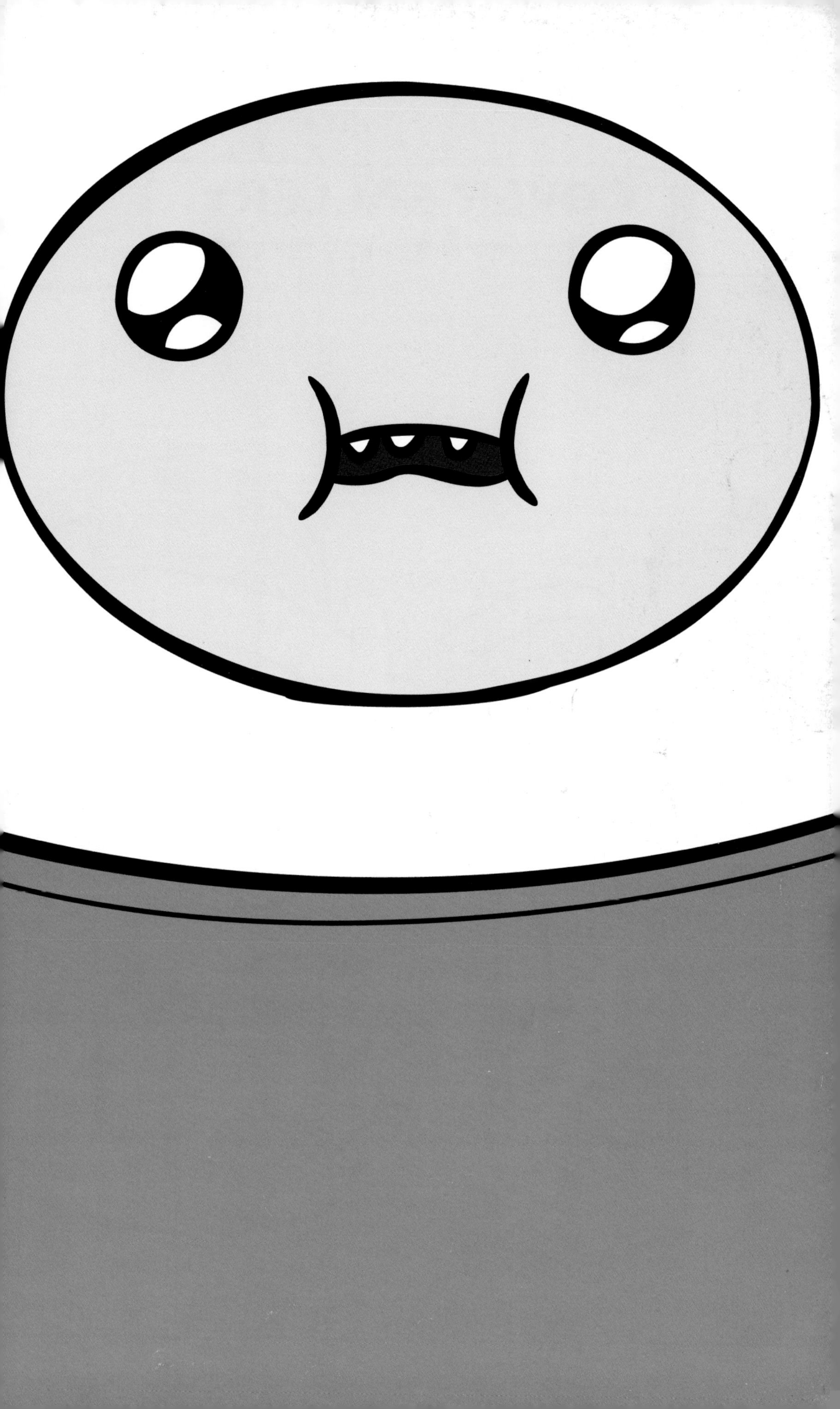

COVER GALLERY

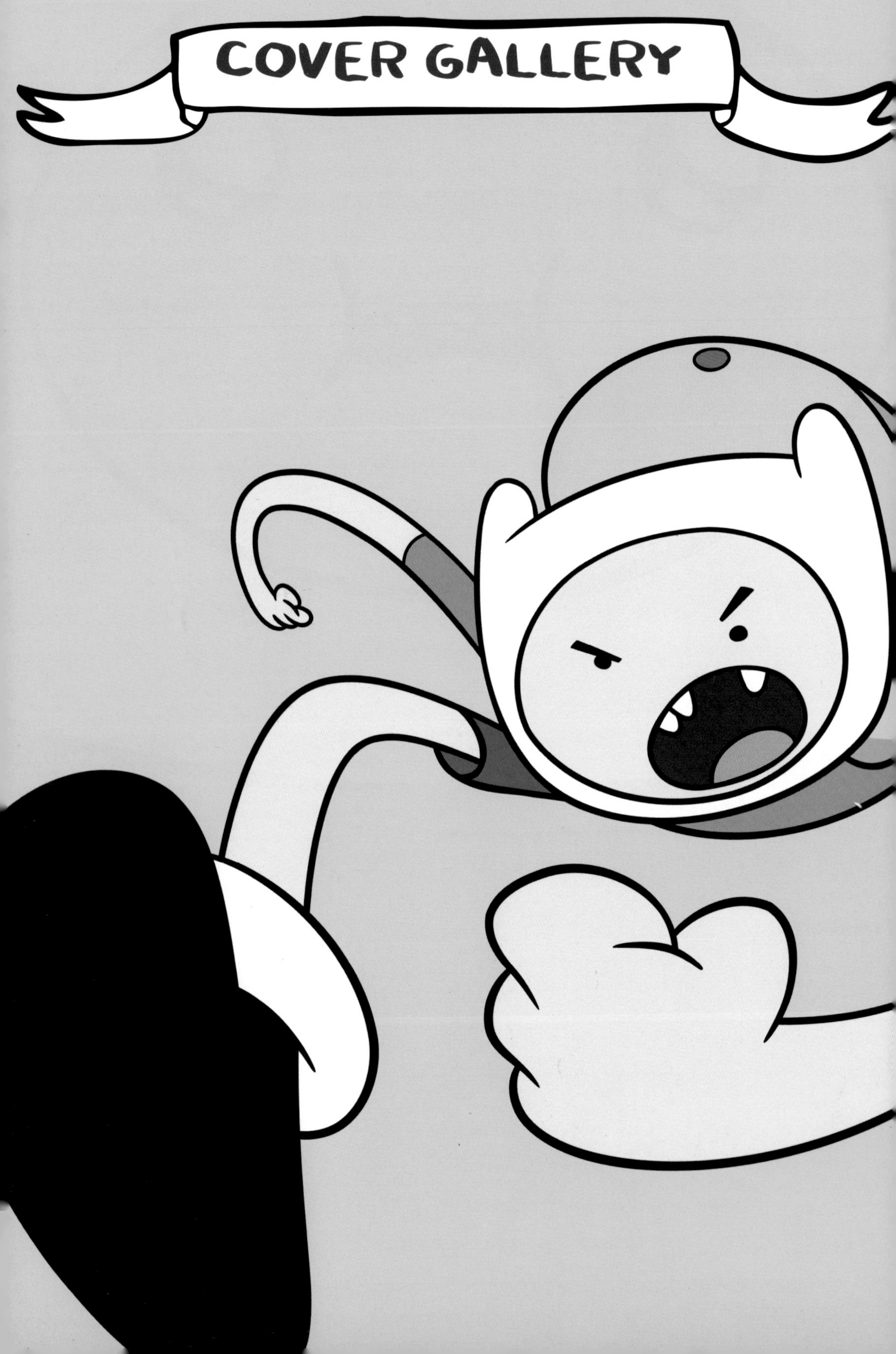

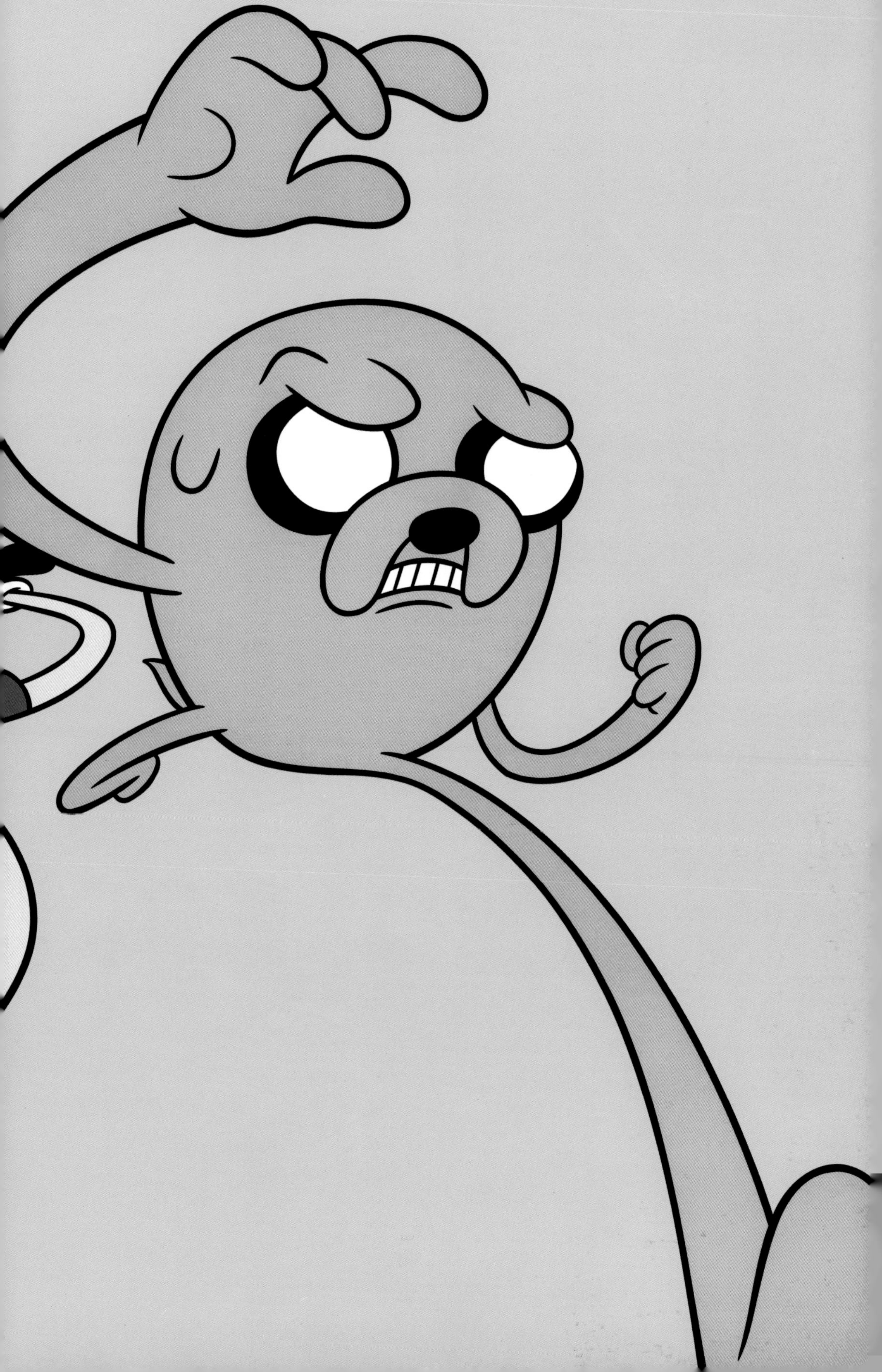

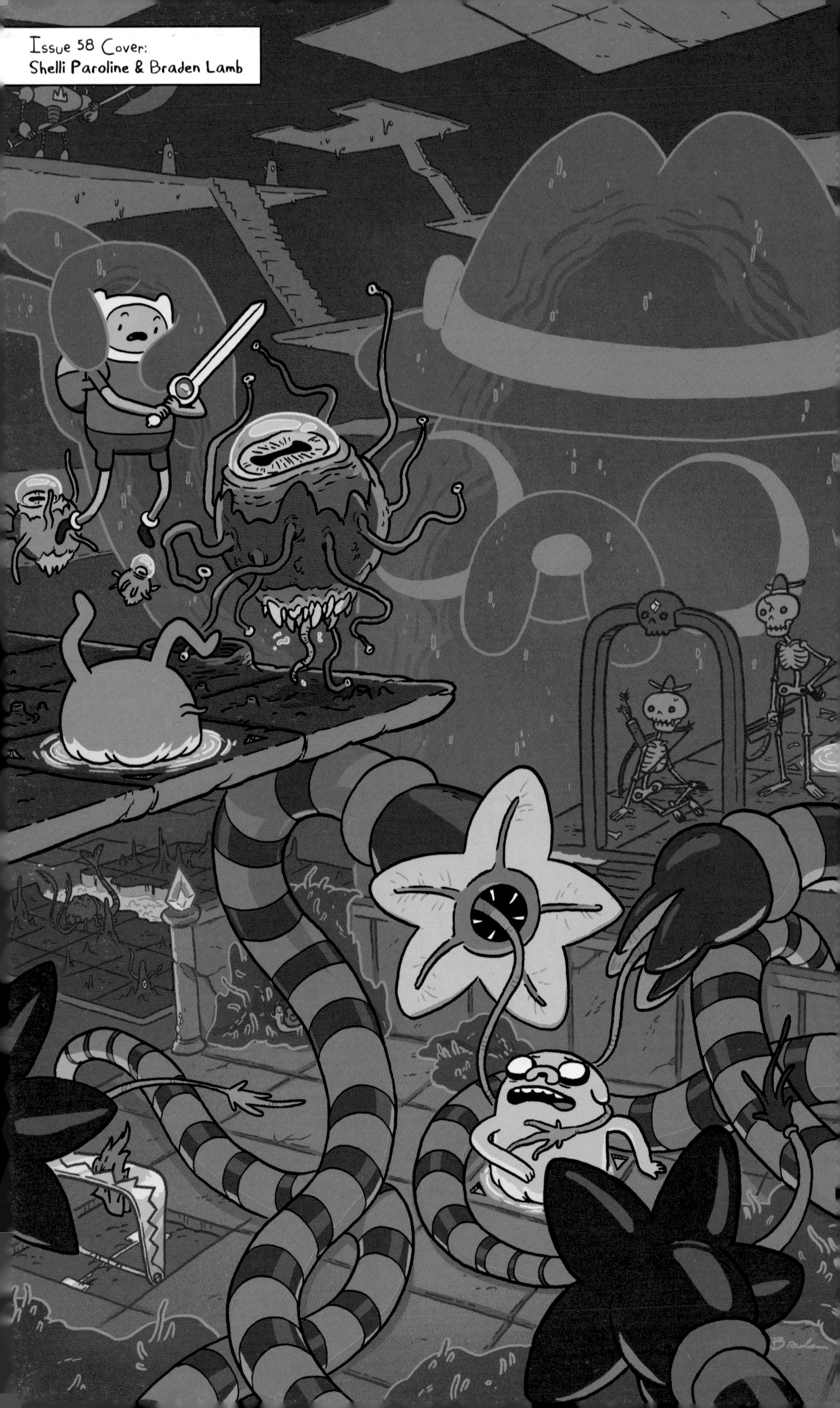

Issue 58 Cover:
Shelli Paroline & Braden Lamb

Issue 58 Subscription Cover:
Emi Jack

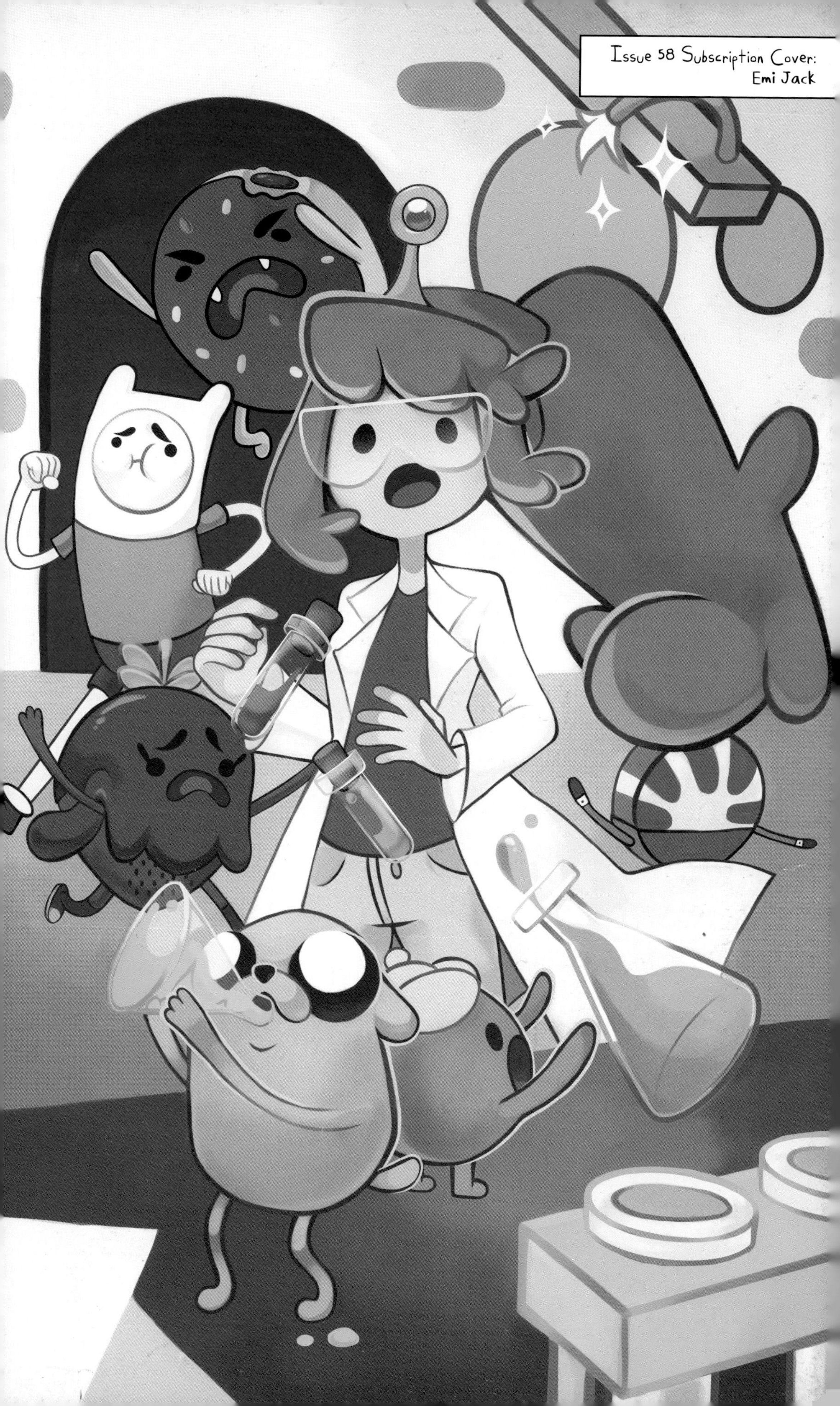

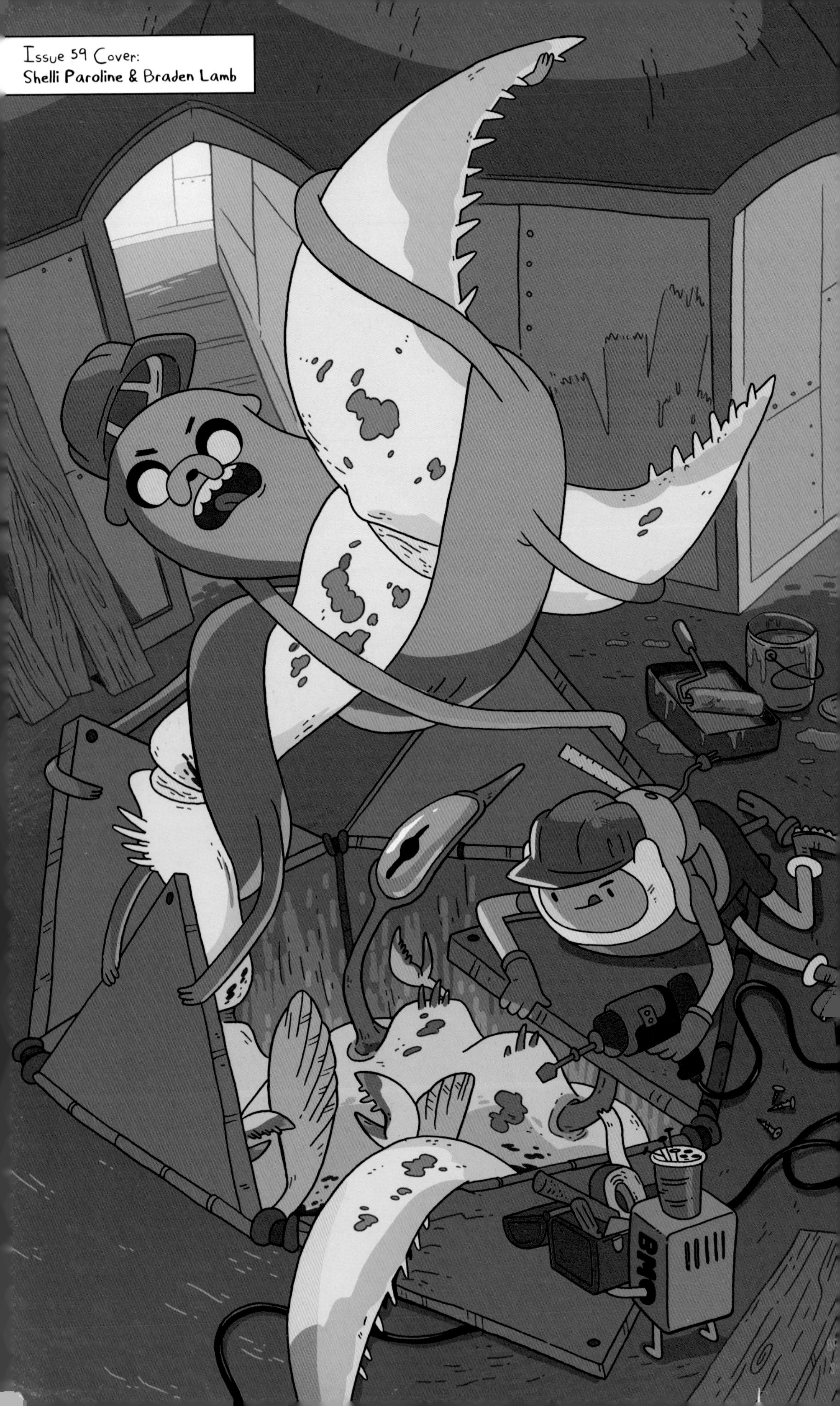
BMO

Issue 59 Cover:
Shelli Paroline & Braden Lamb

Issue 59 Subscription Cover:
Emily Warren

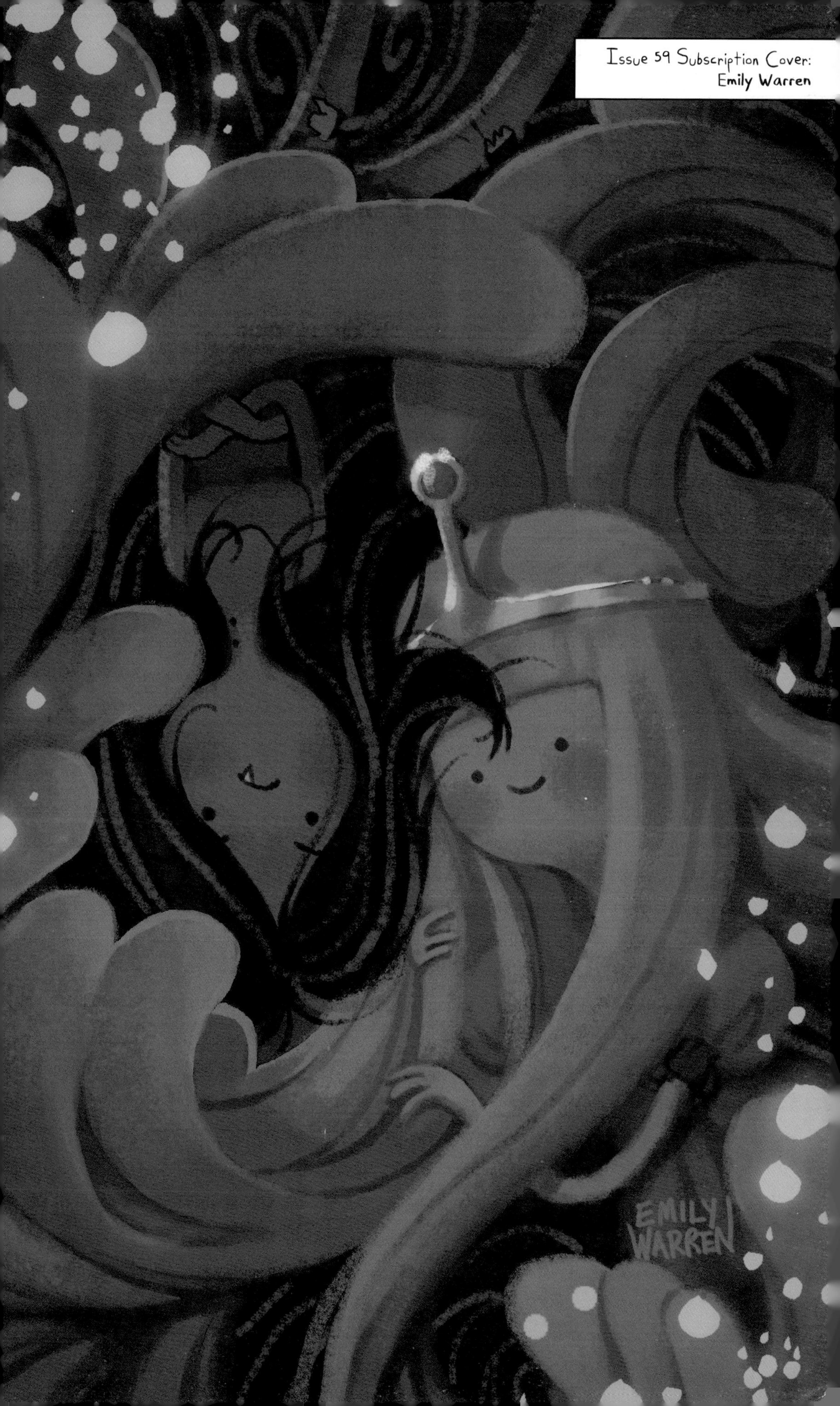
EMILY
WARREN

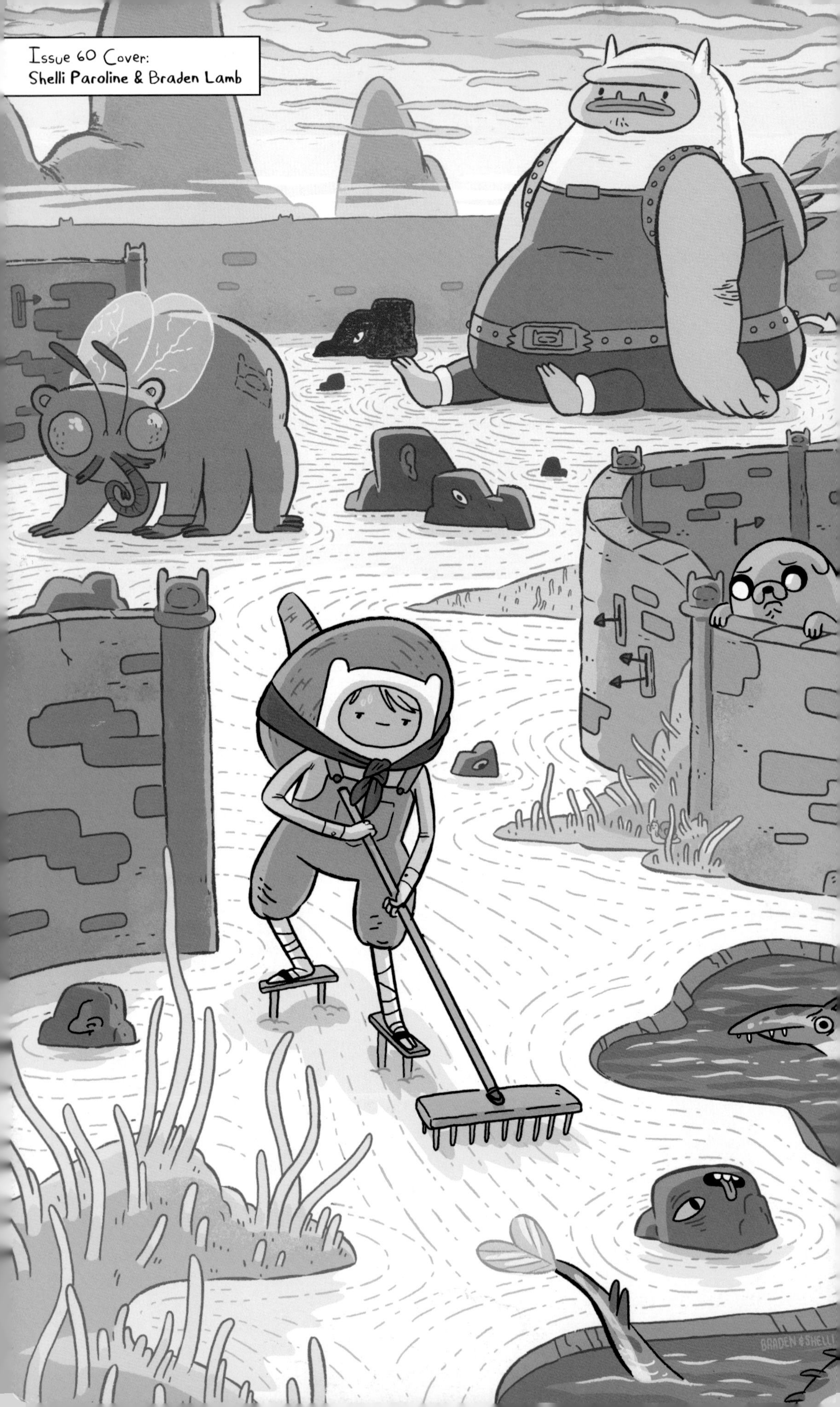

Issue 60 Cover:
Shelli Paroline & Braden Lamb

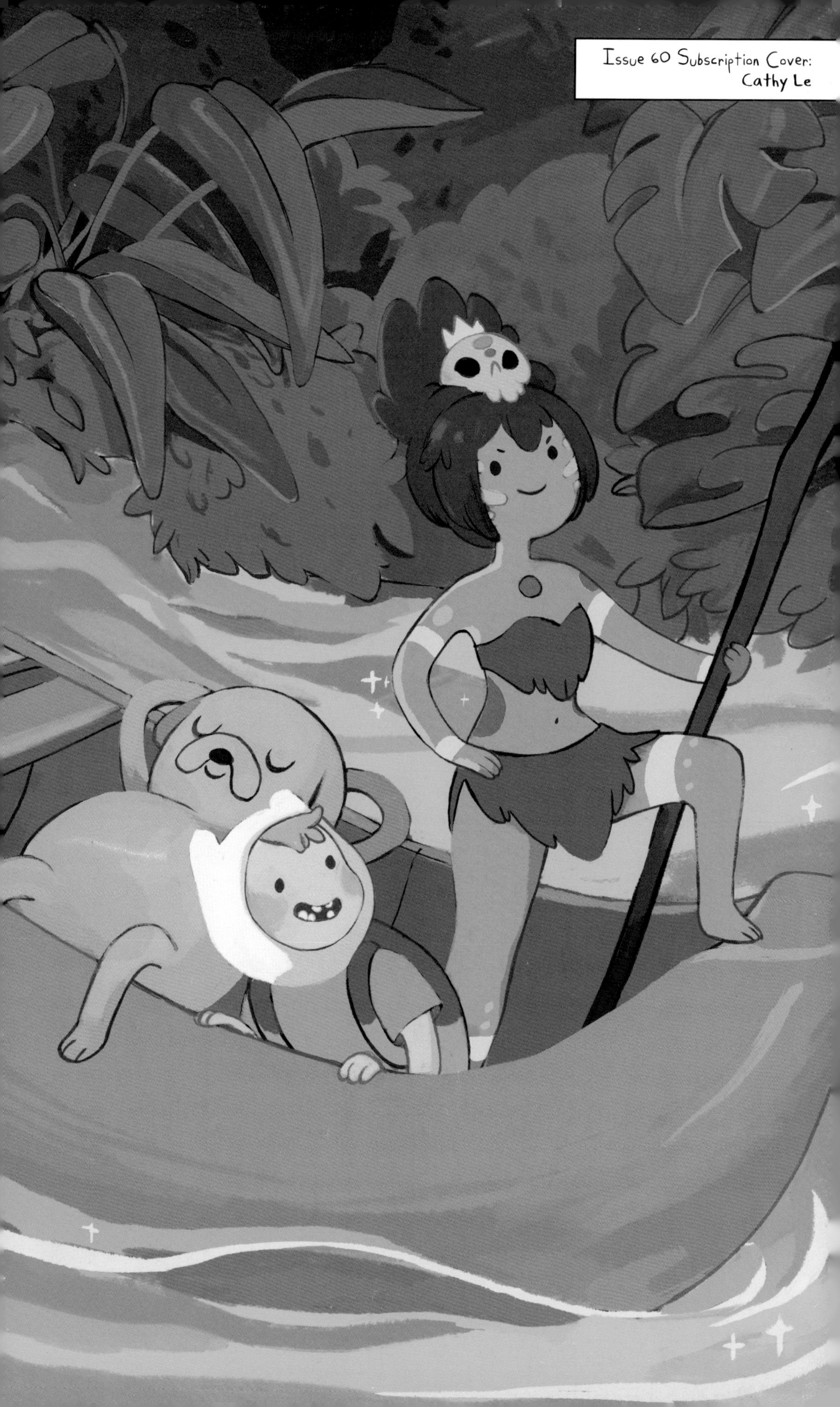

Issue 60 Subscription Cover:
Cathy Le

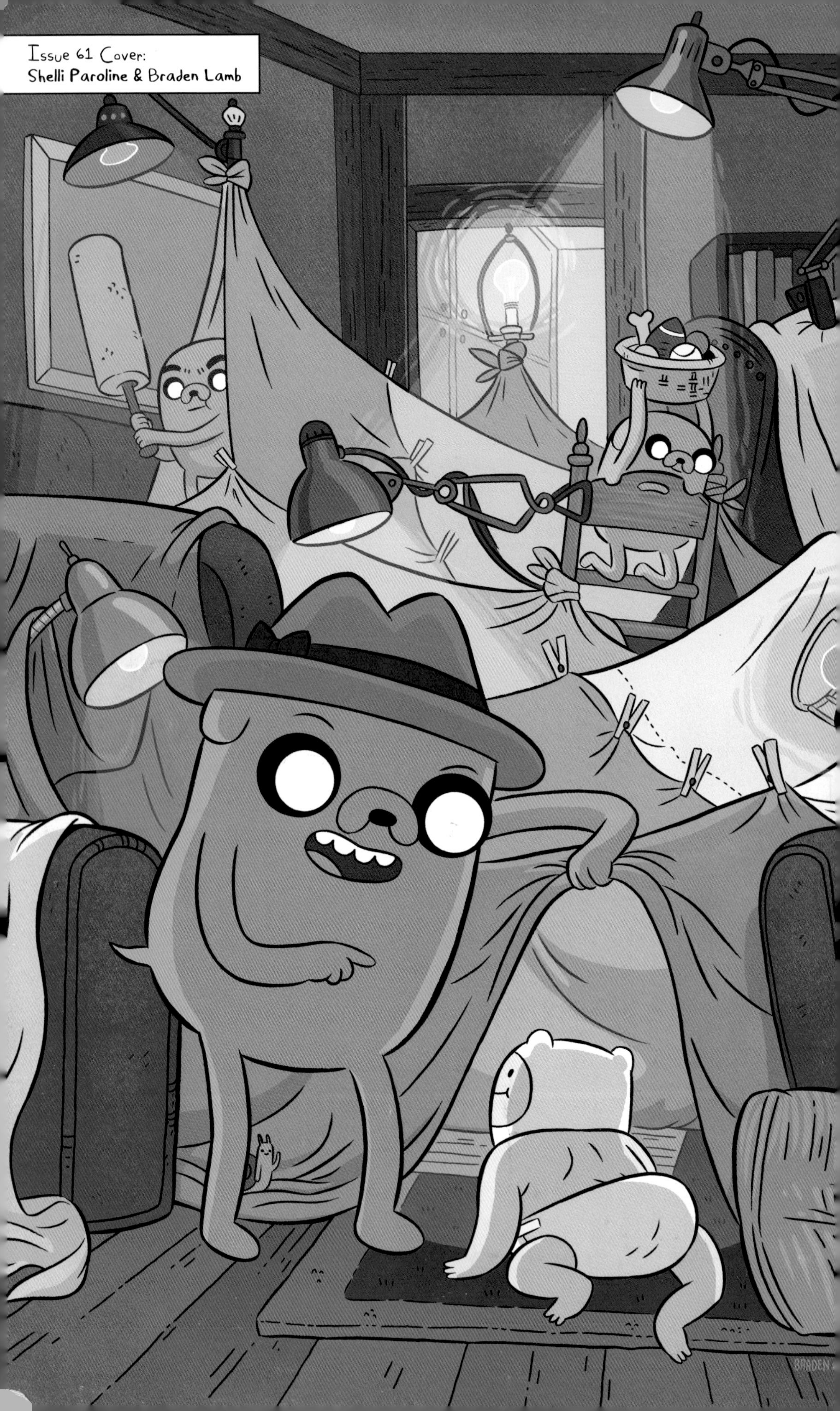
BRADEN

Issue 61 Cover:
Shelli Paroline & Braden Lamb

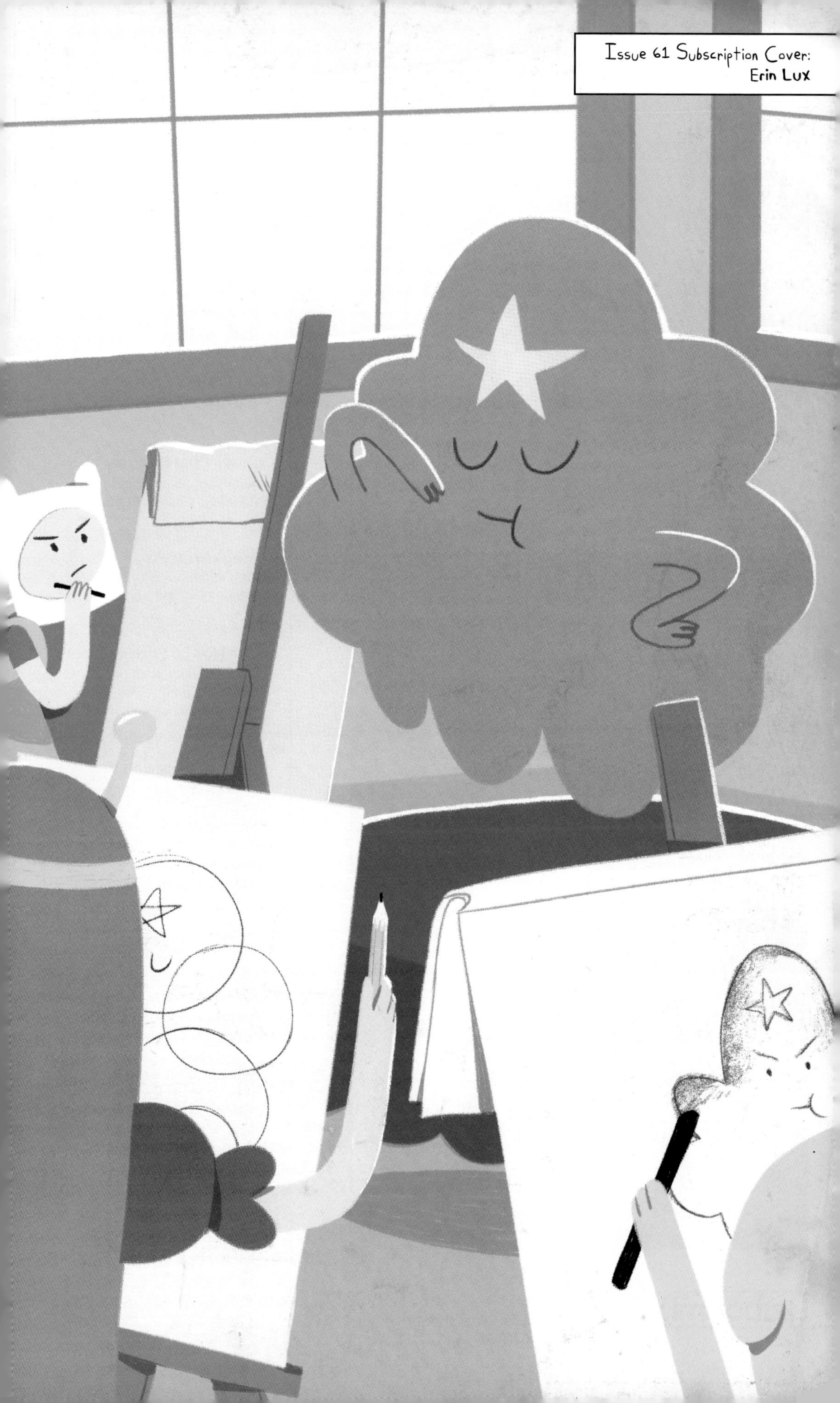

Issue 61 Subscription Cover:
Erin Lux

DISCOVER
EXPLOSIVE NEW WORLDS

Adventure Time
Pendleton Ward and Others
Volume 1
ISBN: 978-1-60886-280-1 | $14.99 US
Volume 2
ISBN: 978-1-60886-323-5 | $14.99 US
Adventure Time: Islands
ISBN: 978-1-60886-972-5 | $9.99 US

The Amazing World of Gumball
Ben Bocquelet and Others
Volume 1
ISBN: 978-1-60886-488-1 | $14.99 US
Volume 2
ISBN: 978-1-60886-793-6 | $14.99 US

Brave Chef Brianna
Sam Sykes, Selina Espiritu
ISBN: 978-1-68415-050-2 | $14.99 US

Mega Princess
Kelly Thompson, Brianne Drouhard
ISBN: 978-1-68415-007-6 | $14.99 US

The Not-So Secret Society
Matthew Daley, Arlene Daley,
Wook Jin Clark
ISBN: 978-1-60886-997-8 | $9.99 US

Over the Garden Wall
Patrick McHale, Jim Campbell
and Others
Volume 1
ISBN: 978-1-60886-940-4 | $14.99 US
Volume 2
ISBN: 978-1-68415-006-9 | $14.99 US

Steven Universe
Rebecca Sugar and Others
Volume 1
ISBN: 978-1-60886-706-6 | $14.99 US
Volume 2
ISBN: 978-1-60886-796-7 | $14.99 US

Steven Universe & The Crystal Gems
ISBN: 978-1-60886-921-3 | $14.99 US

Steven Universe: Too Cool for School
ISBN: 978-1-60886-771-4 | $14.99 US

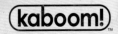

AVAILABLE AT YOUR LOCAL COMICS SHOP AND BOOKSTORE
To find a comics shop in your area, call 1-888-266-4226
WWW.BOOM-STUDIOS.COM